CW01558019

PAULA MCKAY

Piggy in the Middle

S & S

Printed and bound in Great Britain by Ipswich Book Co. Ltd.
Nacton Road, Ipswich, Suffolk.

Typeset by CBS, Felixstowe, Suffolk.

Paula McKay is known and respected for her work as a journalist
and dramatist for theatre and radio. B.B.C. Producer Martin Jenkins
describes her as "one of my very favourite writers". This is her
first full-length book.

DEDICATION

For Brendan, whose idea it all was and
for Ira, so that he will know what his roots are.

WORLD WAR TWO EVENTS 1939-45

September 3rd 1939	England at war with Germany
June 1940	British forces evacuated from Dunkirk, France. (40,000 left dead or captured. 338,000 brought back by British 'home-made' "Little Armada".) Britain waits in fear of German invasion.
July 1940	The "Arandora Star" carrying evacuee children across the Atlantic sunk by German U-boats.
September 7th 1940	Bombing by Germans starts in earnest. Many incendiaries ("fire-bombs") dropped on London, especially in East End docks area.
October 1940	Bombs fall on Balham tube. 64 killed, 550 below injured.
November 1940	Coventry heavily bombed.
March 1941	British troops arrive in Greece from North Africa.
April 1941	British troops leave Greece. (11,000 casualties).
June 22nd 1941	Germany invades U.S.S.R.
September 1941	German 5-way assault on Leningrad.
October 1941	Nine-days battle for Moscow.
November 18th 1941	British army's first offensive opens with Libyan battle.
December 2nd 1941	Hitler orders transfer of some troops from U.S.S.R. to North Africa and Italy.
December 6th 1941	Japanese attack Pearl Harbour.
December 8th 1941	Japanese forces land in Malaya.
December 11th 1941	Germany declares war on the United States.
January 2nd 1942	Manila taken by Japanese
February 15th 1942	Singapore surrenders to Japanese.
March 28th 1942	Bomber Command sent 234 planes to historic German port of Lubeck to try out

	system of fire-raising. Caused fierce German resentment.
April 23-29th 1942	German Baedeker raids on historic cities of Bath, Bristol, York, Norwich commences.
May 11th 1942	"Andes" docks at Liverpool with 1,850 U.S.A.A.F. men.
May 13th 1942	Burma army finished - 800 mile rearguard action to India.
May 30th 1942	1,000 bomber-raid by British on Cologne.
June 20th 1942	Germans capture Tobruk.
September 6th 1942	Germans halted at Stalingrad.
October 23rd 1942	El Alamein, British offensive in North Africa.
November 4th 1942	Rommel's army in retreat.
January 31st 1943	German army surrenders at Stalingrad.
July 10th 1943	First Allied landings on Sicily.
July 25th 1943	Mussolini overthrown.
September 7th 1943	Italy surrenders.
September 10th 1943	Rome seized by the Germans.
February-April 1944	Heavy bombing over Germany by U.S.A.A.F. Heavy losses of men and aircraft.
June 4th 1944	Allied forces enter Rome.
June 6th 1944	Allied forces D-Day invasion of Europe.
June 12th 1944	First V1s land in Britain.
August 25th 1944	Paris liberated.
September 8th 1944	First V2 lands in Britain.
February 14th 1945	Bombing of Dresden.
April 25th 1945	Berlin surrounded by Russian troops.
April 27th 1945	Russians and Americans link up in Germany.
April 28th 1945	Mussolini and mistress shot by communist partisan colonel at Lake Como.
April 30th 1945	Hitler kills himself and mistress.
May 8th 1945	Official ending of World War Two against

	Germany declared.
July 26th 1945	Labour victory in General Election.
August 6th 1945	Atom bomb dropped by U.S. on Japan at Hiroshima.
August 9th 1945	Second atom bomb dropped on Nagasaki.
September 2nd 1945	Victory over Japan. End of World War Two.

YIDDISH WORDS

Word	Pronunciation	Meaning
Shabbes	shah-biss	Sabbath
schlepped	shlepped	dragged or pulled
shikse	shickser	gentile woman
boobahs	boobars	Jewish grandmothers
kishkas	kishkars	intestines
parana	paranar	feather-bed, like duvet
mitzvah	mitsvar	good deed or act, blessing
Pesach	paysoch	Passover holiday, festival
yock	yock	gentile man
goyishe	goyisher	gentile
nuchas	nuchass	joy
miesse meshinas	meeser mershinas	a bad fate or end
schlong	shlong	penis
meshugee/meshuga	mershoogar	crazy
coorvah	coorvar	prostitute
muzzletoff	muzzletoff	good luck!
krenk	kraink	ill or aggravation
schmaltz	shmaltz	chicken fat/over-sentiment
goyem	goyim	gentile
schmakel	shmakell	penis
frum	froom	orthodox
schtum	shtoom	keep silent/quiet
fress	frass	eat well
kayn aynhoreh	kineerhorrer	to cast off evil eye
meshunganah hunt	meshooganar hoont	mad dog
broche	broch	a blessing or exclamation
shlemiel	shlemeele	simpleton
Chivah/shivah	shiver	seven mourning days
shikkereh	shickerrer	drunken
kinder	kinderr	children
fagala	fagelerr	sweet/endearment
choochala/chotchkeleh	chootchkalar	plaything/endearment
barmitzvah/Bar Mitzvah	barmitzvar	boy (13 yrs,) becomes man

CHAPTER ONE

September - October 1940

"Eenah-deenah, abba-dasha, rer-rye, dommanasha, chikka-rakka, omm, pomm-poosh!" Why was I thinking of that - the rhyme we always chanted before choosing who would be 'It' in our games?

"Igaree-eye, igaree-eye, pop the vinegar in the pie, aarom-paarom, pop-schaanarom, skin it!" None of us knew what it meant. I sang loudest - got my tongue round the words cleanest - If you sang loud enough you wouldn't hear the shouts of father and mother, wouldn't see the looks of the others in the ring if you shut your eyes tight and sang out "Igaree-eye, igaree-eye . . ." and father's screams with the windows thrown open and mother's as she closed them down, would sound out and drop into the grey courtyard - bounce, echo and collide with each other and the dark, brick walls and across the heads of the black-haired, black-eyed circle of children singing and playing.

We were away from that now. How long before I'd see them again? Would I ever?

"You don't look scared," I said to mum. I was, though I put on an act - I was eleven after all - I thought she ought to be frightened, we didn't know where we'd be put, which house, family, would have us pushed on 'em, like it or not -

It was a contradiction in her I couldn't make out - not then anyway. Later, with maturity, I could, but sitting pushed up against her in the small bus that shook us round the narrow streets of Kettering on that September afternoon in 1940, I saw her eyes full of sparkle like green lemonade and her little mouth lipstick'd in the careful cupid's bow she liked and I saw a woman ready for what might come - ready and strangely eager.

"D'you think anyone'll want us?"

"God knows . . ." She'd say that when she wasn't sure the way things would go. Grandma, her mother used to say it too, except when she did she had a good idea how they'd go - usually bad.

"Sylvie and Fay got taken in." Sylvie was my best friend. We'd gone to the same Jewish school in Stepney Green and Fay,

1

her mum, was my mum's best friend. She pushed her face to the window, trying to peep through the one patch of clear glass. I hoped we'd have a posh billet like they got except I shouldn't have been envious after what they'd gone through - losing their house in the air-raid and Sylvie's dad buried under the debris so's he was given up for dead and they only went on digging for him 'cause they heard the cat mewing and after all if the cat was still alive and it in the same basement room, then Fay's Sid could be O.K. Now Sid was in the army.

"D'you think dad'll be all right?"

"Nothing'll happen to him, loves himself to madness - always has."

The billeting officer was writing on a clip-board with our papers on - did he hear? P'raps dad would be safe, he said he'd still go down the shelter nights -

I hated Germans, as much nearly as dad from when he was in the First World War - what did they have to bomb us for - try and set all London alight for - ? Dad said it was because they wanted to take over the whole world - 'specially Bolsheviks - dad knew a lot about that - he was a communist.

"I'm tired." I leaned against her. There was still a bit of Evening in Paris scent on her. "It's been a long day," she said. It had, 'cept I didn't mind the train journey - with houses getting less and fields spreading wider and trees willowing like girls with long hair in the wind. The nearer we got to Kettering the more excited I'd become - p'raps we'd have a thatched cottage for our billet like you see on calendars - but as we drove round and round the streets with straight terraced houses the same colour as the tenements we'd left, I wasn't so sure - The bus stopped. "Here we go again," mum muttered.

Mr. Parmer looked scared, scared as I was feeling when the billeting officer asked him. Mum smiled her best actress smile while I tried to look smaller and the billeting officer who was fed up same as us talked fast and before Mr. Parmer could push the front door shut on his 'monastery' as mum later called it, we were his.

He had a face with all his feelings on it - pale watery eyes which he kept rubbing with a red, spotted handkerchief and a nose with the most enormous nostrils. "A pig's snout," mum called it. It

2

was dim inside with a low light spreading grudgingly from the shadeless bulb hanging at the end of the hall.

"What's that smell?" I whispered to mum.

"Paraffin."

And suddenly I could smell it in the shelter - a small paraffin stove Mrs. Connolly would use to heat a drop of water.

Mr. Parmer lifted a steaming, sooty kettle from the fire-grate and poured it over an Oxo cube in a cracked cup. He stirred it deliberately, not looking at us, then took a square of bread, dipped it in the brown water and ate it. I'd never seen anyone do that.

We had the small back bedroom. "Yippee!" I jumped on one of the two black iron beds. For weeks it'd been nights slept on the hard stone floor of Charrington's Brewery where we'd all gone - us and the neighbours - 'cause it was safer in their great deep vaults. Mum was at the window, looking down at the garden. "We've never had a garden mum."

"We did once. You've forgotten." And she brought back when I was very small and we'd lived at the top of a high Victorian house in Forest Gate. "The landlady - right Irish cow - could she drink - had the D.Ts. Terrified I was to go down and hang out the washing - set her dog on me - bloody great Alsatian." She drew the faded curtains, their black-out lining drooping at the hem. "Not much is it?" It wasn't. A dressing-table with oval mirror speckled brown, a single wardrobe, its wood now dulled and a rag-hooked rug of someone's old clothes between the beds. Then she opened the door, stealthily creeping along the landing to Mr. Parmer's room. I followed. She turned his door-knob slowly, peered inside but before I could, closed it. "Yes, we'll soon have that." It seemed right to me - after all, there were two of us.

It was so quiet in bed - no noise of brewery machinery or people snoring or arguing over cards - just mum breathing steadily away.

"Mum . . ."

"Umm?"

"It's not very comfortable . . ."

"Better than being hidden away under that stinking brewery." She joggled about. "Lumpy bloody mattress . . . Stop talking, I'm worn out."

But I couldn't stop thinking. Was dad down the shelter or at home in our small flat on the fourth floor of the buildings, staring at the double bed which me and mum shared and the single one placed behind ours going the width of the narrow room, which was his, his bed where he always slept alone? I smelt the paraffin lamp as Mr. Parmer came up and saw its flicker through the gap at the bottom of our door. Funny he used that when there was electricity on. Mum's bed spring squeaked. She couldn't sleep either.

Mum soon had an understanding with Mr. Parmer. He was old-fashioned and respectful, for wasn't she a married lady even though she hadn't had a letter or any money from her husband who was "hiding away like a rat underground and to hell with everyone!" as mum said over and again. So she acted as housekeeper and we got our food and heat thrown in to make up the difference in the billeting allowance and soon everywhere was fresh with cut flowers about and the hem stitched back in the curtain.

She'd been cutting late roses and now held a salmony-pink one to me. "That don't smell like the brewery eh?" It didn't - it was ever so easy to forget people were still there, coming out in the mornings to smoke that stung your eyes and the sky like it had been set fire to.

"Remember when dad stood me on the beer barrel to do my songs?" He'd said I was keeping everyone from being so scared and that was a good thing but really he liked showing me off - they both did, it was one of the few things they shared with any real happiness. I liked it too and I thought of the old Jewish women who had nudged each other proudly as I sang out, saying maybe there was hope after all and how Mrs. Connolly's boys who always chased me and Sylvie, clapped and whistled.

I wanted and wanted a letter from dad - even though it was peaceful here, just me and mum on our own. He might be dead or have an arm or leg blown off. He'd never be able to use the sewing machine again then would he - ? Mum looked so pretty, standing with the roses - like on a birthday card - would she be glad if he was killed - by the Germans who'd never got him in the First War?

"What's the matter?"

I turned to hide tears that came on their own. "Dad said he'd take me to America when he won the Sweepstake - to his rich brother."

"Oh, that one! I've heard that one, over and over I've heard it!" She made a laugh which wasn't really one. "So what you crying

4

for?''

I couldn't tell her - explain I liked having him around to take my side when she told me off or tell me how clever I was and I'd have to make something of myself even if there wasn't a revolution where everyone'd be equal. She picked at a petal. ''You know you're a 'mother's girl' really.'' She was right - wasn't it me she turned to after each of their fights? And me it was who'd be used as the battering-ram or the peacemaker and it would be ''tell him'' or ''speak with him'' or ''get round him'' and I would be the Piggy in the Middle while they stamped and danced around me in their angry tormented way.

But here it was quiet - Mr. Parmer's house and his mother's before him - quiet, with the 'country' furniture, as mum called it - with no oak sideboard - an angry gash across its middle, reminding you when dad had crashed the brass candlestick on it - (one of a pair welcoming in *shabbes* with white, lit candles), crashed it down, opening and wounding it as he cried out that he was wounded - all 'cause mum was running off with the landlady's lodger - taking me and running off - Here the furniture was old-fashioned, quiet and knew its place.

The best of it stayed in the front parlour. We spent most of the time in the back living-room-cum-kitchen. Here the fireplace was with its black oven - here too the heavy iron kettle sitting on its smoke-blackened hob, waiting to be swung over the flames to boil up for tea or water to wash or to scrub floors. On the rectangular deal table food was prepared and eaten, washing was ironed, newspapers spread, around it four pine chairs with scratched legs. Best, was the rocking-chair in wood black like ebony but not so grand - it had a plush velvet back, patterned, and a seat which sagged for all it had dulled, brass studs tacked round it. ''You'll break that chair,'' mum would warn for whenever Mr. Parmer was at the railway station doing his shift, I'd take it over and rock and rock till its runners almost snapped. All the water had to be brought from the 'barn' as Mr. Parmer called the outhouse - ''That's your job,'' mum ordered, ''I can't carry heavy pails with my inside.'' Since my birth she'd been weak that way. Often she'd gone to hospital, only to come home drawn and thinner - which she didn't mind 'cause she was always grumbling about being overweight - ''They *schlepped* you out with the forceps and nearly ruined me at

5

the same time.'' Whenever she told this I felt guilty like I should have entered the world with a great eagerness, sparing her such pain and everlasting trouble. So soon on I learned about 'rings' and 'flooding' and other horrific 'women's' problems.

"Do all ladies have that?"

"Most," she answered, "but not as bad as me."

So every day before going off to my new school, I'd fetch in two big pails of water and every day after school fill them up again. Worst job was emptying the chamber-pots into an enamel bucket to tip down the outside lavatory each morning. When we had two big Irish navvies lodging with us later, I hated emptying theirs - always brim full, them being heavy-drinking men - I dreaded spilling the bucket all down the stairs. One job I liked - polishing the barley-twist *shabbes* candlesticks, now standing, proud evacuees, on the parlour mantlepiece - one was bent half-way down from that time dad'd smashed it on the sideboard. That was the worst row ever with dad's hands on mum's throat and the landlady and mum's boy-friend pulling him off - then mum's brothers chasing round, giving dad a black eye. I was taken to mum's eldest sister out the way and afterwards dad told the police, so grandfather paid dad a lump sum of money to stop him getting my uncles prosecuted. Grandfather despised dad after that.

The candlesticks were all we'd got from home - our two rooms and kitchenette near the top of the buildings - the Germans wouldn't get it I was sure even though in my nightmares the bricks and stones would be blown about like in the fairy story, "I'll huff and I'll puff and I'll blow your house down!" and the neighbours would be tossed through the spaces where the windows were, on over the roof-tops and little humpty-backed Mrs. Goldstein would be crouching under the table in her basement flat and Mrs. Connolly in the next block would be covering her youngest, Jimmy, with the big bosom we all used to laugh at. Mum said nightmares were a way of getting bad day-time thoughts out of you and the buildings would probably survive another seventy-odd years. "Besides, your father's got to have somewhere to scuttle to when he surfaces from the shelter.''

I thought of how dad laughed when he told of his tricks for getting through the First War, like when he used the brushes for grooming the horses on his own body, hard, after rubbing them in the filthy mud. "Wouldn't catch me shooting my foot off like some poor buggers did - Medical Officer said he'd never seen a rash like it - still, got me sent behind lines for a spell it did - away from those bloody trenches" -

Fay'd got a job learning to machine uniform jackets so mum was able to borrow from her - "I'd work too, but for my inside," mum told her. Sometimes her and Sylvie would come round for a big talk while Mr. Parmer was out the way at his evening shift - what a talk it was - the best bits were in Yiddish which I knew lots of 'cause grandma was always speaking it - my 'facts of life' was got that way and soon on I learned that dad was "useless" in bed but that Fay's Sid was "fantastic" -

"I was a silly cow - ruined my life," mum would say after Fay'd gone. Her and Sid loving each other so much, made it worse for mum. "You know, your father never once looked in my eyes and said, 'You're pretty'. That means a lot to a woman, a little thing like that." Then out would come the romances - the Ethel M. Dell and Netta Muskett and she'd flip the pages, sigh and say, "Why couldn't I have met a man like that?"

It was grandpa was the trouble, him and mum were like petrol and a spark to each other - "Bloody hypocrite - chasing after the *shikses* while mother was having seven children and God knows how many miscarriages in-between - and I'd tell him - to his face!" Mum always came out with what she thought. "All the time in trouble wasn't I? Anything wrong, it was my fault - So, I meets your father - actor that he was, soon as I took him home, that was it - your grandfather said he'd be a good, no, a stable influence, him being older - him - stable! I should never have been talked into it - should have done what *I* wanted!" I wish she had - done what she wanted - no wonder on her wedding day the *boobahs* in the synagogue said what a shame for mum with her pretty, bright manner to be marrying a 'widower' so much older - Mum's eyes would lose their lemonade sparkle whenever she told this -

Same as mum I could mimic and make anyone laugh. Sylvie was in the third year at school, being thirteen, so I made another friend in class, Mary. She giggled at me from the first day - they all did, seemed these country kids liked my Jewish-cockney humour. Soon we'd confided many secrets though she told me more - that's 'cause mum always warned about telling people our business. She'd hated everyone hearing their rows wherever we'd lived - "Thank God, here, for once, I can walk out with my head up."

I was dying to get into an "A" class - I was entitled anyway - hadn't I passed the exams for High School till the war came, stopping me - ? Now I was stuck in 2B and it seemed to me I must show the others what I was made of 'cause even though I was the class comic, sometimes they stared so's I'd feel like a clear piece of glass and once one said, "How long since your tribe left Palestine?" I was definitely going to giggle less.

Mum was reading a letter from dad. "About time." She drew a Postal Order from the envelope. "Is he O.K.?" She handed me the page of familiar short, straight strokes. It hadn't been easy finding work - lots of places flattened - no power or water - 'I've had to do Fire-watching - up all night sometimes but got a job at last machining army overcoats. Go down the Tube when I can but there's plenty arguments if you've got no ticket and people think you're queue-jumping . . .'

"See where he's made himself a folding mattress for sleeping down the shelter?" She laughed, folding the Postal Order in her brown purse. "I can pay Fay back at last."

That evening, as usual after dinner, Mr. Parmer went round his sister's. "Wish I had my piano." Mum's book rested unopened beside her.

"You can sing without it."

"Not the same," she answered, dully.

Grandfather had given it her - she was the only one of the family who could make it come alive so's its rich walnut glowed as she played. Often, in the courtyard my friends would pause as her lovely voice, sad or romantic, sounded over us. "That's your mum." Then we'd eagerly chase each other again and the longing in her voice would go on, unnoticed.

Another letter came from dad. "We might have your father coming to stay." She crunched the pages. "Tells me to ask Mr. Parmer."

"Is it 'cause of the bombs?"

She waited before answering, then threw the letter on the fire. "I s'pose I can see what he says."

Mr. Parmer was terrified. Even the extra rent mum dangled

8

didn't make him easier. He trod about the house like the floor was hot under him. When he got in, he'd go down the 'barn', then upstairs, and into the parlour, seeking dad the 'intruder' -

One foggy afternoon soon as I got in I could smell pipe tobacco. Father was in the kitchen. It was the direct hit on Balham Tube had made him rush away. "Pleased to see me?"

"'Course!" I answered, not looking at mum.

CHAPTER TWO

October - January 1941

The old quarrels soon flared, though at first father was careful when Mr. Parmer was about. By now we had the front bedroom. Mother kept me in Mr. Parmer's big bed with her and same as in London dad had a single bed, spending most of the mornings and a lot of the afternoons there. He said he'd "a lot of catching up to do after all the lost nights with the raids and Fire-watching." When mum mentioned work he told her he wasn't "in any hurry to sweat my *kishkas* out again" -

As long as I could think back there were times when he'd hide away in bed, like he needed to get away from everyone and everything - like he was fed up with it all and couldn't see no way out. "It's a rotten world," he'd say, "the capitalist system eats away at you." I was always a bit unsure what the capitalist system really meant but I felt father must be right if the idea of it had such an effect on him.

Mum said he ought to be contributing something to the war effort, but he quick saw through that telling her he'd done as much as any human being could and had she forgotten his 1914 lot with the shell-shock and trench-foot and on he went till I wished she'd never opened her mouth. Poor mum, worried as always about being short of money.

I'd just got in from school. Father was shaving, mum talking - "It's a disgrace I still borrow from Fay. Why can't you get a job? Go to the Employment Exchange, they'll fix you up with something

. . . anything!''

He threw the razor into the bowl of water. "You think 'cause there's a war on the bosses don't exploit you! Fay . . . Fay . . . cheap labour she is, that's what! They can go to hell! I won't be exploited, war or no bloody war!''

It sounded right to me and fair, but watching mum I could see she didn't think so. "You got no pride. How can you walk about with nothing in your pocket?''

He opened the back door and slung the dirty water onto the garden. She couldn't stand that. "Plenty have to," was all he answered. I remembered the times I'd seen him dig in his trouser pocket for a couple of coppers to give a 'down and out' we were passing. "If all the 'God Bless you guv'nor' I've had come true I'll live to hundred and ninety at least," he'd say afterwards.

Mary asked me why he wasn't in the forces. Her father was a sergeant in the R.A.S.C. - she was always saying about it.

"He was in the First War - and he's been Fire-watching in the Blitz!''

"Not much good watchin' 'em - should have tried puttin' 'em out!''

Dad called her a 'yokel' when I told him and suddenly mum was agreeing with him. For all she seemed to like it in the country, mum wasn't yet really at ease with the locals, except for Mrs. Lee with the dress-shop down the street who was always calling her "my duck" and "my booty", phrases I'd never heard till we came here - and then there was Mr. Evans, the corner grocer who she'd flirt with to get a bit more on the rations, but he was Welsh so it didn't really count.

After a while though father got ashamed in front of Mr. Parmer who'd come home from the railway tired out and dirty. There dad'd be, newspapers spread, studying the printed words - what was happening in Sidi Barrani? - Was General Wavell the man to put up against the Italian forces? For everything he had a theory and a solution, sitting there, the fire cosy in the grate. Mr. Parmer would walk straight past him, out to the 'barn' for his clean-up in icy water and all the while father's eyes wouldn't budge from the papers. One night he announced, "I've got a job, from the Employment Exchange." We waited. "It's not my trade." Strangely, he'd always taken pride in his skill as a machiner of ladies' coats and costumes. "Well?" mum asked, clearing the newspapers impatiently. "I'll need a bike and it's shift work." Mum started spluttering. "Nights? They got sleeping accommodation there have they?" Father got up, snatched back the papers and walked out, banging the door.

"You shouldn't have," I begun.

"Loves his bed more than he loves me. Night-work - it'll kill him."

Dad was in the parlour, in the dark. "P'raps it won't be too bad." He made no answer. "Dad?" His voice came back thinly. "Better than sitting about."

By the end of the week he'd found a second-hand bike, rusty, with high handlebars. That gave mum another cause for hysterics but even he laughed as he tried to ride off the first night, wheels wobbling, the dimmed lamp throwing a shaky beam on the road at the beginning of his long ride to Startaday cornflakes factory.

Saturday we didn't see him at all. Sunday he appeared, eyes black-ringed and a face looking like it had been white-washed.

"What d'you think of it then dad?"

He started. The whole place should be bombed by the first German plane to get through - it was "medieval" - "a killer" - God only knew how he would stick it - the heat was unbearable - the oven trays heavy enough for a horse to lift, let alone a man - while the "foreman bastard doesn't take his eyes from you" -

A new enemy and a new anger took him over. Instead of the old workshop guv'nors who "deny a man the dignity of labour, with the piece-work system, where you never complete a garment right through," now it was the cornflakes factory. He'd get back, sweating from the cycle home, with yet another 'tale' of the conditions or the foreman who kept him at the ovens -

Mum would listen and nod as though she too despised the foreman and the circumstance which brought dad to it but then she'd spoil it by saying he never was too fond of work and had he been talking unions and stirring up his workmates and finish off with the jab - "At least you're too old for the call-up so count your blessings" -

Blessings dad didn't think he had so he eased his lot by reading yet again the works of Marx and Engels which he kept in a scarred leather case under the bed and mum eased her lot by reading yet again from her pile of love-books.

11

So we went on in this new pattern - the war on - us part of it -
the rationing, the blackout, the shortages, the news on the wireless
with cool voices in even tones telling of big events far away and
not so far. One miserable November morning Mary came late to
school. From her blotchy face I saw she'd been crying. "My
auntie Cecily - my best aunt - she's been . . .", she pressed her face
deep into my navy woollen cardigan, ". . . dead . . . killed in the
raids . . .". I wanted to say something wise and comforting - after
all, I'd seen something of bombing and death. "Wipe your nose,"
was all I could manage.

Already the neighbours were "knowing our business" - dad
would always dig up past history in their fights and soon the spinsters
next door barely nodded when they passed on the path between our
gardens.
"Why didn't we ever live anywhere for long?"
"Ask your father," mum answered. But I knew really - she
moved from place to place out of shame, not that dad and her were
the only ones who fought and cursed - it was just that their curses
were so much stronger - more imaginative than anybody else's.
He'd scream - "May your hands shrivel and drop off before you
touch another note on the piano!" And she'd throw back, "You
should stay paralysed in the bed next time you bury yourself under
the *parana*!" But now she wouldn't be able to move anywhere
and that meant I'd be at this school till the war was over and how
long would that be - ? So this'd be my last chance to prove myself
- even if I couldn't go on to High School - "Mummee! Mummee!"
I'd run home after school, calling up from the courtyard. The high-
up window opened. "I've passed! I've got through the examination!"
Curious heads had looked down from black-railed balconies to see
this clever child. "Are you telling the truth?" - How could she
think I'd make that up? -
Dad had been proud. "If *I'd* had a decent education I'd have
gone into politics - an M.P. even." Within a few weeks the war
was on and no-one thought of education or changing things in
parliament.
I liked Saturdays 'cause that's when Fay and Sylvie'd call - Mr.
Parmer would be round his sister's and dad'd still be sleeping and
us four would get on with chatting and laughing and in-between

12

eating mum's bread-pudding fresh made. "Where'd you get the dried fruit?" Fay would ask and mum, with a wink and tilt of her head would indicate the corner shop. Most times Fay would go on about how much she missed Sid and mum would complain about dad - then Fay would sigh, unable to make sense of a Fate which took her husband away and left dad here. P'raps she ought to have married someone lots older instead of younger like she did, then he'd have still been here like dad was with us. Though she was always going on about loving her Sid, Fay wasn't a bit like I imagined a real 'heroine' was - nothing like those in mum's books or in the films - Mum loved films - so did I - as long as I could remember she'd taken me, even when I was nearly due to be born she'd sat with me in her belly watching Al Jolson in "The Jazz Singer". In London we'd go three times a week after school - she carrying a brown, paper carrier bag with our 'tea' in it and this we'd devour in the magic darkness of the Odeon or Rivoli - wherever there was a good 'love' film on.

"Here!" she'd say, poking a rye-bread with cream-cheese sandwich at me and while I chewed she'd cry wonderful big tears and if the film was really moving, sob so loud the usherette would come to our row, flash her light and tell mum "sshhh!" Between the first and main picture if she'd enough money left we'd have half each of a choc-ice. It was always worse for her when we got back from these 'outings' - like she'd left her real self behind, there on the screen with the 'hero' - and the shadow of herself which she'd dragged home would wander from bed-room to living-room, restless, till she finished up playing the piano, singing "Lover Come Back to Me" or "Sweetheart", all of them without the written-down music but which sounded wonderful to me and anyone listening on soft summer nights - I knew dad did love her for didn't he always say, after the worst of their rows - cry and say we both were the whole world to him, but if only he'd be a bit like the heroes in the pictures and tell her soft, loving things sometimes, she'd have been so much more happy - so would he p'raps -

One Saturday Fay called alone. But she and mum didn't laugh, instead mum listened while Fay told in a soulful voice like he was already in his coffin, "My Sid's been posted abroad." She held out her arms. "God only knows if I'll ever lay eyes on him again."

"'Course you will Fay, isn't he charmed? Who else could have lived through what happened with the house?" Fay nodded, wanting to believe it - that Sid was immortal - "He was here, yesterday, wasn't s'posed to be - give him a twenty-four hour pass they did and he wasn't to travel more than twenty-five miles from Worcester. Him and some of the others said "balls" to that and come home anyway." Mum called his C.O. a "cold-blooded bastard". She sounded just like dad.

Mr. Parmer was speaking less and less. He'd get in, wash, eat his meal fast, eyes darting constantly to the door, only to be finished before dad got back or came down from his rest. There was a delicate time just before supper - dad would be brooding about the night-time 'ordeal' before him while Mr. Parmer would sit in the rocking-chair, feet flat and tight on the linoleum, his heavy-knuckled hands gripping the smooth, black arms. Then father would pick on something. Why wasn't the kettle boiling for his shave? Why hadn't mum called him in time for the six o'clock news? She had, she'd snap back. Me and Mr. Parmer would wait - it was the usual game - whose move next? -

Other times dad'd try and get Mr. Parmer in a conversation about the war or politics in general but he would just dab at his watery eyes with the spotted handkerchief, unable to say what, if any, opinion he had. Father would later tell me he was "a typical type - the downfall of the working classes." Poor Mr. Parmer - I felt sorry for him.

One evening Mr. Parmer was waiting silently, as usual, for the meal. Mum had just given dad his packed lunch. He opened it, examined it, then instantly threw the sandwiches on the fire. "That's what I'm supposed to work on! You should try . . . for one night . . . you wouldn't last two seconds!"

"Lunatic! That's half our quarter-pound ration gone!"

"Go wave your eyelashes at Mr. Evans - you always get what you want out of him!"

The cheese melting over the hot bars of the grate and the bread violently, unexpectedly toasting, made me hungrier than ever. "It's the work he's doing," I told mum when the place was quiet again.

"He'll never stick it, you'll see, by Christmas he'll have left there."

But by Christmas Mr. Parmer had moved out. He brought a small lorry and while the snow fast covered its canvas top collected the few bits of furniture his sister wanted and was gone.

It was the first house we'd ever had to ourselves. Now I knew how a feudal land-owner felt or a princess - a Czarina even! No matter we were still tenants, we had it all to ourselves! Now I sat in the rocking-chair as much as I wanted - he'd left that - together with some delicate pieces of china and blue and white willow-pattern plates with birds in pairs and lovers running over small bridges. Mum liked two yellow vases with bold painted-on flowers and twining leaves done in gold paint. Funny he'd left them - p'raps men didn't care so much about things like women did. In his old room on the dressing-table he'd also left a black lacquered glove box which mum said was his mother's - it seemed cold-blooded somehow, him leaving that - mum said I could have it for my pencils - don't s'pose his mum would have minded.

"I'll organise the removers then, to fetch our bits from the old flat." There was an uncertain tone in dad's voice.

"S'pose so," mum answered, not all that certain either.

The first Saturday of the New Year he went to London. "Will I have the back bedroom now?" I'd been watching mum like a cat trying to catch a bird. She started, much the way a bird does too. "No. I'm surprised you asked." She was up and busy. "There's plenty needs doing before he gets back."

"I'll still be in with you when I'm twenty-one!" She raised her arm and I dodged out quick.

On Monday they were back with the furniture. The snow got everywhere as dad and the removal men unpacked. They trundled it in, leaving big, icy pancakes and me and mum followed after them with floor-cloths. "Where we going to put it all?" mum said like she always had.

"We got *four* rooms now mum!"

"Yeh," she said, a bit unbelieving.

At last it was time for the piano. Now she clucked about them till they swore out the side of their mouths. Then it got stuck as they were turning it from the hall into the parlour. "Seems we'll have to get the front window off and poke her in that way," the foreman said. So they panted and pushed the walnut piano back out into the cold street, mum warning, "Careful, it's very special . . ." then dad told her she was getting on the men's nerves and any second I expected a fight. It all brought back those many other times we'd moved when windows had come off on the fourth or fifth floors - you had to start near the top when you were a new tenant - and how the great tackle of hoists and pulleys had been used in a bold show of daring by other removers. I always waited, listening for a mighty crash if and when the strong ropes binding the piano snapped - snapped and let the magnificent creature of music tumble to its death in the playground below.

Finally it was settled in. Mum first put milk in a saucer and set to cleaning the ivory keys, then while dad and the men were still struggling in and out, she set down to play. 'Cause she was happy she started with the comic songs, puffing out her cheeks to whistle like she always did when the family used to gather at grandma's for birthday or engagement parties. Dan the foreman said she was "a dab hand at tickling the ivories" and dad looked proud. Then they sat down for a "fag and a breather" and clapped when mum finished. It was the best day we'd had since we arrived. The rows between them seemed a long way off.

CHAPTER THREE

March - May 1941

My twelfth birthday was born on a windy March morning. The daffodils were just open when I went to the lavatory first thing. I cut one where the sun had warmed it to show its inside and stuck it in the fancy yellow vase. It smelled lots sweeter than bought flowers.

Ethel left me a card before she went to work - she was our lodger. Mum said we'd never had a whole house to ourselves before and we needed the money so why leave the other bedroom empty - ? Looked like I was in the big bed with her for good now. Wished I knew why dad was so hopeless in bed and what men were s'posed to do - p'raps Sylvie'd know -

"Think she's ever had a man?" Fay asked mum once. "A man?

Ethel? Have you looked at her properly?'' The way you looked -
if you were fair or dark, fat or slim, was very important to mum - to
all the family. Her eldest sister was always envied by the other
girls 'cause she was blonde, naturally, and slim and tall - ''real
shikse-looking'' they'd add. Being tall was very important. If they
threw an insult at anyone it would usually have ''bloody short-
arse'' stuck in somewhere. Mum was short unfortunately, but
pretty with a small nose and thick, chestnut hair which was drawn
behind her ears and arranged in a careful row of double curls at the
back. A fringe swept her forehead like the sirens in the silent films
but it was her eyes you couldn't ignore - large, green, they could
change their expression at her instant will. Every morning she'd
take at least quarter of an hour doing her face, most of it spent on
her eyes. There'd be much spitting and rubbing of a small brush
across the mascara block, her jaw drawn down and her mouth
parted in a funny ''O'' while she tilted her head to get at every
lash. Then a combing to separate them with a fine tooth-comb, one
that's used for cleaning your head of lice - then another layer and
more combing-out. She liked her Evening in Paris scent and often
a drop would be tipped on her little finger and dabbed behind each
ear-lobe. Then, at the end she'd tie a ribbon round her hair, fixing
it at the side like the finishing touch on a glossy box of chocolates.

"It was your eyes I fell for'' dad had told her and once, in a
devilish mood, she'd thrown at him, ''I wish I'd looked like this!''
crossing her eyes so's he had to laugh. It seemed she could goad
him to anything - laughter or fury.

Ethel was a spinster of at least forty-five. She dressed very old-
fashioned, with skirts well down her legs with deep hems too like
she was still expecting to grow. She always wore a home-knitted
cardigan, whatever the weather. Her hair was greasy-dark and
Spanish-straight, her eyes also dark though not dull like dad's when
he got in in the mornings. Her job was making boots for soldiers
and airmen and her hands were usually stained and finger-nails
broken. Even though she had the back bedroom I liked her living
with us 'cause she was always laughing. ''God knows what she's
got to laugh at,'' mum said.

Dad didn't go straight to bed on my birthday. ''I've got a
surprise,'' he told me, eagerly, like it was his birthday. ''Shut your
eyes!'' He went upstairs and I heard the case being dragged from

17

under the bed. Great! He'd taken the hints I'd thrown about wanting a dictionary - Miss Gearfield had said I needed one and I badly wanted to come top in my best subject - English - "Open!" In my hands was a large, soft parcel, definitely not a book.

"Here, let me!" He shook free from the folded paper a coat, of light green Harris tweed. My unwilling arms were pushed into it and I was turned and examined while he went over all with his craftsman's eye. "Look, the buttonholes - hand-done. Now, open it so I see if the lining hangs right." Satisfied on that he inspected the finishing on the inside seams. "Taped. Proper. Now, put your arms down straight." I did. "Good. Now with elbows bent." Another check-over. "Perfect. You look like the daughter of a bloody capitalist!" He went upstairs, happy. I went to school. Why didn't he get me a dictionary - him with all his books - he should have understood.

There was a great baking smell in the house when I got back. "My surprise, with the help of Mr. Evans and a friend of Mrs. Lee's who keeps hens." Mum lifted from the oven a small, round cake. Sylvie came round and after tea it was time for the piano. Me and Sylvie begged mum to do our favourite, the "Good-morning, Fraulein Poopah" song. She did it with a German accent and 'cause Yiddish was so like it, made up all sorts of Yiddish-German sounding words, some really rude but as I was now twelve she left all the rude bits in. Me and Sylvie danced a polka to it round the parlour and I felt happy and free. Then I had to do my Shirley Temple impersonation which they never tired of - I could see myself tap-dancing my way through "The Good Ship Lollypop" till I was Ethel's age! "She's like me," mum would always brag to relatives or neighbours, and they would nod, telling each other, "The daughter's an actress and a singer, like the mother - a *mitzvah* it is, something to Thank God for."

"Wish I could do something," Sylvie said. I wished she could too - that would have made up a bit for her facial disfigurement with the right eye-lid permanently half-closed and the right side of her mouth the same. "It's like the poor thing had a stroke," mum would say in an awesome way when Sylvie wasn't there. If only I'd some power like God's s'posed to have I'd have made her lovely and tall as well the way *shikses* are.

Her only ambition was to have a boy-friend and get married.

"Don't you?" she asked. I wasn't sure how I did feel about boys - in that way - in London there'd been plenty, sometimes they'd chased us girls, screaming, all round the courtyard, and when they caught you, kiss you hard and quick and depending on who they were, you'd kiss them back or kick their shins. But I was always careful not to be left alone with boys - my cousin Nigel it was who put me off. Once, when I was staying at my aunt's when mum was in hospital, he'd crept into my room very early in the morning. He was fourteen then and I'd never liked him 'cause he knew I was scared of dogs and he got their terriers to chase me. This time he slid into my bed and began 'examining' me - it hurt - I wanted to tell out but he warned if I did he'd set the dogs on me. I told Sylvie to stop thinking about boys.

Dad came down and announced he wasn't going to work. "It's her birthday, not yours," mum said sharply. "What about us all going to the pictures?" he offered. Mum tried to keep her voice steady. "What about your job?" Sylvie and me waited. "I've not had a single day off since I went there." He looked straight at me. "You want to, don't you?" I couldn't say no, wasn't I brought up on pictures? So he filled a bowl of water and happily soaped himself like he never did when getting ready for work. Mum just sat looking at the splashes all over the table.

It was strange having dad there in the dark beside me as well as mum - he hardly ever came out with us - she always complained about it. "Everyone thinks I'm a widow, always have - Saturdays, Sundays the family go out together - 'Where's your man?' people would ask. What could I say - tell them he's under the parana?"

It was a Charles Boyer film and soon dad was snoring. Then mum complained when he did take us out he couldn't stay awake.

"D'you enjoy yourself?" he asked later. "We'll do it again eh?" But I knew it'd be a long, long time before the three of us went out together.

After that film Miss Gearfield caught me entertaining the class with a convincing impersonation of the screen lover. "I adorrrre you, my beautiful, desirrrable one . . ." They loved it - it was better than experiments we were doing with Bunsen burners. Then there was the time an air-raid warning sounded - the girls were really scared - not used to them as I was - so while we all took cover in the playground's brick shelter I sang them "Bless 'em

All" same as I used to in the brewery. Afterwards dad said it was good I'd showed them "what we're made of."

One day I saw the same small bus that had driven us round and round the town when we'd first come. I knew just how they were feeling, these new evacuees - Germany was throwing everything at us in this spring of 1941. "Got our bits and pieces out just in time," dad observed one evening after the news. "Take this up to Ethel," mum said, handing me a cup of tea. We'd just heard that Ethel's only brother had been killed in one of the raids on Clydeside. She was sitting on the bed holding a framed photograph. "Family always said we looked alike. D'you reckon we do?" I held the photograph, it's frame had a chip off one corner. Why should a strange man in an aeroplane from far off want to drop bombs on people like Ethel's brother and Mary's aunty Cecily? It was the only time I saw Ethel cry all the while she lived with us. Dad said the bombing would get rid of the old tenement buildings in the Clydebank. "It's what they'll do after that matters - give 'em a decent place to live - for the first time."

Mary said the Germans were ready to invade us. One of the girls listening was so scared she was sick in Assembly. "We'd be first, wouldn't we?" I was scared too and mum saw but she didn't answer. That night I prayed. First I asked God to forgive the Jews for not having Jesus for their King. I hadn't considered that much before but now was hearing lots about it in scripture class - not that I really agreed with the idea but if God thought I did he might stop the Germans killing all the Jews off -

"Did you ever believe in God?" I asked dad.

He thought a bit. "It came and went."

"How d'you mean?"

"When I was in the dug-outs with shells whizzing about me I believed and prayed like bloody hell. When the war was done and I was quiet in my bed, I thought all this God lark's another invention of the capitalist class to keep you humble and in your place."

"What you telling her all that for?" mum put in. Not that she was a believer either but soon as he got on about capitalists or politics she'd be compelled to shut him up. Pity she couldn't have been more like Rosa Luxemberg, the Polish communist who was dad's 'heroine'.

Dad said as well that if the Germans were going to invade us "they'd have done it in 1940." I was sure he was right. I didn't tell him Mary had also said how Russia had been our enemy and had made a pact with the Germans. Mum and him had already had a row about that with him telling her it was "playing for time to consolidate their frontiers". I tried hard to understand all he said but it was like he'd swallowed it straight from one of his suitcase books. It seemed awful, him knowing so much yet being stuck in that factory. If only he'd had his education he might have been anything - even now, in the war - a Minister of something - even a spy! He'd have been good at that - what with his cunning and his way of surviving like in the First War. One thing for sure, when I'd read all the books I wanted and got the world sorted out in my mind, I'd never be "exploited" like him - I'd have a position where people listened to me in all my wisdom and I'd be so happy I'd never have to hide away in bed.

"Can Mary come round after school to knit?" I asked mum.

"I'm not so keen on that girl as your friend."

"I like her! We laugh all the time!"

"Much good that'll do you. Look where being a comic got me."

But she gave way - the blankets we were making were for bombed-out families.

"Shall we take our knitting up to your room?" Mary asked. "Yes," mum said before I could stop her.

Mary pointed to the small iron bedstead. "Is that yours?" Then she gawked at the double bed. "My dad's on nights most of the time." Somehow that made it better. Funny thing was, with Sylvie I didn't have to bother to lie.

Ethel gave me two old jumpers "long past darning" to unpick for the blanket squares - poor Ethel, now she had permanent mauvy-brown smudges beneath her eyes. Mum was such a contrast to her, always powdered and attractive even with the constant aggravation and the tears. At week-ends Ethel would try a blob of colour on her face but it would be plonked on making her look like an old-fashioned doll. She was always away before seven in the mornings and at night would disappear after dinner to rub wintergreen oil on her back which was "always giving me 'gip'" - her way of saying it hurt. She told me she'd left Lancashire as "nowt but a bit of a lass and knowing nowt either". Me and Sylvie made up stories

21

about her. "I think she was a poor mill-girl who fell in love with the son of the mill-owner but knowing she couldn't marry him, left home." Sylvie sighed. "You sound just like your mum." P'raps Ethel really had a cousin like Nigel who'd put her off men for ever. Maybe I'd stay put off and a spinster as well.

"You'll never guess what I've been put to doing," she started, one evening when we were on our own.

"What?"

"You'll not let on to anyone?" I shook my head. "Fetch pencil and paper then." I brought my posh glove-cum-pencil box and school rough-book. She began to draw, not very well, an airman's flying boot. "See the heel? It's hollow inside and know what goes in it?" I waited. "A tiny map, rolled up so small and a compass goes in as well and bottom of heel is put back on, all neat and then if they're shot down over enemy country they cut boot down like a shoe and they can get about - stand a chance then don't they?" She looked proud as though she'd thought up the whole thing. Maybe it made it right for Ethel, helping like that, on account of her brother.

Father was moaning again. "That bastard foreman's a lackey, caught me talking union - now he's really got his knife in me."

"I knew this would happen." Mum was like ice.

"What sympathy do you ever give? Want me to lick his boots? Anything for a quiet life? I won't bow before any man!" Out he went.

"He's always tired . . . why can't you . . ."

Her look stopped me. "You should understand - huh! What d'you know - what it's like, borrowing from my sister to pay rent -" She snatched a hankie from her pocket and dabbed droplets of sweat on her upper lip. "I remember one *Pesach*, he hadn't been in work for weeks - I was ashamed, to go to mother's - they'd all be there - the family, children in new clothes. I got work, peeling onions for pickling . . . they brought it to me, sack after sack, up the stairs - we lived on the top then, remember, Brady Street? Know what it's like peeling raw onions - your eyes - the tears - smell all over the place - ?" She paused. "D'you know what worried me most? How to get rid of all those onion peelings."

I remembered - and I could smell the onions, strong, and see mother pushing the fine orange-gold peelings into the small lift-up

22

flap on the wall in the poky kitchenette, pushing them tightly in so's they'd fall down, down the dark, smelly tunnel to the waste-bins in the basement and hope that the caretaker wouldn't know where they'd come from. I remembered too her eyes without the lemonade sparkle, red-rimmed from those onion tears.

By early summer the worst of the raids were over. We hadn't been invaded. I wanted to dance Mary around the narrow streets - just to show her - lift her around the waist and swing her out, the way the umbrella merry-go-round did in the park round the corner - swing her and yell, "The Germans didn't come!" Now I could think about my *thirteenth* birthday.

Dad said he was going to apply for work in London. "They'll release me - much more of this and I'll be in my grave."

"Where'll you stay?" I asked.

"My sister's."

Mum said why couldn't he try for a different job here. I asked him like she said to. "You don't want me to go then?" I shook my head.

He stopped talking about it for a bit. Mum seemed easier. P'raps underneath she really did have some feeling for him. It'd be nice to think she did.

CHAPTER FOUR

May - June 1941

Dad discovered the Working Mens' Club. He got up from bed brightly this Saturday announcing, "Get dressed up both of you, we're going out tonight!"

Mum made an expression as if to say "he's had a brainstorm", put down the collar she was mending - a white organdie that had gone from dress to dress - and asked, half-believingly, "Where?"

In his flowery way when he was on to something, he told of "one of my mates at work - all for unions he is, same as me, well, he's a member see and he's invited us!" Till then we'd heard

23

nothing of this "mate" and mum was just about to give one of her sarcastic comments when she caught my pleading look. "Why don't you go along to Mrs. Lee and treat yourself to a new frock," he said, eyeing the collar too. He lay a pound note and four half-crowns on the table. Mum's mouth tipped very slightly at one side. "I'll see what thirty bob'll get me then."

Mrs. Lee and mum got on well with each other. She knew just what suited mum too. "I've this nice little lock-knit two-piece." She held it up lovingly for mum's approval. She touched it. I did too - it was soft like a baby. "No, not blue." Mrs. Lee tried again, with a green crêpe, beading trimming the neckline and cuffs. "It's a booty of a frock and lovely with those eyes of yours my duck." This, mum fell for, refusing Mrs. Lee's offer to alter it "just that bit easier round the hips dear, ready first thing Monday."

Soon as we got back she started, unpicking the side seams from the waist down, pinning them together, anxious looks in the long wardrobe mirror, then stitching the seams back again, her hands fast and nimble - finally the frock was ironed with damp cloths, banging the steam back in with the back of a clothes-brush, an old trick remembered from grandpa's workshop. "Well?" She stood before dad and me, the dress lay on her body, flattering and womanly. Dad took her all in, a smile just curving his lips.

Then he set to, polishing our shoes, telling again as he brushed vigorously of when he'd done his army boots with dubbin but all the dubbin in the world wouldn't have kept the wet out in the Flander's mud. That done, he put on his best navy suit and a shirt with a stiff white collar which made him look just like a doctor or a headmaster.

The three of us made an elegant entry into the crowded club. "This is more like it," mum announced as we seated ourselves beside dad's mate and his fresh-faced wife - she looking like she'd have been easier in a farmhouse kitchen. Everywhere smelled beery-stale and smoky. "Just as well mother's not alive to see me . . ." mum went on. Drinking and pubs were a *goyishe* practice which a self-respecting Jew and his family - orthodox or not - did not take part in. "A small port then," mum said awkwardly to dad's mate who was 'eyeing' her up and down - Dad and the wife noticed as well. The 'turns' hadn't started and I wondered what they were feeling, waiting behind the heavy, plush curtains, now closed on the small stage. The Chairman, sitting at a table just in front, thumped a large shining bell, "Order! Order!" he called as though he was a sergeant-major. People went on chattering. "ORDER!" he bellowed, now on the barrack square and several "sshhs" went about the place.

The audience were generous with the acts which I didn't think much of - neither did mum. "You knock spots off her!" she whispered, as a girl my age did a song and dance routine. "She can't tap . . ." her voice was louder, ". . . look at her arms, hanging like a puppet!" Dad's mate's wife nudged her husband. I could see she was sorry we'd come.

By the end of the night mum had decided - I was to be a turn at the club. I was terrified. Showing off for friends and relatives was one thing - even singing in the shelter had been more out of fear than confidence but performing on a proper stage, with lights and everyone quiet, waiting for just your voice -

"I haven't got a costume," I protested, knowing as I said it she'd manufacture something. Her mind was decided - her child was to be a 'star'.

Now she was filled with vitality. No more complaints about her 'inside', she didn't grumble about dad's lack of affection - her green eyes were bright and sharp as limes. All was arranged with the club - I would have a 'try-out' and if satisfactory be given regular bookings.

"Can't you get me out of it?" I pleaded with dad. "I thought you were gutsy, like me." He was after fame for me too. So, a piece of fine black-out material was cut on the cross and magicked into a short, full skirt and with it a red and black spotted blouse made with dad's help from one of mum's old dresses. For once, they were working as a team and I didn't like it. She found a pair of second-hand tap shoes and after school instead of going round Sylvie's or out with Mary on those early June evenings, I was rehearsed, prompted and bullied to "Give it more go!" and "Smile!" and "Keep to the rhythm!" The impersonations were done over - W.C.Fields - "My little chickadee, my little prairie flower" - until she was satisfied I'd got just the right nasal intonation. Then Mae West, spitting the words, "C'mon up and see me sometime" out the side of my mouth. "Swing your hips!" And she'd strut around, swaying her own. The dance routine would be gone through, till the sweat was running down me like dad when he got in from his cycle ride.

It was the BIG NIGHT - Fay came, all glamorous, reddish-gold hair done up in three sweeps. Sylvie smiled at me best as she could and mum and dad were like two cats walking the edge of a high wall. I was on following an aged magician. The applause was like desert rain. "P'raps they won't like me either," I told mum as we watched from the wings.

The Chairman clanged the bell. "Order! Order! Ladees and Gentlemennn! For your entertainment, a special young lady, making her DEBUT!" The pianist started my music, too loud. "Go on," mum said. Again the bell, louder than any fire-engine in the raids. I was paralysed. Mother pushed me forward. I pulled at my too-short skirt, tapping my way on.

Somehow I got through. I sang loud and clear, smiled at the first rows of smudgy faces through the lights, mimicked and gratefully took in their laughter, mimicked again till they were at my mercy and after what seemed like hours heard the clapping of an audience well satisfied.

Mum grabbed me, plonking a smacker of a kiss on me. Dad was mopping his head. Fay and Sylvie were in a mish-mash of excitement - Words like *nuchas* and a *mitzvah* spun about the small dressing-room walls while I gulped glass after glass of warm lemonade. Finally, the lady ventriloquist and three singers who modelled themselves on the Andrew Sisters asked up please to GO as they also had performances to give!

How they talked that night. "She'll need a business manager - I can handle that," he was saying. "I'll have to find fresh material, she can't keep doing the same stuff," she told him. Rarely had they been so united.

I fell into bed, feet tingling, my mind darting every way. Downstairs, on they talked, on into the night, sometimes arguing and shouting so that I was disturbed in my dreaming of the family gatherings at grandma's when I would be at the middle of things with my entertainments. And their words rose up with hope, rose up and brushed over me, alone in the big bed, words of the future, plans for us, a family not to be ignored, a family of importance in a world tumbling down. I slept and dreamed and woke and still they'd not come up. It was very quiet - p'raps they might be

26

kissing and cuddling - it'd be nice to think they were.

Mother had a purpose. She sparkled - all because of her talented child. Gone were the moping days, the gorges on bread-pudding. When dad went off to "get the country fed" she'd warn him, "Careful how you go". All because of the daughter who would achieve such fame - who would realise such ability, passed on, passed on through the blood of the mother -

"She'll have her chance," she told Fay, "not like me." And Fay's hazel eyes would go liquidy with sympathy as mother went over the lost opportunity to study singing in Italy because of grandfather. "A chance in a million and he stopped it." So the tale of a visiting relative, hearing her sing, who had in turn taken her to a distinguished Italian teacher, was told again - with sighs and with indignation. "He wanted to train me in voice production, breath control, languages - can you imagine - all for a pittance, so impressed was he -" And Fay's head, as always, shook disbelievingly from side to side at mother's lost world of riches and fulfilment. "And him - that *shikse*-chaser, he stopped it. Why? Because he said Signor Visconti, that jewel of a man, was a white-slave trafficker!" I wished I knew what that meant and why mum got so upset when she said it.

Sylvie also was thrilled by my venture. "Aren't you scared?"

"If only you knew . . ."

"I think you're s'posed to be, all actresses are."

"I'm not an actress! Besides, what do you know about it?" She turned abruptly. "Sorry. Sylvie . . . what'll I do?"

"Do?"

"If I tell, will you swear on your grandma's grave on your father's side not to let it out?" She nodded. "I don't want to go on the stage."

"You don't?"

"It's more than just stage-fright - every time I think about it I feel sick down to my feet!"

She put her arm round me. "Your mother . . .?"

For days I thought about it - how to wriggle free of the whole business. It was my own fault, showing off - never would I fall into that trap again! Even if bombs came and fell all about me I'd sit with my mouth clenched and let someone else keep their spirits all up!

Another outfit was produced - a dress, shorter still, of bright, cyclamen pink with an oversized floppy bow finishing the neckline. "Well?" Mum waited for praise for her efforts. "It's . . . nice," I gulped. It was all so unfair - why should this be the reason for mum being happy again? Why couldn't she and dad be like other parents? I bet Mary's mother and father didn't carry on like this - and Fay and Sid - they didn't expect Sylvie to be anything but Sylvie, with her twisted eye and mouth. Why couldn't I be the same as them - just ordinary?

The house smelled all over wintergreen oil. Ethel wasn't just rubbing it on her back but her chest and sprinkled on her large hanky so that even night-time it crept through the crack at the bottom of the bedroom door till you forgot it was summer and a time of nice-smelling things and thought it was sudden winter with smells of fog and sooty chimneys and leather shoes drying off by the fire. Ethel had a cold. Her whole body went about with a droop to it. "Hot milk with onion in," dad recommended. He knew all there was to taking care of yourself. Ethel tried, after work - all day Sunday. "It's jusb no good," she croaked, blowing again from her swollen nose.

"Don't hang around her, you'll catch it and with your booking next week-end we can't take any risks." I almost hugged mum - unknown she'd saved me - innocently, she'd set the idea into my quick, wicked mind. From then on I was a nurse, a ministering angel to Ethel - all behind mum's back.

"You off to your reading again?" she complained. "What about going through your new routine?" But it'd be out the room and up the stairs, book under my arm, to the quiet of the front bedroom and soon as it was safe to do so, creep into Ethel's.

Never did an invalid have such attention - I smoothed and tucked about her, leaning close to her mouth - when she sneezed I inhaled the spray of germs as though they were all the flowers of the garden in bloom. Yes, Ethel would be my Saviour, just like they were always going on about in school assembly. Suddenly I knew why a Saviour was such an important thing.

"Oh no!" mother cried as I sneezed for the fifth time in a minute. "I warned you. Didn't I say be careful?" Gradually I was turning into a shivering, sniffling mess - happier than I'd been in weeks! Best of all my voice was a croaking whisper - but mum

could be determined. "I'll get you right if it's the last thing I do."
I was put to bed with water-bottles and extra blankets and then the
cures really got going. As there were no lemons I was denied one
of my better-liked pre-war cures - juice of lemon in honey and hot
water - now it was swallowing vile-tasting balsam. Then while
Ethel was being cursed to hell I was smothered in the borrowed
wintergreen till the bedroom smelled like Ethel herself was stamped
into the four walls. "Don't stick your head out the covers. I'll be
up every half-hour!"

I lay there, a happy prisoner, planning my future life - doing
nothing but studying so's I'd get successful through my head, not
my stupid, tapping feet! I'd show mum - she and dad would be
proud - just as if I was Shirley Temple herself!

"This'll fix you." It was the cure I loathed most - Russian
tallow, an old remedy brought from there by my grandmother when
they'd fled the country at the beginning of the century. A white
candle-like substance, it was melted, poured onto brown paper then
placed immediately onto your back, chest or throat. She stood over
me, steaming paper glistening with the runny tallow. "Lift your
nightie up to your chin." I couldn't even yell without a voice.
After work dad came up.

"How's the sick girl then?" I clutched at him. "Please! Tell
mum to stop using grandma's cure!" What was I hearing? My
voice - it was back.

"It's worked anyway. Good. You'll be O.K. for the week-
end."

"I don't want . . . to . . ." I was crying bitterly.

"What is it?"

I told him - my fears - my determination to do well at school -
"like you always said -" and I begged him to talk mum out of it.

"Pity. You're good at it. Shouldn't throw away a chance." He
sat on the bed, misting over the opportunities he'd let slip - if only
he'd grabbed them when they were there we'd all have had a better
time of it. "Not hard enough, that's my trouble - too much
compassion for my fellow men."

But you're a communist, I thought, you're supposed to care
about them. I didn't say it out though 'cause he was being so nice
and understanding.

"I'll have a go," he said and went off to "work on" mother. I

29

heard her yelling but for once it was only her voice filling the house.

I never went back to the Working Men's Club. Sylvie said I was a fool.

CHAPTER FIVE

July - August 1941

"Didn't know he had so much life in him," mum said resentfully, against the open window, trying to catch what air there was. Dad had gone off again, up early, pannier bags of his bike filled with leaflets, to the market square, there to stand at the British Soviet Society stall, telling anyone who might listen of the mighty Russian nation now at war with the Germans.

"Is your dad a communist?" Mary had asked. "I see him behind this stall with a great red cloth draped over it - my mum seen it too - she told dad and he said it'd be a good thing if the Russians and Germans killed each other off."

"Don't ever let my father hear you saying that!" I'd walked off, leaving her on the swing with no-one to push her. Pity Sylvie was working now - we could have spent the summer holiday together -

"Do you remember Russia?" I asked mum.

"I was a baby when they ran away."

"Why did they run away?"

"Jews are always running away from somewhere."

"Why?"

She opened the door. I stood beside her. There was no breeze.

When I asked dad about communists he just smiled. He didn't smile a lot. He'd laugh, usually when mum said something cheeky but mostly he kept a serious, almost unhappy, searching look to him. Now, as he started to explain, his face went sunny and he blinked fast to help the words out and told of "Man's injustice to man" and "equality of opportunity" and as he spoke he got faster like the wheel on the sewing machine. I concentrated hard, because

30

I wanted to understand but mostly because he was so eager, almost grateful and I thought if this is the way he tells it on the market stall anyone would believe him.

"What you doing?" Mum stood there.

"Talking."

She began cutting at a loaf with strong downward thrusts. "Don't start filling the child's head with all that."

"I'm not a . . ." I started, but my words got buried under a mighty exchange of accusations, denials, events past, torn up, scratched up and flung again with fresh hate. "Stop it!" They quietened at once. I must have screamed it louder than I knew. "You're the children, both of you! There's a war on and people getting killed - the Germans might invade us and all you can do is fight with each other!"

"The Germans won't invade now . . ." father began.

"She's right! What d'you think of, day and night? Politics! We're living on the edge of death and the best you can do is sell pamphlets in the market!"

"You tell me! I sweat my *kishkas* out keeping us fed - keeping the country fed - you -" He was clenched up, the spittle spilling from his mouth. "Why aren't you in a munitions factory eh? That's what you need - get off your arse and do something instead of burying your head in that rubbish you read!"

"How can I?" She was crying now, cutting the slices faster, spreading them with fish-paste as though that was the most important thing in the world. "I'm not strong . . . since the birth . . ."

He grabbed the sandwiches, pushed them in his jacket pocket, unwrapped, and went out, slamming the front door so that the heavy knocker banged twice against the chipped green paint.

She went about, nun-like, closing windows - except they'd already heard - next door - opposite - then she started the piano but there was nothing from her voice.

All dad's talk about inequality got me thinking about how things were before the war - me and my friends never thought of ourselves as "unequal" with anybody. We had enough to eat and our parents never were turned out for not paying the rent though mum said we came "near to it if it wasn't for grandma helping out with a few shillings . . ." - Some families were - mostly gentiles and as we watched from doorways Yiddish whispers went about of "that's

31

what drink brings them to . . ." - But mum was always frightened when dad got thrown out of yet another workshop for "starting revolutions" - even in grandpa's place he told his fellow workers they were being exploited, till grandpa caught him at it and nearly had a fit before throwing him out too. Whenever mum got scared I'd get scared as well and even though mum and dad didn't drink, wonder what it'd feel like, being on the street, our furniture in a wooden wheelbarrow and nowhere for it or us to go.

But we never were so I could just go on playing and daring the others to throw the ball higher and joining in "eenah-deenah, abba-dasha" to see which of us would be first into the turning skipping-rope - to jump in - feet close and tight and when it was my go I'd leap and tell those turning, "Faster! Faster!" P'raps dad didn't play out much as a boy and that's why he had such a worried look about him and was always thinking such serious thoughts -

She'd stopped playing the piano - the terrier across the street was yapping to be let back in. Mum watched it, frowning, through the curtains. "Fancy coming to pictures mum?" That always made her feel better - sitting in the dark three times a week you didn't think of what you didn't have or bugs in the wallpaper that crept back even after the fumigating people came in - sitting in the dark watching Ginger and Fred dance their flickering black and white movements it didn't matter that dad never kissed her - and after, when we got home, I'd put on her dress, the old one with the helter-skelter of fringed beads, from shoulder to hem - in georgette it was, shaded pale green to stormy-sky greyish green - she'd worn it at aunty Sophie's wedding - I didn't care it was torn, when I wore it and did my mouth in a cupid's bow I'd swing and sway before the long wardrobe mirror just like Ginger with her white fox trim around the bottom of her skirt.

"Another time p'raps," was all she answered.

Ethel knew there'd been a row as soon as she got in, same as I always knew - it'd be like the house had been bruised by a heavy wind. We both ate, silently. Mum was all amove, the way she would be for hours following a fight - first upstairs, then into the garden plucking dead heads from the flowers, watering everything even though it'd just rained. In winter she'd rake at the fire till the hot coals were put to rest in the ash-can beneath long before they'd finished their life. Now she was scraping the dirty plates till the sound grated on our ears as much as the anger grating inside her.

"Best get supper things washed," Ethel offered as mum took herself away with a new Ethel M. Dell. "It was a nice meal. Your mum's good at doing things so's you don't know what's in 'em." Then she laughed at what she'd said. I did too.

"Why you always happy?"

She went a dullish pink. "Don't know as I am."

"Is it 'cause you're not married d'you think?"

She laughed again and the front of her dress trembled against her as she did. "Some married ones is happy."

"Rich ones p'raps, like mum's eldest sister - she lives in a posh house and has blue Wedgwood vases everywhere and a woman comes to clean three times a week. She seems happy."

"She might just as well have been if he'd been poor."

"No!" I said quickly. "D'you think everyone'd love each other more if they were communists?"

"I'm not sure I know answer to that one."

"Dad reckons they would."

She frowned, considering it. "Happen he's right then."

That night I wished very hard that a miracle would happen to make mum love dad - really deeply, the way Fay loved her Sid. She'd loved him even when he'd gambled away the bit of money he got as a presser, even though "he's promised a thousand times to stop . . ." as she'd tell it to mum. Then she'd throw *miesse meshinas* on the heads of his pals who kept him out nights playing pontoon and repeating her mother's words - what can you expect if you marry a younger man - Fay was seven years older than her Sid.

Sylvie ought to have had lots of brothers and sisters but none of the babies would grow properly in Fay's belly. I don't know what happened to them - all those babies still so small you couldn't see the slightest bump. Sometimes she and mum would whisper very low and once I caught mum telling her, "be ever so careful 'cause if the woman gets caught we'll all be for it". Fay seemed scared and said that's what loving a man brings you to -

There was one time Fay had dragged herself up to us on the fourth floor and nearly fell in the door - her face was white as the chalk my teacher used and there was blood down her legs - it was scary - I asked should I run for the doctor but mum said "No!" very sharp, hauled Fay to our bed and propped pillows under her

33

hips and legs so's she was raised all down the lower part of her body. When dad got in he told mum "not to get mixed up in it . . ." but mum said he was a fine one to talk about compassion for humanity and she'd help Fay out any time!

Often I'd look at Sylvie with her poor eyelid pulled down and her mouth which could never fully open with laughter and I'd think what a sad and cruel thing it was that of all the babies Fay'd lost the only one left to her should be like that.

It was raining. Storming summer rain. Mum was having "a little talk with Mrs. Lee" and I'd been instructed to "peel the potatoes and wake your father twelve o'clock sharp!" This was when I hated being evacuated - without plenty of friends to play with - in London it didn't matter if it poured, there were the landings and stairs for Hide and Seek and Kiss Chase and what screams and giggles would rat-a-tat into the stern old walls - Now I sat watching the water spilling over the wash-house gutter where it was cracked.

"Where is he? Didn't you call him?" Mum was back, her hair wet, face dark as the sky. I galloped upstairs, two at a time. Dad was smothered with bedclothes, even the bald top bit hidden from sight and sound. I pushed at the heaped body. "Dad! Get up!" A moan of displeasure and pull up further of covers was all I got. "Dad, you're on three to eleven . . . it's almost twelve and mum's got to give you dinner . . ."

"I'm worn out . . ." came the voice of an old man. Mum was calling. I took a chance and did what I'd seen her do many a time - pulled the bedcovers right off him. His body squirmed with anger. "What the bloody hell . . ."

"He's coming!" I yelled down.

"All this not going straight to bed - standing at that sodding market stall . . ." On she went - "Where's the rent coming from if he loses this job? War-time or not if the bosses want to chuck you they find a way round regulations." Then it was "a disgrace I have to take lodgers in when you should have your own room - why do I do it? Ask him, ask that father of yours!"

"But it's . . ." I stopped, from saying it wasn't it - the money just - and didn't we all know, even Ethel, she needed the excuse to keep me in the big bed with her.

Dad snapped the wireless on, then moodily poked at his food. "That's right. That's right," he'd repeat as though he'd known,

34

long before the information came from the mouth of the brown, wooden box. Now and then he'd clench up, turning his head into his chest and all the while I watched carefully, for through him I knew how the war was going.

The results of the summer exams came and Yippee! I was to pass into an "A" class in September. Mum said nothing. Dad said he'd been expecting it. I nearly said what about my dictionary then but had already decided to save up for one myself - there was something about words - not just having them so's you could make the world better like dad said - all the most interesting things were spoken about or written down in words with long strange sounds, words which could frighten you like a row of upright soldiers with rifles down their sides or curling above and below the lines of papers and books in a self-important and mysterious way. Some day I would have them all - then I'd be something to be reckoned with.

Mrs. Lee must have read into my mind 'cause the next time me and mum went to her, out she comes with, "I shall have to find someone to give me a hand with odd jobs now and then. If you know one my duck, send them round." At once I said, "What about me?" Already the dictionary was in my hands - mum was about to protest thinking how she needed me but Mrs. Lee's dimples went even deeper as she smiled a grateful, "That'll suit fine - alright dear?" this to mum - "Just for the time being till I get someone permanent . . ." I could see why mum liked her. She was a widow and told mum it was the best thing that could have happened and "what a wonderful thing insurance policies are . . ." all this with a cheeky wink - I wondered if mum had dad insured -

So I made tea and unpacked dresses, I held out the pins while Mrs. Lee turned up hems and when she went to do "a quick little errand" I was left importantly in charge. "My little business is thriving, thank the good Lord", she'd say, 'cept it wasn't the Lord but the war that was making Mrs. Lee rich - even with clothes now on coupons working women had their own money to spend and with many it went "on their backs" as Mrs. Lee happily put it.

Soon I had my dictionary. I went through it in alphabetical order. "Have you ever been in a state of acrophobia?" I tried on Ethel but when she looked at me with the face of a baby, I felt

35

ashamed at being so big-headed. But it didn't stop me - I pestered everyone with sounds unfamiliar, most of which were pronounced in an over-loud, self-conscious manner. Sylvie was interested in any words to do with reproduction. I was as amazed as her to find out a boy's dickey was named a "penis" - a *schlong* we'd heard of but a "penis" was something again. Soon we had a private joke, getting each other going saying aloud, "Peanuts!" But now I could also read the daily papers with better understanding and follow the news from the Russian front just like dad.

"I'm scared." I put the paper down. "What if the Germans reach Moscow?" Dad blinked hard. I waited - for him to tell me it wouldn't happen - wasn't he always saying that at the market stall? His fingers tapped on the shiny surface of the American cloth. A fly came and busied itself about the table. It settled on dad's hand. He didn't even notice.

Mary invited me to tea. Mum wasn't keen for me to go. "Alright, but keep your mouth shut if they start pumping you."

Their garden had more flowers and green things about than even Victoria Park! There was an enormous plot stretching deep back so's you didn't see other houses or people's washing - just pear and apple trees. Most important was the allotment her father had dug out before he went in the army. Mary strutted between furrows of potatoes, cabbages and carrots, proudly pointing them out for I didn't know one from another.

"Are they sweet-peas?" I asked, trying to be knowledgeable. It was a row of high criss-crossed canes with curling snake-like stalks twirling round and up. "Dope! They're runner-beans!" She marched about, a General on the battlefield. "Look." She crouched. "Ssh!" Down behind the raspberries was a hedgehog.

"It's not in a ball. I thought they went in a ball when humans were near."

"Watch." She pulled at a stiff, dry blade of grass, leant over the creature and touched its snout. "You have a go." I stayed still. "It don't hurt it." I knelt but instead of tickling its snout I touched its spines, just to see how sharp they were. I thought they'd prick like a needle but they didn't. I slid my finger down the spines till I touched its underside - its belly was soft - the spines here darker brown and silky. It made no movement but stayed crouched, same

36

as me. "C'mon!" Mary called.

Her mother was cutting marigolds the colour of oranges. It reminded me how I missed eating them. She wore a blue, straw hat and as she came nearer I saw the same slant eyes of Mary - "Chink-eyes" they called her in school. She twisted a scrap of string around the stems then pulled from her pocket a pair of white, cotton gloves. It was Sunday - she must be going to church. "I'm off to the cemetery. Behave yourselves." She went through the gate at the end of the garden.

I asked who was dead. "No-one special." It wasn't an answer. "Tell." Mary was stretched long on the grass, eyes closed. "A German, what was shot down."

At once I thought of father - a German - "What?"

"Why shouldn't he have respect when he's dead same as anyone?" Her eyes stayed shut.

"They're our enemy!" I stood up. I wanted to go home. At that second Mary was my enemy. "What would your father say?" I slung at her. "And what about your auntie Cecily who was killed?" She turned on her side away from me. "Mother and dad are both . . ." I waited. ". . . Christians." She said it softly, half-embarrassed, half-superior.

Well, if that's what Christians do, I thought, I'm glad I'm not one of them.

"Well?" mum said when I got in.

"Nice. It was nice," I told her. And that's all. That night I dreamed I was laying flowers on a grave - I didn't know whose - and as I knelt my tears fell on the marbly slab so's it crumbled and suddenly a helmet rose up, straight and hard from the depths - then the stiff body of a German soldier and without seeing me he jumped out in his high, glossy boots and began marching over the other gravestones, all the while goose-stepping, his hand stuck high in a salute and each time he brought his foot down on a gravestone it cracked open so that I saw the skeletons underneath and they moved, slowly sending up moans, getting louder and full as though the whole of Europe was moaning. Then mum was shaking me and asking why I was moaning out.

There was just one week left of the summer holiday. All I seemed to be doing was reading or going through my dictionary. I'd be glad to get back to school.

"You've a face long as a kite." Me and Ethel were alone, washing-up. I hadn't seen Mary since that Sunday. "Ethel, how would you go on if someone who calls themselves your friend says something which you know is wrong and shows them up for being narrow and stupid?"

"In whose opinion?"

"What d'you mean?"

"Well, if it's your opinion they're narrow and stupid you might be wrong. Happen they're thinking same - that it's you are the narrow, stupid one."

"But I'm not! I know Mary and her mum are wrong having sympathy for a shot-down German!" Ethel listened, her face serious as I told it.

"That's a rum story . . . a German airman." Was she thinking of her brother? "Still, he's dead and done with 'ent he? And if he's six foot under he can't do no-one more harm." She stopped wiping a plate. "No, I s'pose a bit of compassion, to the dead any rate, don't come amiss."

I wanted to say that dad's idea of compassion - to the living - seemed to me a much better idea.

CHAPTER SIX

September - Christmas 1941

My first morning back to school I asked dad to wish me luck. "Ssh!" was all I got. He pulled his chair closer to the wireless. "If Leningrad falls it'll be goodbye to us before 1941's out."

Three months - twelve weeks - please God, don't let Leningrad fall, I've only just started my "A" class. I asked my old teacher, Miss Gearfield, if Leningrad was a big place. "Yes," she answered, gravely, "lovely city - formerly the Czarist capital of St. Petersburg."

"If it's big doesn't that mean the Germans will have a worse chance of taking it?" She didn't reply, just frowned till two straight lines formed a neat cross in the middle of her forehead. "To be honest, I just don't know."

Miss Arnold, my new teacher, was very fat. She rolled rather than walked. Her eyes were 'poppy', which the girls said was because of her goitre. I didn't know about them and decided to look it up the minute I got home. She taught mainly English and that first lesson got us going with "Oliver Twist". When she asked me to read aloud I did a Fagin which had the taste and feel of a living man. It was the same with Bill Sykes - my cockney accent and acting abilities charged out like a galloping horse - they were my victims on that soft September morning and battles and bloodshed were far from our young minds.

When I asked dad that night to help with my arithmetic, all he could say was, "Ask your mother." He was so haggard, worrying over what was happening in a land he'd never been to and probably never would. The wireless was switched on and off - papers read and re-read - one moment they were "an invincible Red Army!" - the next the headline 'FIVE-WAY ASSAULT ON LENINGRAD' was said aloud like a funeral oration. So it went for the next few days and, fog-like, the fear spread about - our house - into the street - Mr. Evan's shop - so that women getting their rations would stop their chatter of what meals to get and men returning from work walked with a heavier step.

"Keep out his way," mum warned. I was having breakfast. "What happened at the market stall last week-end?" So - he hadn't told her. "Is there any more sugar?" She snatched my cereal dish away. "Don't change the subject!" So, though I knew dad wouldn't like her knowing, I let out how he'd been going on about the brave Russian army when a man whose soldier son had been taken prisoner in Greece turned on him. I'd listened, holding tight to dad as he threw out his misery and anger. When he'd done he was trembling - so was dad.

"So . . ." She rubbed her fingers back and forth across her chin. "Still, he does ask for it . . ." She stopped as dad came in. He drew a penny from his trousers. "Go get me an 'Express'." I left at once.

Minutes later I ran back in. "Dad! Dad! They've done it!" I stuck the paper in front of him. "Look!"

He read the words - at first silently, mouthing them, then shouting out, "Nazis retreat at Leningrad!" Then a jump from his seat - a laugh, gay - relieved - "Didn't I tell you? Now who says the

39

Russians won't last three months? Now who's going to push back the German bastards eh?'' He poured tea - it didn't matter it was lukewarm - and swallowed it like it was champagne.

The garden was autumn-yellow and untidy. Mum brought in the last of the michaelmas daisies and long, bronze chrysanthemums so that each room in the house had its share of the last of summer. Dad watched her from behind his pipe and she knew he was, though making out she didn't.

The storms had kept the harvest late. There was anxious talk of "gettin' it in over the week-end if the weather holds . . ." Mary had asked if I wanted to come to her uncle's farm to help. "It's a good lark after . . ."

"Can I, mum?"

"There's too many accidents on farms - 'specially to children."

"Dad . . . can I?"

"She's old enough to be sensible, aren't you?''

"You both heard me. It's too risky."

"But . . ." He didn't take up the plea in my voice, just went on smoking. Coward! I wanted to yell, you're always ready to have a go at her over your precious politics! What about now - sticking up for me!

That night I kept right away from her, sleeping almost on the hard bar of the bed-spring. Why did she have to keep me to her like a baby? always scared for me to do anything - Mary would know why - "I couldn't bear it if anything happened to you" she whispered, "you know that." I lay rigid and silent. "Don't you? Don't you?" she repeated.

We were doing revolutions in history class which was much better than kings and queens. When it got to the French one I really let go - dad had told me lots about the risings and the terrible Robespierre and surely and confidently I repeated all this knowledge while everyone listened open-mouthed. Somehow it made me forgive him a bit for not standing by me - yes, it could be useful at times, having a revolutionary for a father. When I told mum history was now my second-best subject she did a "Ummm . . ." then started on her "lost chances" again and how "the family always bragged about me . . ." then added with a voice bitter as an orphan, "Much good it did me, being clever . . ."

40

It seemed to me that dad at least knew why he was a victim - he had something outside of himself to blame it all on - but mum could only keep it tight inside her like a spring, except the spring would often snap up, out of control - then it would be, "I've thrown my life away . . . ruined it . . ." and grandfather would be cursed to hell, he, that "old bastard who gave mother - an angel - hell too and God alone knew why she went on loving him - bearing him child after child -" It seemed at those moments she hated all men, even Mr. Evans with the lift in his voice who let her wheedle him and flirt with him and who'd tell her, "You're a terrible woman indeed and get me put inside yet!"

There were hard December frosts now in the mornings. Outside was all fairylandish - not for dad - he'd get back from night shift, eyebrows like Santa Claus, feet and hands white with cold. I'd poke the fire hard in sympathy while mum got hot tea in him, both of us waiting to see how much longer he'd stick it.

I walked the slippery pavements to school, so much more sparklier and sharper than in London, my knees chapped where my socks ended - p'raps I'd end up with chilblains like Ethel. At school it was all talk of Christmas and the excitement of it caught me too so that I began counting the days till the twenty-fifth - I didn't see why I shouldn't, Jesus was a Jew, so in some ways I had more right to him than they did.

"Can we also have a tree for Christmas?"

"Don't see why not." Dad had no conscience about it - he was as critical of Jewish "capitalists" as Christian ones. Wasn't he always going on about Montague Norman, a Jewish Governor of the Bank of England - ? "I've only got one religion," he'd say, "and that's a belief in the equality of all men."

So I set to making decorations for the first time ever while dad, his pipe tight in his teeth, followed the events of war in north Africa and Russia and mum mixed flour and water paste for the paper chains, all of us snug with our new-found Christmas, far from guns and shells and men in the cold and men in the heat and all of them wishing they too could be away and back in their ordinary homes.

We were eating 'dad's' breakfast flakes when it came sudden out the wireless - the Japs had attacked Pearl Harbour. "Now the

Yanks'll have to come in it with us,'' dad said.

"All it'll mean is a lot more people being killed,'' mum said, pulling me to her. "Thank God we didn't send her to America after all.'' She was thinking they'd be bombed by the Japs same as the Jerries bombed us. Dad said she knew nothing of strategy - they couldn't bomb the Yanks - he didn't explain why not. Just the same I was thankful I hadn't been sent off to dad's rich brother Morry in Philadelphia. It was in June 1940 dad'd written asking them to take me for the war. It hardly seemed real when a letter came back - "Sure we'll have her . . .'' I thought of all those films and practised an American accent but just as mum was crying over me and my friends envying me, the Arandora Star was sunk by Germans while carrying internees across the Atlantic. "Not meant to leave her are we?'' dad had said. He meant how he'd come back to England after trying to "make it good'' in the U.S. same as uncle Morry. "Just wasn't cut out for business - too soft.'' Mum said it was because he "lacked initiative and was too bloody trusting.'' I didn't say, but I was pleased he had failed. Even so, dad wasn't envious of his brother - even proud he'd made it - p'raps uncle Morry was only a very small capitalist -

"Be handy if they sent another parcel in time for Christmas,'' mum said. Mum and me would get so excited, tearing apart the bashed-about box with Customs stamps and our address written over big three times - we'd poke about the second-hand clothes looking for the chocolate though why they sent chewing-gum I never could make out. If only they wouldn't wear such bright-coloured things with big patterns - dad said they might be rich in America but England was the place for taste.

All he was talking about was why Churchill wasn't getting on with the Second Front in Europe. It was on his lips mornings, evenings, Saturdays at the British Soviet Society stall. He put up large posters and played Russian marching music, calling out in his thin voice, "Open the Second Front!'' Mr. Evans said dad should "think on our poor lads losing their lives on the convoys taking tanks and guns to Russia - wicked the way them U-boats is picking them off . . .'' When mum repeated this dad said war was "a bastard - always has been - always would be.'' It sounded so bitter - so without hope, which wasn't like him 'cause he always knew just who was to blame and how it could all be put right.

42

"It might be an idea to ask Fay and Sylvie round Christmas day," mum announced.

"Smashing!" I danced round the kitchen. Straightaway me and mum got busy to make it a real celebration. She mascara'd her eyes and did her usual on Mr. Evans so besides the extra sugar and fat allowance for Christmas she got enough to do an extra special big cake. We iced it to look like snow shovelled up and stuck a red Father Christmas on top. It was a cosy feeling preparing for it in our small house - the first we'd ever had all to ourselves with us the landlords and having a lodger - Ethel wasn't going away now she'd lost her only brother and when mum told dad he'd be "the only cock among the hens" he did a funny "Cock-a-doodle-do!" in a silly voice till I nearly wet my knickers. He and mum started laughing also - it was so nice to hear I wished we'd all discovered Christmas years ago.

I told Mary about our preparations. "I didn't think your people celebrated the birth of Christ Our Lord."

"He was ours before he was yours!" I spat back at her. Mum was right. I should stick to just one friend like Sylvie -

Christmas morning mum got dad up early to chop wooden boxes for firewood and I set out my home-made cards on the mantlepiece. Ethel was looking bright after mum said how pleased she was with the knitted cardigan and "hadn't realised you'd such good taste" - then Ethel opened my card and told mum, "She's reet clever, your lass." It seemed it was going to be a good day with all of us being nice to each other.

Dinner-time Fay and Sylvie arrived, Sylvie very grown-up, her hair swept up each side of her ears and tottery on too-high heels. "D'you like working?" I asked. "Better'n school . . ." She never was keen on learning. Fay sat glum, missing her Sid like always - Dad started on about the war soon being "done with now the tide has turned in the Soviet Union" and mum actually agreed with him.

Mum done us roast chicken and a proper Christmas pudding with tiny silver threepenny bits in - Ethel nearly broke her false teeth on one and me and Sylvie set off giggling like always. Ethel was knocking back a good bit of beer, getting unusually chatty, then she fetched her brother's photograph. Now tears spilled between the blobs of rouge leaving channels of white beneath the bright coral. "Look," she showed Fay, "d'you reckon he's like me?" That set Fay off weeping. Mum gave Ethel a filthy look. "I wouldn't have upset you for anything," Ethel apologised, crying for all she was worth. Fay sobbed and dad sat repeating "The only good German's a dead one." Our happy day seemed vanished.

"Why don't I read us a real Christmas story?" I offered. No-one answered. I fetched the book Miss Arnold had loaned me. "A Christmas Carol", and read aloud with all the feeling I could. Before long they were with me, me and the writer in our world of fantasy yet not so different from real life.

"That's a story with a moral - shows the emptiness of greed," dad observed when I finished.

"Wish I could read out books like you do," Sylvie said.

Dad got up and banked the glowing wood with damp slack from the bottom of the coal bucket. We sat closer to it while he said how lucky we were compared to all the people in occupied Europe and those away from their homes. That set Fay off again. "He ought never to have been sent!" mum said, indignant for Fay. "After what he went through." Then though we'd heard it many times - how everyone thought Sid was dead after their house had been bombed, she went over it like she was telling it for the first time ever -

"The cat it was saved his life - Sid'd never come down the Anderson shelter with us - said he'd take his chances indoors. This evening - I'll never forget it till the day I die, him and the feller who lived in the single room stayed in the basement kitchen playing cards - go to his grave playing pontoon wouldn't he? The two of them it was, and the cat, staying there, playing bloody pontoon - bombs screaming down everywhere -" Ethel wetted her mouth - a splinter of wood in the fire sparked - "I knew it was a direct hit - our house and next door's, flattened - gone - and Sid underneath . . ." She paused and now she licked at her lips. "We finally come out the shelter - the rescue people says there no chance - they was all there - bloody Pathé Gazette filming away - no-one could survive under that they says - says we was lucky to be alive - lucky - I begged them - remember Sylvie how I screamed at them? It was no good. Then the cat crawled out, covered in dust but unhurt. Never in my life was I so bloody pleased to see a cat. That did it - they went on digging through the small tunnel the cat had

44

come through. When they get to him the other feller's dead, stretched across Sid's left arm, pinning him down - all night he'd been like that. When they finally get him out - his hair - it was white as the snow falling outside now.''

Dad poked at the slack and the rush of air whipped up a jaggedy flame. ''What's he doing in the front line eh? King's bloody Royal Rifles! That's what I want to know!'' Mum was angry for Fay and Sid. She bunched her mouth. ''Know what? I'm gonna' write a letter for you - to his Commanding Officer. I'll put what a disgrace a man who went through what he did should be in the front line!''

We all said what a marvellous idea. Everyone knew what mum's letters could do - hadn't the family always got her to compose letters when they'd needed things sorting out? We cheered up. Dad said ''What about a tune on the piano?'' So mum played and I gave my impersonation of George Formby singing ''Limehouse Laundry Blues'' which Ethel said was ''reet good''. Dad then rolled up his shirt-sleeves, placed his hands behind his neck and twitched the muscles in the tops of his arms so's they jumped up and down - at the same time he wiggled his hips in a belly-dance just like the buskers in the Mile End Road. Me and Sylvie clapped and yelled for more - Fay and mum said he was mad while Ethel watched everything just as if she was having a wild dream - Mum suddenly decided to get things really warmed up with a traditional Jewish wedding dance so while she led us from room to room, waving a white handkerchief, me and Sylvie sang out at the top of our voices - goodness knows what the spinsters next door must have thought - we hadn't heard a thing from them all that Christmas day.

CHAPTER SEVEN

January - May 1942

Mary asked what my New Year Resolution was. I hadn't got any idea - ''*I'm* going to save every bit of used-up paper for salvage collection.''

"Already do that,'' I answered, smugly, "and cardboard and when mum does soup I make her save the bones and put them out - it makes glue for aeroplanes . . .''

"And fertiliser for putting on crops, my uncle Bill says.'' She never let me get the best of her in anything -

I asked dad what his resolution was. He just lifted his Daily Express higher. I read the bold page one headlines, 'MANILA IN JAP HANDS'. I asked him if that was bad for us. "Bad for the Yanks but it'll be worse if Singapore goes.''

I hadn't thought much about the Japs - as for hating them, I didn't know if I was supposed to or not - dad had always gone on about us "buying cheap goods from them at the expense of the unemployed here . . .'' but that didn't seem a real reason to hate them - "Listen to this . . . 'American Expeditionary Force ready and equipped to join British Forces in direct assault on Germany coming to British Isles in next twelve months'. What's the good of that? Twelve months! *Now* they should be here, to get the Second Front started!''

"They can't be in two places at once,'' mum put in.

"What d'you know - It's all part of capitalist strategy - war or no war - they don't miss a trick - we sit back while the Nazis *schlep* the *kishkas* from communist Russia and they take out the guts from the German military fighting machine - ah! Churchill's a shrewd fox - suits him this way - suits all the capitalists - I know what I'm saying!''

"You're *meshugee* . . .'' mum started.

"Wait - once the war's over it'll be another story - now it's our courageous Russian allies, but the minute it's finished - you'll see - the Red-baiting . . .''

"Long as it's not Jew-baiting . . .''

"Ach! You're a fool when it comes to world affairs.'' He scraped his chair into the table and went out to the lavatory.

"Is he right mum? About Churchill? On the wireless and the newsreel they're always going on about the brave Russians . . .''

"Don't you start, for Christ's sake - I have enough with him!''

Now that I was turned thirteen I tried mum again about a room to myself. "We don't really need Ethel's money do we . . .''

46

"So - you don't want to be in with your mummy anymore."
Her voice was teasing but I saw really she was bothered. She
looked hard at my plump, emerging body - the small breasts just
rounding out - the eyes growing wiser by the day. She placed her
hands either side of my face. "Be very careful."

"What of?"

She sighed - a sigh I knew from the beginning. Nothing more
was said about my room. In the long January nights I snuggled
close to her and tried not to think about it. Then, without warning
an old bed arrived. It had a deep mesh spring and over it a grey
and white striped feather-bed of real down. Dad seemed pleased
for me and after Ethel saying she "wasn't much bothered" in I
went with her.

I thought I'd got used to Ethel's wintergreen oil - it was different
trying to sleep with it. She was always rubbing oil somewhere. It
seemed that even the wallpaper was rubbed in oils and the rag rug
between our beds. After she'd gone to work I'd lay there mornings
pretending the room was just mine, then I'd think my most secret,
fanciful thoughts, not scared for a second mum might wake and see
straight in my mind. She was careful though to see that dad still
kept in the single bed, always up and dressed early before he got
back from nights. Ethel didn't get bothered the way Mr. Parmer
did when they fought - she'd just stick a bit of cotton wool in her
ears soaked in camphorated oil. When mum begged him, "What
about Ethel?" so's he'd control himself, he'd curse her in Yiddish -
I knew them all - *coorvah* meant prostitute - ladies who got wages
for taking their knickers off. I'd seen them, standing outside
Woolworth's on Aldgate corner - vivid hair they had, of red and
gold and they wore shoes with spindly heels and straps round the
ankles. Me and Sylvie wanted shoes like that - Mum didn't look
like one of them. When dad's raving got really bad she'd get the
piano going, desperately singing operatic arias. Goodness knows
what the unmarried ladies next door thought - "Man-haters they
are - wonder if they're Lesbians," I heard her telling Fay. I'd
quick looked up that word and next time they were out in their
garden, gave them one of my 'examining' looks. Me and Sylvie
had a big talk about it. We'd never 'experimented' like some of
our friends did. One, Katie, whose parents had a toy shop with a
flat over it would take us up to the bedroom while they were busy

47

selling teddy bears and some of the girls would take their clothes off and kiss and touch each other - not rough like Nigel did but slowly and gently. "Did you ever want to?" I asked Sylvie. "I want a boy-friend really," and she let free a choked kind of laugh. I hoped and hoped she'd maybe get one.

"Mum's saying about going back to London, getting a transfer." Sylvie picked at the jagged cuticles around her nails. "She's all the while worrying about grandma on her own." She looked sick as I felt.

"Fay? Leaving?" Mum was combing her hair - she threw the comb down. "How d'you know? When? She said nothing to me!"

"P'raps Sylvie got it wrong . . . you know sometimes . . ." She picked up the comb and pulled it through her hair again, tugging like an angry child.

Two weeks passed - we saw nothing of either of them. Mum was all the while picking on me and dad. Even Ethel kept out her way. One blustery afternoon I walked straight to Woolworth's - I had to find out what was happening. Sylvie's counter was cosmetics - it was odd she was chosen for that, what with her mouth stuck down at the side and her eye looking like she was always giving you the wink. Mum said the manager was either a fool or soft-hearted.

"Where's Sylvie?"

"Who?" There was a tall, thin girl where Sylvie should have been.

"She always serves at this counter."

She didn't answer, just straightened the rows of lipsticks rolled out before her. She used her hands very carefully, guarding her over-long fingernails. "What's she like?" I said nothing and went to the next counter where a woman was measuring off tape. "Oh her - with the funny mouth and poor eye all pulled down, she's in London. Went off with her mother."

I walked home drearily. What did she mean - "went off"? - Mum was waiting - I was late - there were "soldiers in town" and "you're growing up now" and "what would I do if anything happened to you?" - After supper I escaped to bed. I'd got "Little Women" out the library. Dad approved because it was about freeing the slaves in America.

"Why you hiding away?" He wasn't on till morning shift and was relaxed for a change.

"Dad, you ever had a close friend?"

He sat on the side of the bed. "Come to think of it . . . don't think I have . . . not what you'd call a proper friend."

"Why not?"

"Never stayed anywhere long enough I suppose." He picked up my book. "Why you asking?"

"I wish I wasn't the only child!" It came out like a pen-knife blade. "Why couldn't you and mum . . . I mean . . . I wish I didn't have to need a friend so much!"

He got up, awkward now. "It was the way . . . things happened . . ." He twisted the door-knob. "Times haven't been easy . . . a family costs . . ."

I didn't read anymore - instead I thought of Fay and Sid and all those brothers and sisters Sylvie nearly had.

When I pulled my bedclothes back next morning there was a blood-stain on the sheet. "Mum!" In seconds she was there. "Look!" She stared at the mark, then pulled me around, spreading my nightdress wide. Then she slapped my face.

"Oh!" The tears came, quick and hot. "What's that for?" She put her arms round me. "Sorry . . . it's the custom . . . you're a woman now . . . my mother did that to me . . ." Then she gave a short talk, not looking at me - pulling off the sheet - fetching a fresh one - at the same time telling how a baby starts from a seed and that the blood you lose every month is because the seed hasn't been made into a proper human - When I tried to get in with I knew all that 'cause Sylvie'd told me ages ago, I couldn't get the chance, so fast did she speak, eager to get it done with -

She left. I examined the old bed-sheet. I couldn't see any seed. The following day the blood stopped. I thought more about mum and all those "floodings" she was always talking about - just as well I wasn't going to take after her.

"Yesterday . . ." she began, uneasily. I waited. She fetched cups and saucers and inspected the sugar bowl. "Won't be enough till next week." Still I sat. "Men will want to . . . touch you . . ." The kettle let out a gush of steam and the lid started its usual rattle. She lifted it, pouring deliberately into the tea-pot. ". . . never let them put their hands . . ." now she came and placed her hands on my small breasts, "here . . ." she pointed next to the place between my legs - "or there . . . that's how you get a baby." She filled cups, lifted hers and drank deeply seeming not to notice how hot it was. I sipped at mine. "Soon you'll be leaving school . . . going out into the world . . . watch them . . . men . . . watch their every move." She drained the cup and now held it, her hands around it like a fortune-teller about to see into my future. "I was a girl, my first job. The boss flattered me, told me how pretty I was. I liked it . . . flirted a little . . . it meant nothing." Her lashes fluttered, just as they must have done then. "One evening he asks me to stay, do extra typing" - she was blinking hard - "the next thing he'd got his hand down the front of my dress - I didn't think he'd do that - I pushed him off - he was tearing at my dress - I thought he'd gone mad - I screamed, again and again" -

"Don't . . ." I took her hands from the cup - I didn't want to hear - I didn't want to know of this 'grown-up' world - "Thank God, the caretaker came - still there - the old man" - She wiped the sweat from her face. "I told mother - she tells my father . . . What does he do? He's going to sue the boss - d'you hear that? Thought he'd make himself a millionaire out of me - never mind what happened - a rich man - out of me!" Upstairs I heard father dragging the suitcase from under the bed, then the books pulled out, stacked neat on the floor. "Then what happened?" - now I needed to know. "The court hearing comes - I tell it just as it was. When it's the old man's turn, he crumbles - my only witness - I couldn't believe it - he was to say, he'd promised, how he'd found us - me and the boss - struggling -" She took a long, deep breath. "We lost the case. Afterwards the old man comes to me - 'I'm not young', he says, 'who'd give me a job after this? I'm sorry', he says. Sorry! Your grandfather went mad - says I brought it on myself - I wasn't any good -"

"Grandma?"

"She knew I was telling the truth." Again a sigh. "So - you see - how careful you must always be -"

"I will be mum - I promise -" I wanted to add something to make up to her for what happened all that time ago, but I didn't know what to say.

It'd just been announced that we'd done "a thousand-bomber raid on Cologne". Dad told me Cologne was a beautiful place but the raid was in retaliation for the German's bombing our old cities like York and Norwich. "Mind you, this time it was us got this lot started." I asked what he meant and he said as how the British had let loose a load of incendiaries on the ancient port town of Lubeck, almost burning it to the ground. "Why?" I asked. "Why?" he repeated. "War's war, that's why."

I kept thinking about it - how beautiful cities like Cologne which took so many years to grow, should have to be bombed on and what did the airman think when they pressed the buttons on a fine May day, that dropped the bombs - and even dad, who hated the Germans more than anything, seemed sad as he spoke of Lubeck.

I'd just left the house next morning when the postwoman handed me a letter. "Give it to your mother dear, to save my legs." I was late but this was special - from London. I ran back.

Mum tore the envelope in an uneven pull and scrapped out some lined paper with Fay's thick, careful handwriting.

"Well?"

"They'll be back at the end of the week, with her mother. The old lady's been very ill."

"Yippee!" I gave her a tight hug and hurried off. Horrible bosses and bombings on Cologne seemed a million years away -

CHAPTER EIGHT

May - July 1942

"You coming to see them?" Sylvie asked. The town was curious - 'specially the women. Spring had come and gone and the Yanks had arrived. The U.S.A.A.F. really. "In Wickstead Park they are, everyone's going."

I asked mum. "You're too young."

"Sylvie's going."

"Americans all think . . ."

"What?"

51

"They're lady-killers."

"How d'you know?" She went into the garden and pulled weeds the rain had sent up.

When I asked dad it was, "Yeh! We'll go -" Then he went on, like I'd not heard before, of when he was with uncle Morry and got into bootlegging during American Prohibition to make money - "In the bath we did it . . ." For the moment he was back there, enjoying the quick-silver living instead of being just here, working round the clock making cornflakes and "sweating all the while like a pig".

"Look at 'em - like flies round a jam-pot." They were - mostly women, some worn, a few with babies sucking on dummies, unaware of their mother's new interest. Others hovered in bunches, curious and trying not to show it. Bold ones called back at the Americans offering chocolate through the park railings - some went across and took the offerings then ran back to show their friends the goodies of soap with sickly-sweet scents, already seeing themselves lathered and naked and excited at the very idea. Lots of the servicemen looked young - not much older than me and skinny too with crew-cuts which looked like the evacuees who came from London lousy, some of them - and had all their hair shaved off.

Dad called out, "Any of you boys from Philadelphia?" A red-haired one pushed forward, grinning. "That's my place mister!" Dad and him were really pleased with each other and shook hands while dad jabbered on about places he'd stayed and the Yank said, Yeh, they were still there and dad said what about that and I kept tight hold on him, all the while looking round for Sylvie.

Going home I kept thinking none of them looked much like any of those stars I'd seen in all those films. Mum was reading when we got back, in the rocking-chair, a dark, red cushion behind her head. She turned as we came in so that it slipped down her back. She wasn't interested in my chatter, still away in her own mystery of fancies. Dad said they were "a bit green and don't know whether they'll be up to a real scrap." Mum turned a page, asking who was he to talk. At once his good humour was away.

"I had my bellyful in 1917! What d'you know - mud - the horses - up to their - and men - bodies - I had shell-shock -" He clenched and unclenched his hands. Now he was started he had to go on - the officers were criminals - incompetent bastards (worse than the Germans) from the British ruling class who should have been put up against the wall and shot. Then there was the time he'd been "insubordinate" and for punishment was left tied to the barrel of a field gun "for hours - in the cold and wet - without food - bastards - didn't break me though - I got through!" -

Mum had escaped - unpegging washing - humming - careful not to look towards the house. There was no tea - I poured a large dose of coffee essence in a mug - he liked it strong. At last he stopped still and sat down to drink, gulping the dark, sweet liquid, his fingers, slender for a man, clasped round the purply-blue mug. Now and then he looked up and swore at mum's small, round body, still outside -

"What's the latest news dad?" He kept silent, re-filling his mug. "Dad?" Suddenly he was off - General Alexander and the retreat from Burma - the Japs were "artful like a wagon-load of monkeys" - but it was without his usual eagerness and soon he was quietly sullen again.

Sunday, Sylvie called. "You seen 'em yet?"

"The Americans? Dad took me. What d'you think of them?" She held up her leg. She was wearing golden-coloured nylons in place of the gravy-browning stain which went all streaky when it rained. Sylvie hadn't wasted much time. "Smashing. How'd you get them?"

"I've got a boyfriend!" Her face was both soft and excited. "Guess what - he's from Texas!" Her mouth strained as always, to make a proper smile.

"Is he a cowboy?" I could hear it was a childish remark. The gap between my thirteen and her fifteen seemed suddenly awkward and enormous.

"How old is he?"

"Just nineteen."

"Does your mum know?"

"A bit."

"What's 'a bit'?"

"She knows he came in Woolworth's and we talked."

"What d'they kiss like?"

"Nice."

"Sylvie!" She'd gone straight into my trap. "You're too young!"

"Don't be daft -" She sat, crossing her legs, admiring the

golden sheen. "Still want to know what they kiss like?" I nodded. "Not wet and he didn't stick his tongue in my mouth."

I shuddered. I would never let a boy do that - French kisses they were - "Your mother'll kill you!"

All that evening I kept looking at Sylvie - she kept looking at her legs.

"Were they nylon stockings Sylvie had on?" mum asked when she'd gone. I told her yes. "Where'd she get them?" I shrugged, my lips tight. "I'll have to talk with Fay. A girl like Sylvie needs special watching."

I knew why she said that - on account of her face. It wasn't fair - why did women always have to be good-looking? And would Sylvie be extra grateful to her Yank for treating her like any ordinary girl?

Dad said did I want to go with him to the market stall Saturday mornings - the Daily Worker paper was out again and he was selling it like he'd written every word himself. Sometimes he'd 'grab' a customer and start off a political discussion, then his dull face would glow and his language become rich with special words while his small, brown eyes glimmered as a bird's does when it pounces on a worm. He knew every detail of every battle, 'specially in Russia and I got used to names like Marshal Zhukov, and places like Smolensk - General Alexander and General MacArthur - Singapore and Hong Kong - suddenly my geography lessons at school became real - I even lectured the girls on the Urals and how "they were strategically vital to Soviet defence".

One sunny, June day, while Miss Arnold was out of the room I heard myself addressing the class in dad's words. After lesson she kept me back. "Tell me, do you think you would like to go to Russia after the war?" I'd never thought about it and said so. "It's not like here you know, in England every man and woman can speak freely - we have a democracy - that's what we are fighting for - the defence of democracy."

I told dad what she'd said. He said it'd be a good thing when I was fourteen and could leave that school.

Like I expected, Sylvie was all taken up with her boyfriend. I missed her - lots - I went to Woolworth's. She was at her usual counter but instead of customers she had her face upturned to a lean serious-looking American. I knew he was her cowboy. He had a straight thinnish body with shoulders hitched up like a puppet and the strings stretched tight. He ran his hand through his hair and I could make out a ring with an "H" on it - I nearly called across "Hi, Hank!" except Sylvie wouldn't have laughed. If only he'd disappear and things could be like before. He grinned suddenly, showing a blob of gold on an upper tooth. Dad was right, they must all be rich.

At last - end-of-term exam results and Yippee! I was second from top in English and third in History. That night in bed, before Ethel came up I said aloud a slow chant like the Rabbi does in synagogue - "Oh, next year, if it please you, oh Lord, next year, before I leave school, let me come top, oh Lord, let me come top." Mary came middle. "I'm not bothered, I'll work at my grandpa's shop till I get married."

"D'you want to get married very much?"

"Silly. All girls do."

"I don't."

She tilted her head sideways, her elfish chin jerked upwards, not really believing me. Let her work in her grandfather's fancy shop - let Sylvie stay in Woolworth's till her Prince Charming arrived - I'd never be trapped like that just waiting for some boy to set me free - except what was free - mum wasn't for certain - What would I do when I left school? Most people hated their jobs - always thinking of Sundays and Bank Holidays and "won't be long now till Christmas . . ." P'raps I ought to have taken the chance at the Working Mens' Club -

"Fancy coming to Fay's, mum?" I wanted to share my good news with Sylvie. "Yeh, why not?"

They were billeted in a big house with a crunchy drive leading to the front door. Mum pushed a polished brass bell. "Like a park eh?" It was, with firs like Christmas trees gone madly high and laurels with polished leaves - a bird was singing from somewhere in a rhododendron bush - not singing really - more like a regular hammering on a metal anvil -

"Can't call you in," Fay said, "mother's upstairs." She led us through a side gate and we settled beneath an oak tree. "What's the matter?" mum asked. Both of us had seen the wretched look of her at once.

"He's dead!" She stared beyond us, interested it seemed in a sparrow tipping about all grey and brown.

"Oh, Fay no!" Mum was quite white.

"I'm sure he is! I'm certain!"

"Fay!" mum struck out. "What have you heard?"

"It's never been this long for his letters . . . oh, my Sid . . . I've never looked at another man . . ."

"The letters are just delayed - it's war-time . . ."

"He's had it, I know - he always said every bullet has a number on it -"

"But he's not in the front line Fay - for God's sake be reasonable!"

"What d'you know! The C.O. ignored it - the 'brilliant' letter you wrote that'd keep Sid from the front line - after all he went through, buried alive under the house - now God only knows where he's buried!"

Fay convinced me. I was sure too that Sid was dead. Hadn't Tobruk been captured by the Germans and wasn't Sid in north Africa and wasn't that where Tobruk was? She sat, rocking back and forward on the grass, beside her the evening rays slanted through the branches, a spotlight just missing her.

Death and war - it was becoming all so familiar so's even though I didn't want to, I was accepting it. I thought of when grandma died, all her children, sons-in-law, daughters-in-law, grey-faced, whispering about and we children made to be quiet in the basement kitchen with all the curtains closed and crying and wailing kept in. But grandma had died properly, between sheets, grandfather clutching her hand and she forgiving him his many sins during their life together. That was death as it ought to be, orderly, with each person taking his part like in a game with rules.

Now Fay was shouting, stamping on the soft grass, a wild woman - "Who are you to tell me . . . know nothing about caring for someone . . . not fair . . . he should have been taken . . . yours!"

Mum, trembling, pulled me to go. How could Fay say such things? We hurried away home.

Dad was at the table, his head down. I touched him, glad he was here, not away in the war same as Sid, even though him and mum were always fighting. "I'm tired." He stretched his back, ironing it out. I put my arms about him and for a moment he rested his head against my chest. "Bloody worn out."

56

Mum stood watching then got out the bread-bin and board. "Don't bother," he said, not looking up at her. I waited for her explosion - she was haggard too with mascara smudged on her cheek. She sat opposite him, staring as though at a stranger. He was thinner and the stains beneath his eyes seemed permanently smudged on the way Indian women put charcoal round their eyes. "I've got to get out this job - get transferred back to London -"

"You'll be killed!" I shouted, remembering Fay's death-wish.

"The raids aren't bad now - I'll find a job - doing uniforms -"

That night, through the wall, I heard her crying. She was still depressed in the morning.

"Why don't we go to the pictures this afternoon?" I tried.

"Fay . . ." the rest stuck in her mouth like stones.

"She'll come round, just wait. Go put on your flowered dress, the green, and make your eyes lovely."

"Who's going to see them in the dark?"

So we sat, side by side in the cinema on firm plush-covered seats - red - nearly always red - around us servicemen, Yanks mostly, their arms looped round girls. The film was a love story, with spies in it and one of the lovers, in the French Resistance, got caught and was shot. We both cried and when we came out mum said she felt a lot better.

At home dad hadn't been by himself. "Come in here both of you, I've got a surprise!" An American in U.S.A.A.F. uniform stood by him. "This is Albert. I met him in the Working Mens' Club. And guess what - he's Russian." Albert held out his hand. "Pleased to make your acquaintance," he said, with an accent a bit like the spy in the film only less.

What was a Russian doing in the American Air Force - ? And for certain Albert wasn't gangly and young like the other Yanks - he seemed nearly as old as dad. "Albert's interested in politics, same as me." He gazed at him in a true comradely way till Albert smiled also, his startling blue eyes crinkling small and his broad nostrils stretching wide into his cheeks. Mum was giving him a good look - at his toughened lined skin - the way navvies have and his lips held in a smile. He told us his people were in farming - "I was till all this - all our people were back in the old country - well, not much more'n serfs I guess you'd say" -

"My parents were born in Russia," mum said.

57

"I was a kid when mine left," Albert said.

"Isn't it a small world?" dad said.

Albert visited often. Dad perked up and didn't say more about London and I was really grateful to Staff-Sergeant Nervosk and even grateful to his mother and father who'd left "the old country".

Mum would sparkle whenever he came - with 'goodies' like tinned chicken and ham and peaches and she said what a pleasure not to have to go "wheedling to Mr. Evans". Sometimes he'd sleep over on the parlour sofa and dad always made sure before he left for night-shift that Albert had his own old overcoat to cover himself with. Even Ethel glowed when he was around.

"Wouldn't it be smashing mum if Albert married Ethel and took her to America after the war?"

"Don't be ridiculous! What could he see in her?"

"She'd be alright if she wore shorter skirts and plucked the hairs from over her lips - I bet she'd be pretty . . ."

"Pretty?" Mum laughed. "Her?" She tied the bow of her collar, white and fluffy, and spread its fullness carefully over her own generous breasts. "P'raps she would at that. Poor Ethel."

"Why'd you say that?"

"She'll never know love." She flicked at the bow again. What about you? I thought but I didn't dare say it.

CHAPTER NINE

August - 1942

Fay wrote to mum. At last Sid's letters had got through. "I'm not running round to her - she knows where I live," mum said, independent now she'd got a new friend - Albert. So when Miss Arnold invited me to tea - something she did each summer for the girls getting high marks, mum said straight away, yes - "It'll be nice for you and Albert's coming round later so I'll have company." I was really thankful dad had discovered Albert.

Miss Arnold lived on the posh side of town, where shopkeepers and solicitors lived. The house was on four floors with chimneys all over the roof. "This way," she said, leading past a shadowy room where I could just make out an oldish figure writing at a desk. "Father's busy . . . always into something new . . ."

"Can I use the lavatory?" There was one thing I knew - posh houses always had bathrooms - I had to see what Miss Arnold's was like. She wobbled her way to the staircase and pointed up the stairs.

It was big. Bigger than grandpa's and mum's rich sister's. There was a heavy wooden lid on the lavatory seat which you had to lift before you could use it - Miss Arnold for certain came from a very refined family.

"While we wait for the others would you like to see some of my books?" Nowhere but the library had I seen so many. There were volumes of leather-bound Jane Austen, Thackery, Dickens and all of Shakespeare. "These are the sonnets," she said, smoothing her hand across them. Till then I didn't know he'd written anything but plays. "Have you read all of them?"

"I'm still trying to," she answered lightly - almost girlish. "Books are . . . my life . . ." She poked at a loose pin in the twist of fine hair at the back of her head. "I love them the way some people love another human being." She sounded half-apologising. "It's quite selfish of me, I realise I should clear them . . . for the war . . . at least the less important ones . . . what's less important . . . d'you understand?" She waited and I gave a nod. "I read such a moving thing in the paper recently." She moved across the room and I watched her hips shake. She pushed herself into a brown, leather armchair and I sat too. "It seems the Japanese were very close to Kuala Lumpur - in Malaya you will remember," she added in her teacher's way. "A Briton who had lived there most of his life and now about to leave as part of the evacuation, concentrated on smashing up his home - his cherished possessions. He had on the wall a priceless hand-painted vellum of Kipling's "If" and this he recited bitterly, punctuating the verses with blows from a hammer." She stopped, closing her eyes and I became aware of the clock ticking politely on the bureau. "Imagine, destroying something you value so dearly -" She pulled herself up. "Let's go and see if the girls have arrived shall we?"

I told mum about everything - the lavatory lid, the father, the books, except I didn't say about Miss Arnold loving them like people - didn't think she'd want me to -

"P'raps it'll be a blessing if he does go." At once I was back in our world - gracious houses and book-lined rooms forgotten.

"Dad?"

"We'll manage . . . we did before he came . . ."

"Maybe he won't leave now . . . Albert . . ."

"Albert . . ." She half-smiled.

"Dad's happier with him here."

She let free a trill of a laugh. "Thank God for Albert!"

Then dad fell off his bike. It was on an early misty morning and he'd swerved to miss an army lorry. Off he went in a commotion of self-pity and accusations, at the same time ordering us, "make two hot-water bottles and fetch the embrocation oil and rub it here and oh! not there . . .!" We dashed round each other like bluebottles at a dog's bone in summer - At last he was away in bed.

"Pshew . . . he's the biggest coward on earth - mark my words, he'll have the rest of the week off." But it was to be more than that - Friday night he announced, "That's it - the accident's finished me, they can go to hell, cornflakes or no bloody cornflakes!" Mum strained to hold her mouth. "I'm going to London tomorrow and see what I can sort out."

So Saturday morning he left. On Sunday, Albert called. He listened disbelievingly as mum told sorrowfully of dad's 'abandonment' - He looked long at her, his eyes warm with appreciation. "I got an idea! It's a swell day. Why don't we fix us a picnic and take it along to the park?"

"All of us? Ethel as well?"

"Sure kid. Go tell her." I hated him calling me "kid" -

Ethel perked up at once and blobbed her rouge on. "Why don't you put lipstick on, like mum?"

"I don't have looks like your mum that's why." She didn't seem sad when she said it - p'raps Ethel wasn't bothered about not being good-looking -

Mum sliced the Spam Albert had brought and we stuffed sandwiches in his big khaki bag and off we went. Me and Ethel sat together on the bus while Albert, by mum, talked away in his American mixed just a bit with the accent like I remembered it in grandpa. Mum seemed to have forgotten to be miserable -

It was fresh in the park. Except for a few soldiers and airmen with girls - on the grass - under full leafy August trees - it was mostly older men and women throwing crumbs to the birds who didn't know there was a war on. "Fancy a ride on the lake?" Albert offered. "I'll say!" I answered, all American. We got in the wobbly row-boat, mum and Ethel laughing, young, nervous girls both and then mum called Albert her "gondolier" and he rowed till the sweat made rivulets down his forehead. I held his uniform jacket on my lap - it had his smell on it - cigarish - I traced the upside-down stripes on his sleeve with my finger, suddenly wishing dad had made it in America and smoked cigars instead of his old pipe. "Enjoying it Ethel?" She had her hand trailing the water. "Aye, I am that," she said in a softer way than I'd ever seen her.

Afterwards we had our lunch then walked slowly like we was all on holiday and I said in mum's ear what a nice person Albert was and Ethel was a bit ahead, listening carefully to Albert and mum said yes, Albert was nice and all the while watching the both of them.

At home mum did a big fry-up of left-overs, like Bubble and Squeak. Albert said it was "real good and we don't have nothin' like that in Montana." Then he rocked a bit in the chair of Mr. Parmer's mother, lit another cigar and the bends and twists of it went over me and mum and Ethel.

"Fancy some music?"

"I sure would," Albert answered mum, looking a bit too long at her I thought - so mum did her impression of a French cabaret lady singing "Zuzette" and when she got to a certain line she winked her eye devilishly and Albert slapped his thigh, saying she was "a goddam star turn!" Then she switched to "Dark Eyes", a special, sad Russian song she'd always done at family get-togethers. So much feeling would she put in this everyone would cry. Now Albert was gazing at her, his Russian soul clear in his face.

She didn't ask me to do my turns - still cross about the Working Mens' Club - instead she asked Ethel, "Any party pieces?" It was wicked of her 'cause she must have known Ethel couldn't do a thing. "What about 'She's a Lassie from Lancashire'?" We all looked towards Ethel who went deep red down to her neck. Mum played a chord and we waited.

It wasn't that Ethel couldn't sing in tune, it was just she didn't know where to put her voice - soprano or low down - it wavered about, sometimes wildly like a fish trying to get off a hook. I joined in the last bit, singing loud to snuff out her sound. Albert said it was "a real experience" and at that mum exploded with laughter - I nearly did as well and ran out the room.

Albert must have been sorry for her 'cause that evening he gave her lots of attention till she glowed like a paraffin lamp that's just been cleaned. Then it was cards. Cards were in mum's blood and she was lucky. Now it was rummy with Ethel and Albert losing every hand to mum. I dreamed away in the rocking-chair wishing Albert would see beneath Ethel's plain face and fall in love with her so's they'd live happily ever after same as in the films -

The front door slammed. I stopped rocking - Albert dropped mum's hand - Ethel had gone to bed - Dad was returned from London.

That night I dreamt a long dream. All my dreams were vivid and this one just like for real. I wanted to tell Ethel about it in the morning but she'd left for work - "Ethel, you got married to Albert", I wanted to say to her, "your hair was done short and curly, your lashes mascara'd to thick fringes and you wore a long, white silk dress which rustled as you walked and I was your bridesmaid and carried your enormous lace train very carefully as we walked down the aisle, everyone in church smiling, and Albert was waiting at the end, his blue eyes startling with light and happiness. Then the minister started the ceremony but he wasn't a Church of England minister - he was Jewish and we were in a synagogue under the canopy and we couldn't understand the words he was chanting and at the end Albert trod hard on the wine-glass after you'd sipped from it and everyone shouted "*Muzzletoff*" for luck." I lay there watching the morning sun catch the uneven ridge of the out-house roof. Then I remembered the end of the dream - where mum was watching alone from the balcony above and when they had all called "*Muzzletoff*!" she'd shouted, "Bad luck to the pair of you!" Then she'd let free bitter tears which had fallen on the heads of the men and women beneath, like heavy rain.

"You're late getting up." I looked at mum to see if she was still crying. Funny how strong dreams are.

"Is dad . . .?"

"Your father's gone to work. Albert's back at base. Ethel's

62

already left. Now -''

"Is he still going - dad? Did he say?"

"I don't know - oh, let him live with his long-faced sister - see if she'll put up with him and let's hope she's a bed strong enough to take the strain!" She drew the curtains wide. "Move yourself now, it's a good day to do out this room."

I well knew this habit of hers - when she was upset it'd be a thorough turn-out of the house - sweep and scrub everything clean, polish it all away, like the more order in the place the less the muddle in your life seemed muddled. So I set to, doing out Ethel's and my bedroom. I rolled the rag rug and threw it out the window, ready to beat across the washing-line. Fresh sheets were put on both beds and while I worked I thought about Sunday and what did dad think when he found Albert here again - didn't he ever remember that time she'd nearly run off with the lodger?

I swept under my bed, then dragged Ethel's case from under hers - there was an awful smell coming from it.

"Smell? What sort of smell?" Mum was upstairs, down on her knees, sniffing at the case.

"You look like a dog -''

"Stop laughing - I think I've got a key to fit." Before I could say Ethel wouldn't like mum going through her things, she was away.

"Oh!" I pinched my nostrils tight. Mum had removed a brown paper bag from the now open case. "What is it?" With her nose screwed up she opened the bag, looked in and immediately twisted it up tight again. "Dirty bitch!"

"What?" I repeated.

"Her dirty sanitary towels."

Poor Ethel. Why should she feel ashamed to burn them on the fire or put them wrapped in the dustbin like me and mum did - "What when she gets back?"

"I'll speak to her - Don't look so worried - I'll be careful."

For the next few days I watched Ethel - listening for the case to be pulled out - peeping from beneath the bedclothes, but she seemed never to want to use the case again - so far she didn't know we'd discovered her secret. "Have you said about it to her yet?"

"No," mum answered, a bit uneasy too - p'raps she liked Ethel more than she let on.

63

Dad was busy with his transfer to London. First there was the doctor's certificate telling of his '. . . long-standing back condition aggravated by the heavy lifting at work . . .' Mum read it with a very wry face but I thought of all the times he'd dragged himself to bed, hot-water bottle tied round his back with an old neck-tie - He tried to sound enthusiastic about the next job he'd be "sure to get" and the "big money" he'd be sending. She listened, holding in the taunts and jabs till I almost wanted her to have a go at him 'cause her quietness I knew was keeping her fears inside of her. If only I could tell him - "You're always saying you love her - at least after the worst rows you do - then why are you going?"

But before he went, Ethel was gone. Without any of us knowing she'd packed her few things and crept away. "What made her do that?" dad asked. Mum gave a slight lift to her shoulders, her expression said nothing. A letter came for us to 'please post on my ration book'. And that was all -

The back bedroom was mine! I should have thought about poor Ethel but no matter how hard-up mum might be, I never wanted us to have to have anyone in the house. It was my room - my own, special private place and it was right it should be - I'd waited long enough -

The night before dad left there was a parting row - he said she wanted "a horse not a man!" She came back with, "You're eaten up with yourself and don't deserve a wife and beautiful child!" On it went - ". . . family warned me not to marry you!" - "Liar! Your father begged me to take you off his hands . . . you caused him and your mother nothing but *krenk*!" - "*You* lie! Who blackmailed me into marriage? Only a worm would go into a woman's handbag and take a letter from another man . . ." - "And what a letter eh? No wonder you were terrified I'd tell your father!" - "Blackmailer!" - "Coorvah!" - "Louse!" - "Cow!"

She sat alone - upstairs, doors and windows rattled as father thumped about, searching for clothes, books - "It'll be alright mum."

"Think so?"

"P'raps you could - find a job?"

"Me? With my inside trouble?"

"Shorthand-typing - you'd be sitting -"

"My speed - who'd give me - ?"

"You could try!"

64

"You're like him! Without feeling!" I got the endings of the hurt and anger. At last she was still - upstairs was quiet also.

"We'll soon get another lodger," I told her.

I loved my room - now I would be losing it. Last night I had taken all my clothes off and looked at myself, long, in the dressing-table mirror - this way and that I had turned, seeing the shape of my breasts and the shadow of soft hair over the place mum said never to let a man touch.

Before dad left I told him be careful but really I didn't believe anyone could be careful if a German high in a plane decided to drop a bomb on them - "Got through the First War didn't I?" He buttoned his best suit jacket and was gone.

Albert was surprised dad had left so soon. "I'd have liked to wish him luck," he stuck on the way people do when they think they have to.

He visited lots now - helping with jobs - bringing in the water - "You're real tough, puttin' up with such goddam backward arrangements" - What would he have thought of some of the places we'd lived in in London, with the mice and bugs?

Mum told him she'd be looking for a job - dad wouldn't have much to send us after he'd paid his sister. "I'm slow now but once I was so fast I could take dictation straight onto the typewriter."

"Is that so?" Albert said. She stood by him, her lashed eyes heavy with the mascara she'd never give up and he leaned nearer, catching a wisp of the Evening in Paris - I could see he'd do anything to make her road easier.

By the end of the week he'd found us two boarders - great Irish labourers working on lengthening the runways at the airfield. "They get good pay so charge 'em plenty," he told her with his peasant's nose for getting the most out of something. I was back in the front bedroom.

Paddy and John were handsome in a big, tanned way with appetites like "oxes" as mum put it. She'd set them down to a pyramid of a dinner with four pounds of potatoes between them and endless suet puddings and dumplings to fill out the little bit of meat ration. They kidded each other and joked a lot - it wasn't so bad having them. Now Fay had started visiting again. She and mum would put their heads close and the old talking would flow and I caught whispers of "the Yank" while their faces took on the 'mother's of the world' look. All mum'd repeat after was, "Sylvie needs special watching" -

Mum seemed happier than I'd ever seen her. What with Albert there most week-ends and dad sending some money and the 'big' board-money, she was rich - and best, no rows, no curses, no swinging moods from father, so that the house got to knowing itself and we in it got to be expecting to be calm and content and it was a new thing for me and I got to liking it too. Then there was the adoration of Albert. I saw it. Fay saw it. Everyone saw he was daft about her. And mum enjoyed every crumb of his love. Her eyes sparkled bright as stars - she sang like a song-thrush in and out of the house. Even the spinster neighbours smiled as they went down the outhouse path. I was happy for her - and yet - if only she could have been that way with dad. I thought about my prayer - the one I said so many times when I was little -

> "Dear God, please make mummy and daddy love
> each other so's we can be a proper family,
> but if they can't then let them get divorced
> and both find two other people to love and who
> will love them and then they can get married
> again and we can all live happily ever after.
> Thank you God, Amen."

It looked as though God was finally getting around to answering at least half of my prayer - but what when dad came to visit - for sure he'd see what was happening. Fay said he was "a fool to bring Albert home . . . handed you to him on a plate . . ." She was right - it was one thing loving humanity but how long would dad go on loving Albert when he saw what was what? That night before mum came up I said a new prayer.

> "Dear God, now you've found someone to love
> mum like she wants, do you think you could hurry
> it up and find someone for dad? It might help
> if you could make her a communist, like Rosa
> Luxemberg, if that's not too much trouble.
> Thank you God. Amen."

66

Albert seemed to be getting a lot more sleeping-out passes, even though the small sofa in the parlour was hard. I noticed that whenever he stayed over mum was late coming up to bed.

CHAPTER TEN

Late August - 1942

It was a safe feeling having Paddy and John there. Paddy told me, "Watch out for yourself with all these 'solders' about." They came from the west of Ireland and after an evening's drinking would set off singing about hills with the mist on them and girls with the bluest eyes ever - I wanted to ask why they were helping us in the war seeing as how dad'd told me Eire wasn't on our side - not that he was surprised seeing as what the British had done to them - just the same I was glad they were here. Mum made certain they knew they were just lodgers, most of the time keeping to their own room and when Albert was there him it was who sat in the rocking-chair, flicking his cigar ash in the grate.

Fridays was when the drinking got started proper. They'd wake me coming in late, stumbling up stairs, dropping a shoe - then there'd be enormous pees through the night in the chamber pot so's it seemed the walls were tissue paper.

One Sunday after they got back from mass Paddy found me with "a face long as a kite" - his own was calm and bright at the same time. "Want to see some Irish dancing?" he offered. I followed him to 'my' old room. They rolled away the rag rug and while John whistled and clapped his hands, Paddy tapped his feet, not moving from the one spot, arms rigid at his sides. "Want a try?" I followed his instructions, but just couldn't keep my arms still. "Down girl! Keep 'em down!" he shouted. It was no good - all the training mum had given me to use my arms stayed with me. It felt like walking backwards on a moving staircase.

Mum rushed in the bedroom, angry and flushed. "What the hell's going on?" None of us answered. "The ceiling's nearly falling in and what are you doing in here? Get downstairs at once!''

I heard her above me talking low but fast - then Paddy's voice - I bet she was turning them from me - I'd never forgive her -

"Don't ever do that again - go in their room -''

"We was only dancing.''

"You spend too much time with the pair of them - you're almost a woman now - you must watch yourself -''

"You should talk!'' It came out quick - she lifted her hand. "Don't you dare!'' I yelled, every bit up to her.

Her face was white. "If you ever speak . . . to me . . . like that again . . .'' Her voice watered down - I moved near to her. "It's your father . . . if anything happened . . .'' She was weeping now - ". . . he'd take you from me . . . Remember, what I said, never let anyone touch you . . .'' I nodded. She took trembly breaths, trying to calm herself. The next time I played dominoes with Paddy we stayed down in the kitchen.

"Cat got your tongue?'' he asked, as I sat uneasily watchful since mum's warning. He was looking down at the dominoes, the tip of his lashes curly as a girl's. "Your move.'' I lifted the black, oblong piece of wood, feeling him looking into me - "Huh!'' He slapped down another piece. I stared on at the fortress of wood with its white spots spreading train-like across the deal table. "Your move,'' he repeated. Now I looked up at him and a strange stirring vibrated through me like I was a musical instrument.

He took to bringing in water. At night he'd empty the slop bucket after washing-up - and best, he'd empty his and John's chamber pot. "Fancy a game of cards?'' he'd offer when mum was off out with Albert or "What about a bit of a sing-song?'' He wasn't much of a singer but John had lots of Irish *schmaltz* as mum would have put it and Paddy and him would get all soft-eyed as John's tenor voice went through the place.

"It's a pity you like your beer so much,'' I said once after one of these 'concerts' - They just laughed. Mum said they were "Irish fools giving the publicans most of their hard-earned cash'' but lately it was her going to the pubs with Albert. She'd never done that - it was something Jewish women didn't do - go to the public house like the *goyem* while the children sat outside on the step. Dad always said they did it to forget their rotten lives but would he be as understanding when he did find out?

68

When mum got back from these outings she'd be gay and excited, not just from the alcohol but from being at the centre of things with her piano-playing and the servicemen and their girls crowding around her - it was far from being an opera star but mum was loving it. The happier she got the more I thought about dad. Was he miserable? Was he missing me? Was he safe?

"Peaceful without your father isn't it?" mum said.

It was almost time to return to school, the last September ever that I would. I didn't want it to end - it was scary - the world was frightening, not just because of the war - it had always been, just like dad said, with everybody scrapping to get by and treading on each other while they did so.

"It's nice out. Want to help me tidy the garden?" Mum had on her loose smock, flower-patterned - nearly all her clothes had roses or daisies or mixes of flowers. This one was rust and gold same as the colours in the garden. So we raked and gathered and stacked ready for a bonfire and when the flames did whoop through the leaves, cracking them into a last bit of life, I whooped inside myself too and it didn't seem so bad that the world was scary -

"You two are busy."

"Dad!" He was in the open doorway, the flames making an unusual rosy glow on his face.

"Where'd you come from?" Mum's voice was even.

"Wrote. Didn't you get it?" She rubbed her arm across her forehead and went into the house. "Wait till you see what I've brought you!" I tried to smile. Mum was washing her hands, scrubbing her nails hard. "Soon be back at school eh? Good. Learn all you can . . . How's the Irishmen?" - this to mum - "Not giving any trouble?" He pushed a parcel at me. "Undo it." I unwrapped a skirt, of neat, grey flannel of the finest quality.

"It's . . ."

"Well?"

"A lady's skirt."

He smiled. "You bet your life it is." He leaned forward, untying the laces in his well-cleaned, black leather shoes. "Bond Street you'd have to go to find one to match it. Got it made up special for you in my workshop." He stretched his legs. "Better." Now he set a small box of chocolates on the table. Mum wiped her hands hard with the towel. He pushed the red box with curly gold edging to the middle of the table. She paused - twisted her wedding ring. ''Thanks.'' He took his jacket off and carefully spread it across the back of his chair - then he took out his pipe. ''Dying for a good smoke.''

''How long you staying?''

''Till Sunday,'' he answered her.

''I'll get the single bed made up for you.''

''She can do that,'' he told her.

I felt I ought to be sending a prayer up to God thanking him for keeping Albert at the base this week-end though I wasn't sure God would approve of my reasons why -

Much later the sound of John and Paddy, laughing and chatting with the good temper beer brought them, drew nearer the house. Then the familiar bumping up the stairs - ''sshing'' each other - then the heavy snoring of men with drink in them that I was getting to recognise - and all the while me and mum and dad, still, in our room, listening to the breaths of each other in the darkness and trying to guess from the beat of the breaths what each was feeling.

In the morning they went to early Mass as always. Mum was up - dad's bed empty. The black-out curtains were drawn back and I could see grey-blue smoke from the chimney opposite. Already it was chilly - there was something about Sunday morning chillness, p'raps 'cause there was more time to notice it. Downstairs they were talking - mum's voice, fast, not waiting for answers - on and on - Now, loud, I heard her clear - pleading - ''. . . we're not living together . . . why hang on to me?'' Then him - ''I'll never let you go!'' I got out of bed and went to the top of the stairs. The lino was cold under my feet. What would Paddy and John think if they came back now? P'raps I should yell down, say stop, before Paddy and John got back, at peace with themselves and the world. Now he was begging as a man might before being hung - ''Don't!'' I wanted to call, ''Keep some pride. She'll hate you more this way!'' Then my name - the old tricks out of his hat - ''Think of her, she needs a father . . . love her . . . love you both . . .'' ''Love?'' she mocked, ''You don't know the meaning of the word!'' She flung it at him as though the whole world had done her an injustice. And then he wailed - I covered my ears - the wail had all the agony of our race in him and she kept herself apart and cold

70

like the hardest of Christians when they call "dirty Jew!"

I sat on the top step, my face tight against the bannister. "I won't cry! I won't!" The front door opened - last night's drink smell was still on them. "Go away! Go back to your church and priest who says you marry and stick it to the end, even if you hate each other!" But the words were only in my head and anyway, were their priests so different from our Rabbis who also said you should stay together for the family and for tradition? Oh, why did Paddy have to hear it all - and why oh why daddy, did you ever bring Albert home?

There came a loud crash - mother's scream - Paddy and John were in the kitchen before me. Father's hands were around her neck - her hands pulling at his. The weight of Paddy threw dad to the floor. He stayed there, looking like an old tramp - John brought down whisky "Hold her head still," he told me. She was shaking so's it trickled down her chin. "Get your mother to bed." Paddy ordered.

I lay on the bed with her, patting her like she was a baby. In the parlour beneath, Paddy and father were talking. Now and again a big sob came from him - On it went - all that morning and none of us thought of food or the world and the chill Sunday slipped away till it was regular Monday morning again and dad had gone.

First day of autumn term - it was good to be back at school. "You're working like a beaver," Miss Arnold said as I stacked books away after the others had gone. I wanted to tell her, "It's my last chance Miss - to get all the answers to the 'why's' and 'how's' 'cause once I'm out there, there won't be another chance."

"Don't get locked in by the caretaker," she warned, heaving herself off. It was still in the room - just rows of desks, ink-stained, slanting down from the back, same as in a music-hall. What was it like being a teacher? I sat on her chair, before me rows of big-eyed girls, attending to me, taking good note of what I was telling them. They didn't chatter or giggle for I spoke of useful, sensible things - things to help them in the grown-up world - things that would stop them being tossed this way and that so's they wouldn't end up in a trap of a job like Sylvie or have to wait for a revolution like dad was still waiting. There'd been no word from him since that last awful Sunday but still each day first thing I did when I got home from school was to look at the mantlepiece -

71

just in case a letter was there.

There wasn't. Just Paddy home early. "Have I done something to upset you?" Since the fight I'd hardly looked at him. "Would you have time for a small surprise?" He was away upstairs, two at a time so's it was like a thunderstorm in the place. As quick he was down. "Eyes shut," he ordered. He poked a box at me. "Open!" I tore the paper off a cardboard box tied with string. I pulled at it but it went in a knot. Paddy stretched it with his navvie's hands till it snapped. Inside the box, stately and important was a leather writing-case. "Open it then," Paddy said. There was a zip going round three sides - I slid it smoothly open. It was lined with green moiré silk with pockets for paper and envelopes and a special small one for stamps. There was even a little loop for a fountain pen.

"Paddy . . ."

"She's lost for words for once is she?"

"Thanks."

"It'll suit then, seein' as you're to be the educated one?" He tapped out a cigarette from an American pack then lit it with deep, drawing breaths. "And mebbee when I'm back in Kenmare after this show's done, you'll scribble me a bit of a note."

I reached up and put a kiss on his rough cheek. The colour flushed into his face. Awkward, he stubbed his still-new cigarette out. John came in and took him off out of it.

I sat at the table, before me my posh present. P'raps I should write to dad first - p'raps he was waiting for that - for me to let him know it was alright - I was still his - his little girl - no, not that - big - no, nearly grown-up, yes, grown-up daughter who was in her last term at school and who was going to do so well she'd show everyone. 'Dear dad,' I wrote, 'this is the first letter I'm writing with the paper from my new writing-case that Paddy got for me' - but that wouldn't do - soon as I mentioned Paddy he'd think of that last time when he'd lay on the floor crying like a hurt animal. If only it hadn't been Paddy - probably he was just sorry for me - that's why he'd given me the present - it was just a present given in sympathy - I screwed the top back on my fountain-pen.

Mum was in the room, breathless and crying. "She's a cow! Cruel!" She scruffed her face with her sleeve.

"Who?"

72

"Her opposite . . . Mrs. Allen . . . the bitch! Who's she to call me names? Wait till Albert hears!"

She had been in Mrs. Lee's - ". . . chatting and laughing we were - two neighbours up the road as well - Mrs. Lee was sorting me out a dress without coupons - on the quiet - in she comes, this Allen one - never liked me has she - worse since Mr. Parmer left - in she comes - 'Morning,' she says to the others - stands chatting to them - then all of a sudden out she comes with it, says no wonder some of us have cash to throw around with the Yanks paying - looking at me all the while - The others went quiet - everyone knew what she meant. I says, 'Just what are you saying Mrs. Allen?' And out she comes with it - says I was a tart! Calls me that! Without blinking an eye!"

"Oh, mum . . ."

"I ought to have hit her, Mrs. Lee said afterwards."

"You should have!"

"How could I . . .? I couldn't . . ."

I found her one of dad's old white handkerchiefs. She had a big blow and another go at Mrs. Allen, the "bitch and jealous hag who couldn't get a second look from a dustman let alone a fine, generous man like Albert." I listened and sympathised and on she talked. The darker it grew the worse it seemed. "They all speak about me." She moved across the bed, pulling at my nightdress. "I've seen them, staring, each time I step up the street with him."

"They don't . . ."

"You don't think bad of me? Put your arms round me. You love me?"

"'Course I do."

"Say so."

"I love you mum." She held to me. "Mum, I think it's better if we don't tell Albert any of this."

"Alright, if you say so." She fell asleep. Yes, Mrs. Allen was a hag and a cow.

At the week-end mum told Albert everything. He took her out and got her a large solitaire diamond ring. She'd never owned anything like it. "D'you know what I'm gonna' do? Knock on Mrs. Allen's door and shove this right under her nose!"

"What about you kid?" Albert asked. "What can I get you?" Mum was upstairs, changing into a fresh dress for him. "He won't free her - d'you know?'' It came out before I could stop it.

"If I was your dad I guess I wouldn't be in too much of a hurry to let her go either." If only Albert wasn't so nice about everything - "Maybe I should go see him . . ."

"No! That'd just make it worse!"

He wrinkled his eyes so tight they almost disappeared between his forehead and chin. "You know, your mom and you'd like it fine in Montana." I stayed silent. "You'd have a horse for yourself. Mom too."

I laughed out at the idea of her on a horse. "We're Londoners. I wish you came from New York." At once I was back in all those films - Broadway, with Eleanor Powell tap-dancing down a winding staircase - Streets with every nationality and eyes and noses all shapes - "We're not country people - we're here 'cause of the war - we'd be no good in Montana."

At last - a letter from dad. '. . . you and mummy are everything to me . . . all I've got . . .' There was a ten-shilling note for me. Mum read it. "Trying his emotional blackmail again is he?" She went to the mirror, leaning close to it. "Trouble is, I should never have let myself be talked into marrying him."

"No."

"Between him and my father . . . may his soul rot in hell -" She found a wayward curl and pulled it into place.

"Lots of women stay single."

"Yeh, those left over from the First War." She anchored the curl with a hair-grip. "I wasn't cut out for a spinster."

She wasn't. Her with the bright face and saucy wink when she did her French songs. "D'you love Albert?"

"No."

"You still want a divorce?"

"'Course." She peered at her face again. "There's still time - for me to meet someone." The diamond flashed as she twisted it. "It's like a loan really. I'll have to give it back sometime."

All of a sudden I felt very sorry for Albert.

CHAPTER ELEVEN

September - December 1942

Albert was moved to Polebrook, fifteen miles away. "It won't make no difference," he told her. "I'll get to see you every chance I can."

Soon she was moping around. Maybe she didn't want him for always but she'd got very used to the attention of a man who didn't care about the whole world seeing his love.

For the last half-hour she'd sat by the piano - picking out the body of tunes with one hand. "Everyone says 'Mrs. Miniver's' smashing, fancy coming?" She shut the piano lid. "May as well -" she finally answered.

So we watched the story of a courageous family unlike any family we'd known, getting through air-raids, sipping tea made by well-spoken Mrs. Miniver, all false-eyelashed - and mum whispered so's everyone heard, "She's too bloody good to be true" - Then the newsreel showed the Allied forces in the north African invasion and I asked mum if Sid'd be with them and she said she hoped not 'cause remember what Fay was like when she thought he'd been killed and for sure a lot of them'd get it this time -

Next day, as I turned the latch-key in the door I heard mum singing. "Albert's written - he's off this Saturday." She was ironing a dress, carefully tipping the edge of the iron around the curve of the collar. "That'll be nice," I told her. "Great!" I thought, with relief -

When I got back from the library on Friday mum was talking away in the kitchen - Albert - had he got away sooner? But it was Fay, ashen and crumpled, half-listening to mum talking on and on, saying words of now and of years gone by, words in English, in Yiddish, to bring Fay back to us, to stop the staring at the floor, the wall, to bring her to us - me and mum and Sylvie, who sat watching it all like it was on the films - I knew before anyone said that Sid was dead.

"It's a shit of a thing - war -" Fay said at last. "Thought he had gambler's luck didn't he?" Her head shook a bit forward and then back like she was on a spring. I'd seen my grandma do that - often.

Much later mum walked them back home. I'd said nothing to Sylvie. There were late October marigolds still holding on in a vase on the table, dark orange and large - African marigolds - did they really come from there and would Sid have seen them - Sid who'd never had a holiday even as near as Southend-on-Sea, Sid, pressing away all the weeks of the years at suits and overcoats with the heavy black iron. S'pose all armies are made up of Sids, even German ones -

I poked the fire and a small dagger sparked up - it twisted, yellow, then purple, all the while alive and changing. "I want to stay alive!" I said it out. "Please God, don't let my dad be killed or any more of our soldiers and let the Russians beat the Germans at Stalingrad so's the war'll get done with quicker and everyone can be with their families again . . ." If only I could have said my prayer in Hebrew I'm sure God would take more notice. I kept my eyes shut - How much longer would mum be with Fay?

Paddy was near me - I could smell his own smell. "Put the light on!" But he knelt by me, covering my hand with his hard one. I stayed, like a rabbit, fixed - His shape against the half-light was of stone - this not the Paddy of dancing and laughter but of hills far away in the west of a far-off land. He took my hand to his mouth. "Don't," my voice, a poor weak thing, said. A sweetness tremored through me, new and exciting. Paddy also was new and a stranger to me. "I'm lonely," he said. "The money means nothing - d'you know?" I didn't and wouldn't ask what he meant. "D'you understand?" he was pleading again. He dropped my hand. "Ah, you're just a kid after all -" He rested his hands on the mantlepiece, keeping his back to me, at the same time kicking the fender several times with his foot. I left him alone.

I was still awake when mum got into bed. "War's a shit of a thing," she said, repeating Fay's words. I fell asleep thinking of that.

I woke suddenly. Bells were ringing, loud, one after the other. "Mum!" She was sitting up. "The invasion!" She threw the bedclothes off and rushed to the window. If only dad was here - he knew all about fighting Germans -

"What is it?" mum called through the open window. Mr. Evans' voice sounded back through the morning street. "They're victory bells! For Al Alemein - what you think of that then?" She stayed where she was, the bells filling the room till the bed itself seemed to be trembling. "Poor Sid," she said. Down in the street Mr. Evans was calling out the news, trying to match his strong, Welsh voice against the sound.

It was November damp - the misty sort that finds the secret bends in your body. People were walking into it - grey, determined ghosts. Someone called my name. "Sylvie!" She was beside me, her nose red at the tip. "Fancy a cup of tea?" she said.

It was steamy in the cafe - a man who looked like he'd just come off a long, dirty shift clung to a big mug. Sylvie ordered tea.

"D'you still go with him?" Better to talk of anything except her dad.

"Who?" So - she didn't want to share her cowboy. The tea was too strong.

"I've lots to tell you." My voice was over-gay.

"Yeh?" She sipped hers, staring deep into the cup. I told her about Paddy and the time before the fire. "You haven't told your mum?"

"Nothing happened."

"Not this time." She sounded so experienced - if only I could have told her something - mysterious and exciting - like kissing right up my arm, not just my hand and my neck - "You won't tell your mother?" She shook her head and sipped more, watching me over the top of her cup, waiting for me to get to the real thing - to say how terrible it was about her dad but all I wanted was for her to tell me it was O.K. - that I didn't have to say anything. She pulled on her gloves - there was a hole in one of the fingers - Sylvie never was very neat. "Bye," she said, moving to the door.

I got off my stool. "Come round soon?"

Albert brought us a turkey for Thanksgiving Day. I asked mum what they were thankful for - she said she didn't know and stuck it in the oven quick. Albert sweepingly asked Paddy and John to join us - mum wasn't keen, watching Paddy with an eagle's eye but Paddy refused for the both of them.

"You know what I'd really like right now?" Albert said, when the turkey bones lay, gnawed clean, on our plates. "A little music." Mum started up "Dark Eyes" - he'd go all soft whenever she

77

played that, saying it was his favourite and was "my old man's favourite to . . ." and it seemed that Albert's father also liked suffering in "the real Slav way . . ." Then Albert cried a bit - he was the only man I'd seen cry besides my dad. When she finished Albert placed his hands tenderly on her shoulders and I could see for sure she still enjoyed his adoration, even if it was only for the time being.

When Sylvie called I eagerly escaped - mum, for a change not asking where I was going. It was quiet out - just one girl bouncing a ball up and down on the pavement.

"Remember our games?"

"Yeh." Sylvie's face softened.

"Eenah-deenah, abba-dasha, rer-rye, dommanasha . . ."

"Chikka-rakka, omm, pomm, poosh!" she finished. A lady passing gave us a questioning look. "I'm not Eengleesh!" I called after her. Sylvie giggled - it was good to hear again - We walked on, past the tidy houses. Sylvie nudged me. Walking towards us were a couple - he was a G.I. - black, very - the woman was large and big-boned with home-bleached hair - patchy -

"I couldn't, could you?"

"What," I asked her.

"Go with a black man."

"What d'you mean, 'go'?"

"Could you imagine one kissing you?"

"Yes!" I said back, suddenly thinking she sounded like Mary. "I'd like to feel those thick, juicy lips smack on top of mine!"

She stopped and put her hand on my arm. "D'you mean it?"

"'Course!"

"You . . . can't . . ."

"Why not?"

"It's not . . . right . . ."

"Why not?"

"I dunno' . . . it just isn't . . ."

We didn't talk for a bit. What about that time dad had brought a G.I. to the house - he was black too. Dad and him had chattered non-stop - of Mafia-run politics, boot-legging days and tap-dancing in the streets and even though the soldier was too young to remember a lot of that I was glad dad had someone to really listen to him.

"You should be more broad-minded Sylvie." She kept silent

78

for two whole streets.

"I . . . miss my dad . . ." I stopped still. "Mum'll never get over it." Tears wobbled down her pan-cake make-up. Soon she was sobbing the way I'd never seen her. Two small boys running past stopped to watch. I pulled her into a shoe-shop doorway. There were high wedge-heeled shoes in the window, a different colour on each wedge, five coupons a pair. "Your mum might . . ."

"What?"

"She could . . . meet someone . . . she's not that old."

"A step-father!" She blew her nose very hard.

"It mightn't be so bad." She leaned against me, letting out a small "oh" of a sigh. 'Course, it was more likely I'd be the one ending up with the step-father - "D'you like them?" I pointed to the shoes.

"All right -" she answered, dully. We walked off, through a windy rain. "Remember in the brewery how cold it was on the stone floor even with blankets under us?"

"And we cuddled to get warm," she reminded me. "And when Mrs. Connolly screamed out 'cause a rat jumped over her?"

We hurried on, steps together. "Bless 'em all!" I sang out, "Bless 'em All! The long and the short and the tall!" There was no-one now to join in but Sylvie - we marched on, through the look-alike streets, singing out loud so that several pairs of lace curtains opened as we passed. After we said goodbye I had a funny thought - p'raps Sid getting killed was God's way of punishing Fay for wishing dad dead that time -

Albert had left - now mum was asking "What do you and Sylvie find so entertaining walking round the town?" I opened a book - "Put that down - listen - you haven't forgotten what I told you - about men?" I began reading - "Wuthering Heights" - Miss Arnold had suggested it.

"What do you want to do when you leave school?"

"Something exciting!"

"God only knows where you'll find that round here." Again I thought of the Working Mens' Club - after all, Shirley Temple must have started somewhere. "Mrs. Lee had a suggestion. D'you fancy hairdressing? That's creative -"

"What's it got to do with her?"

She was decided - dad was written to, to 'pay out for her

79

apprenticeship if we find someone to take her on' - He wrote back sharp - they both took this work bit seriously. Yes, though he'd hoped for 'something better for her' he'd pay out even though he was 'against the principle of getting cheap labour under the banner of apprenticeship'. I tried to put the thought of me as 'cheap labour' to a dark corner of my head - meanwhile I'd try and get to the top of the class while there was still time.

I was in the public library. It was fuller than usual, probably 'cause it was so cold out and the library was often warmer. A woman, dark, and with heavy spectacles sat opposite me in the reference room. She was reading a newspaper - her eyes didn't move at speed the way dad's did but carefully, right down the column. The same as dad's her skin was - olive sallow, not unlike the pages in the old books at Miss Arnold's.

She looked up at me - a direct look, followed by a smile which warmed the parchment-like skin. She seemed younger than Miss Gearfield but not as old as Miss Arnold so I worked out she was about thirty-something. She had a prominent, firm nose, not wide across the bridge the Slav way Albert's was but slightly 'beakish' as in a strong wild bird - a Jewish nose it looked and I found myself searching for other signs that she was one the same as me. The lips were full and she held them with the firmness of someone who's been through a bit and managed to get out the other end. I'd seen that kind of mouth in some of the stall-holders in the market stretch of Mile End known as The Waste.

"It is . . . not so cold in here." She spoke quietly but still pulled her coat up around the neck. Her accent was like one I'd heard once - someone old. She turned the long page, her fingers those of a lady, finely tapered and the nails cared-for. "Where are you from?" She answered at once, ignoring my rudeness, "Poland."

"That's where Rosa Luxemberg comes from."

"Rosa Luxemberg? You know of her?"

"My dad does."

She seemed about to say more but looked down again at the paper. Now the book held no interest for me - better to know of the lady opposite with the skin the same as father's and the nose of a Jew.

"Why are you here?" I asked, straight out again.

80

"The war." Quietly she added, "I am Jewish."

"Me also!" Why was I so happy to tell her?

"That is nice." She stretched her lady's hand across the table, placing it over mine.

"Yeh!" I said too loudly so that the librarian watching us came across and told me to keep my voice down.

"I should leave," my sudden Polish friend said. She got up, shutting the clasp of what looked like a home-made tapestry bag. I stood up also.

It was frosty now on the library steps. "Will you come here again?" I asked. She brought one of her deep coat lapels across the other, like a Czar's guard and the colour beneath where it had been was a deeper blue than the rest of the coat. "Perhaps," she answered finally. "My train - it will soon be arriving."

"Train?"

"To London." That's why I hadn't seen her here before. "Perhaps you wish to come with me . . . to the station?"

She walked with long steps which surprised me for she wasn't tall - I had to do one-and-a-half to each of her strides. All the way down Station Road I asked questions - pushing them out before she would be away and again, on the dim platform, more I asked, knowing she wouldn't be offended for wasn't she one of my kind and didn't we understand one another?

Her husband had been English - ". . . in the Air Force - shot down - a good man - not a Jew. His parents I visit here, they are elderly, I stay a little just - then in the library I wait, until a train." She was like a book and it was better than anything Miss Arnold told about. The brim of her felt hat was pulled down and what with the darkened platform lighting I could hardly see her face. She was telling of Poland - before the Nazis - the anti-semitism and while she spoke, quickly, whether from pain or because the train would soon be here I wasn't sure - but meeting her memories, my own came - of fascist meetings and when Blackshirts tried to march through the East End where us Jews lived and how all our buildings came out to stop them while us children stayed with the older women watching from the balconies, and saucepan lids and rolling pins were banged against the railings and as the *boobahs* crashed the lids they threw down curses of *meisse meshinas* and later there were bloody faces to wash and broken bones to mend, but the

81

fascists had not passed -

- and her father had been a comfortably-off businessman - had travelled even to Germany. "Friends there warned him, early on, to leave Poland - he refused to believe - called them scaremongers." She lifted her eyebrows, "Sometimes your own can be stupid . . . at last, from mother begging, arguing, he made bribes, got papers and said for me to go."

"By yourself? When?"

"Wait. I would not leave alone. Around us events were like . . . what is the word? Quicksand - people running like robbers, from homes, possessions, others trying to make quick the contacts with cousins, aunts in America -" She paused. "Is that the train?" I hoped it would be late as always. "What then?"

"The end is - I left."

"Your parents?"

"Still there for all I know, God help them."

Now the train was coming. "Will you write?"

"Write?"

"Please!"

I held the small pocket torch she gave me and she pencilled the address I gave her - Sylvie's - This would be secret from mum.

"You certainly love that library," mum said as I threw my damp coat on the chair. She had a bit of a pout to her so's she looked like some old screen 'siren'. "I thought we might have gone to pictures." P'raps I should say - tell her, what right had we to think of nothing much but our own problems - run off into fairyland in a darkened building when people like Anna and her family had been through so much. Mum thought she knew all there was about suffering - her marriage the greatest tragedy anyone could know. She should be told of Anna - but then she couldn't - Anna was just for me.

The letters did come and Sylvie passed them to me. She was curious but I said nothing, only to "get up quick as the postwoman comes so's your mum don't find out". Anna wrote well - the spelling mistakes didn't matter - it was like she was with me, face to face. I wrote back, telling her of mum and Albert, Sid and Fay so's she could see I too knew of killing and trouble. I told her also of Sylvie and what good friends we were - until her cowboy. And I told her about dad. Now at nights when all was asleep I'd lie awake thinking of what she wrote - about a small child in Poland, a child from a well-off family where the servant brought to school in the middle of the day a dish of good things to eat and how 'the food stuck in my mouth like sand for some of the poorer children had a dry crust only . . .' I wrote back, were these gentile children - for surely no Jewish mother would let her child to school - in Poland or anywhere - with nothing but a crust - ? The answer came - they were the same as us, Jewish, the school was only for Jewish children. It seemed to me Poland wasn't a good place to be, even before the war.

"D'you know anything about Poland?" I asked mum.

"Your father's mother came from there."

I'd forgotten that - that my grandmother was a Polish Jewess. It made me closer to Anna. I wrote, telling her. She was surprised and pleased that I also had 'a link with my country'. Funny how she put 'my country' - would she feel that after years and years?

Sylvie kept bringing the letters - dying to know the "secret" - "Where'd you meet him?" She'd never understand - for her a boyfriend was the only thing worth having a secret about.

The last letter I read over and over - Anna was a communist. Same as dad. But she came from a rich family - what would she get out of a revolution? 'My father says the communists are the party of the working masses' I wrote back. What did that mean - ? I s'pose people like Ethel and Mr. Parmer and Sid and the felling-hands in grandfather's workshop. She answered, 'Your father is korrect . . .' it looked funny with a 'k' - 'but fully to appreeciate . . .' the rest I couldn't make out - words like 'intelligentsia' and 'dialectical', even though I looked them up in my dictionary. What was she thinking about, writing to me like that? S'pose she thought I was cleverer than I really was. 'Dear Anna, could you please keep your letters simpler because even though my dad is a communist, it isn't him you're writing to -' P'raps she'd get offended and stop writing altogether -

Everything was excitement at school for Christmas. I was to be one of the Three Kings in the nativity play. "Thank God they didn't give you the part of Jesus," mum said, "or your grandma would have come from the grave and *schlepped* you from the school!"

"It's funny about Jesus isn't it?"

"Funny, how?" mum asked.

"The way the gentiles celebrate him and yet really he's ours."

"Ours?" She poked the tip of her tongue around the side of her mouth. "I s'pose in a way, yes, really he is."

But it was more than Jesus being born a Jew - it was about how dad always said that Jesus was the first communist. I wondered what Anna would say about that.

CHAPTER TWELVE

December 1942 - Easter 1943

Mum now liked preparing for Christmas. The puddings were long done, with stout to keep them moist like Mrs. Lee said to - the cake was made and maturing with a precious drop of Albert's brandy. I was cutting long strips of coloured paper to make into chains for draping round the years-old wallpaper.

"Wonder what dad'll be doing." The usual Postal Order had come but no letter with it.

"He's brazen enough to just turn up again on the doorstep." I saw she was bothered - Albert was hoping to get an extra long pass.

"What's he do? For the war? Albert?"

"A mechanic, for the bombers - helps maintain them."

"Do many get shot down?"

"Plenty."

I often heard them, droning high above on their way to occupied Europe or Germany. What did they think about, cramped in their planes, bombs neatly stacked, ready to fall on Germans, people same as us, women and babies and old men - I could still remember the screams of falling bombs - s'pose they made the same scream when they fell on Germans.

Christmas Eve I heard from Anna. I'd posted her a gift with my letter, a needle-holder in blue felt I'd made in school. The white stitches holding the material together were uneven but Anna wrote it was 'beautiful, what a gennerous girl you are . . .' Next, the part I was waiting for - 'About your father. You may be korrect when you say he would make for me a good friend but my life now is in

84

its own pattern. Sometime you come to London and we talk like before . . .'

It'd seemed such a good idea - Anna and dad - they'd have got on so well. P'raps I could go to London - p'raps I could make it so's they just met. Now mum was saying fetch extra water in, in case the pipes "freeze again tonight."

"Know what I'd like for Christmas mum?"

"No?"

"A bathroom. Same as grandma had and auntie Sophie."

"Her? She can keep her bathrooms - with a husband like she's got."

Mum never did have time for Jack, even though he was a yock and had been circumcised so's grandpa would let him marry his eldest daughter - Sylvie explained what they did when they circumcised someone and I thought he must have loved mum's sister a lot. The family said so too and that it was a real test having a bit chopped off your *schmakel*.

It was bitter in the out-house. I turned the tap on full, still dreaming of soaking in a bath with water brimming to the top and thought of all those times in the bath-house with the attendant calling out, "Hurry up number twenty-two, we got plenty people queueing to have a scrub same as you!" I bet if dad's thoughts for everyone being equal came about, we'd all have bathrooms. I carried the bucket very carefully - the path was already frozen.

"Dad!" There he stood, in the kitchen, presents spread about like he never remembered the last time when he'd tried to choke the life out of mum.

"Surprised?" he asked, cheerful and normal. Mum got me alone in the parlour. "What the hell am I gonna' do? Albert'll be here any time!" She slipped the diamond ring off her finger.

"He likes Albert." I tried to keep the panic from my voice.

"How did I get into all this?" Dad was calling for "someone to have a cup of tea?" I went. Mum kept where she was.

"So - what have you been up to?"

"I've . . ."

"Not like you to be lost for words - come on then -" he insisted.

"I've . . . found a friend!" This would be just the moment to tell him of Anna - never mind she wouldn't meet him yet - if I kept on every time I wrote - about how clever he was and what a great talker . . .

"A friend. That's nice."

"Not for me." I'd tell him now - she's like Rosa Luxemberg and that'll make up for anything - Albert, and mum never loving him and the rotten guv'nors and the First War. There was a familiar double knock at the door. Dad got up, master of the house. I waited.

"Albert! What a good surprise! Come in, come in!"

Albert stood in the parlour, a ridiculous snowman, boots awkward and apart, snow uncaking from them onto the polished floor. He hadn't spoken. Neither had mum. Dad took his heavy, khaki coat and cap. Albert stumbled out, "Just called by to drop off a couple of gifts." Dad said "swell" the way he went all American whenever he was in the company of one of them. "Why don't you stay over?" he offered. Mum went back into the kitchen. I followed.

"What'll you do?"

"You tell me."

"You won't tell him . . .?"

"What can I tell him? He's either a complete lunatic or just playing a clever game."

"I s'pose he just . . . don't want to admit to it."

"He must! I won't let it go on!"

"Ssh!" I put my arms about her waist. "How did you get into this mummy?" I said, repeating her own words.

We had supper - the four of us. Albert opened his wine and we drank it like it was tea. Dad talked non-stop - mainly about the battle of Stalingrad and Albert picked up the mood and kept wishing him "zdarov'ya" - Russian for "good health". Mum sparkled with a mix of excitement and tension and I waited - watching them all -

"What about cards?" Mum had a dangerous look to her. She suggested pontoon, which Albert called blackjack and in the first ten minutes I saw she was cheating both of them.

"Where'd you learn to play like that?" Albert asked.

Before long she was challenging them to "double up the stakes?" Neither could resist. The pile of coins stacked beside her grew higher.

"Where's those mince pies?" Dad was playing the hospitable host. I brought them in. "Here - here -" he shoved the plate at

Albert, sitting between them - all old 'buddies' - chatting, teasing each other, mum flashing those green eyes at both adoring slaves. Just as well John and Paddy had gone home for Christmas - what would they have made of all this - what would anyone make of it -?

We stayed up till past midnight then dad saw Albert settled in Paddy and John's room, Albert more than 'merry' wishing dad many more "zdarovya's". Mum was 'out' to, letting free small snores in our bed. It was bitter cold and I got further down, warming my feet on the stone bottle. Soon father was giving out deep breaths from his old corner of the room and I lay there wondering what it would be like in the morning.

I was up first and doing my usual job - checking if the outside water had frozen. I shoved hard against the back door. Snow had fallen heavily and was pushed right up against it. Everywhere was white and perfect - just a curve of bird's footmarks through the garden. It all glistened - a big, sparkly Christmas card.

I soon had a pan of porridge made. "Umm, I'm hungry . . ." Albert was down, trying to act normal. Mum was next, a red ribbon around her hair. She wore no rouge and looked slightly tragic as though aware now of her position. She didn't speak. "Shall I make my way back to base?" Albert asked her.

"Please yourself."

I dished out the porridge. Albert opened a pack of Lucky Strike, lit one and blew the smoke through his wide nostrils. Like a dragon waiting for battle to begin - Dad came in, his 'comradely' mood of the night before gone. First he asked mum how long were the lodgers away - did they pay full rent in their absence? - did they ever bring drink back? - was I ever left alone with them? All was asked in a seemingly reasonable way, the responsible husband and father. Now and then he looked at Albert, waiting for his acknowledgement, one man to another, that he was doing his duty, his man's proper duty. Albert was chain-smoking. Mum answered in abrupt sentences.

"Have some porridge?" I tried. Again he turned to Albert. "It's never been easy. There should have been a revolution here - Ramsay MacDonald, he was the bastard - we could have had a Soviet England!" It sounded funny that - I'd never heard that before - "I've never gambled - tried to get work - some of the sweat-shops I could tell you about - Jews or not, I'd have stood 'em against the wall and shot 'em. D'you appreciate it?'' - this to mother - ''Did you ever appreciate - for you and her . . .''

''He doesn't want to know!'' she screamed out.

''Don't you think we should get ourselves together . . .'' Albert tried.

They were off. Forgetting Albert, forgetting Christmas day, forgetting everything.

''It's Christmas!'' I screamed, my voice a mad girl's. They stopped - and for a few moments were quiet. ''Mebbee we should all have a little talk,'' Albert said, not looking at father. Dad looked at mum then at Albert - a wild thing caught in a trap. More words foamed from him, packs of mad wolves keen to get at something - anything - to sink their fanged teeth into - to jab and hurt -

I got out the room - upstairs - I covered my ears but the accusations and curses in Yiddish and for Albert's benefit in English also, banged against the doors and windows till they rattled - till even the walls soaked them up so that they were a strange infection spoiling about leaving their dark stain. What would the neighbours think? What would the street think? That we were doing it on purpose? What did Jews care for their Holy Day? P'raps I should open the window - let the cold air in and yell out, scream out like father, ''I like Christmas!'' over and again, ''I LIKE CHRISTMAS!'' There was the familiar crash of breaking crockery. ''I LIKE CHRISTMAS!'' If I shouted it over and over p'raps everyone'd believe it - that was it - shout it - again and again -

Everywhere was quiet. I waited. Still no sound. Maybe they were all dead - stretched out in pools of blood same as in the Greek plays in Miss Arnold's library. Who had killed who? P'raps father had knifed mother, then Albert and finally himself? Or maybe Albert it was who'd killed dad? Then again mum might have done the pair of them in -

I sat on the edge of the mattress, shivering. There was the creak of the back bedroom door - in a little while the sound of dad's crying came through the walls.

Albert was sweeping the broken china into a dustpan. Mother held open her arms to me. ''When will it end - does anyone know?''

''He's unhappy . . . and frightened . . .''

"And me . . . what about me . . .?"

Albert went to phone for a taxi to take me and mum to Fay's then he went back to base. Fay's mother was *frum* - December the twenty-fifth was another day in the calendar. I was miserable there.

When me and mum got back Boxing night dad had gone, together with the candlesticks - the barley-twist ones mum had kept up the *Shabbes* cleaning of even though she'd stopped lighting the candles. On top of our lonesome Christmas tree the fairy smiled on, wand in hand, looking as though she hadn't heard a thing -

Mum wrote to Albert. She didn't want to 'continue their relationship'.

"A bit hard isn't it?"

"Think so?"

I read out the rest of her letter - '. . . you're not a man. You should have told the raving lunatic how you felt about me . . .'

"Why let it all out on Albert?"

"He's spineless! Another man would have gone for him - all those foul things he called me - how could Albert have stood by with his mouth *schtum*?" She licked the envelope and stuck it down hard - then she went straight out to post it.

"You're going to miss him," I said out loud.

Mum made a New Year resolution - to forget Albert and have a good time. She and Fay started going out nights, though Fay wasn't sure about visiting pubs. "What else is there to do here?" mum asked. "Anyway, you've got to make some life for yourself Fay. What's happened has happened, nothing'll bring Siddy back." Fay nodded, her moon-eyes filled with sadness. So, Fay's mother was left alone to read by her thick glasses while Fay went 'pubbing' with mum and Sylvie was off with her Yank.

"It'll be a relief when she's turned sixteen," I heard her tell mum.

"Does he know her real age?"

"I told him, and warned him not to put a foot wrong."

"A hand's more like it," mum put in. They talked on, of girls already "in trouble" and I hoped like mad Sylvie really did know whatever you had to for "looking after herself" -

I asked her next time we met - "How do you keep from having a baby Sylvie, supposing you let a man near you?"

"They . . . wear . . . things . . ."

"What things? Where?"

"On their . . ." She was giggling now and very pink -

"Sylvie!" She was laughing so much the tears were coming. I got more impatient. "Sylvie!"

She sniffed a bit, stopped, then whispered into my ear. I must have looked amazed. "It's true."

"You're making it up!"

"I'm not! You go to Wickstead Park - there's lots there - on the grass - used ones - I'll take you!"

Whoever could have invented such things? Whatever did people first think when they heard about them? Did they laugh too? I couldn't wait to go and have a look for myself.

Albert wrote back to mum - hurt and angry - 'Keep the ring . . . when your daughter's a bit older and this show's all through you can send her out to me in Montana . . .' Mum's bottom lip pushed against her upper one. "Bastard!" she said quietly. I wish I could have said it as well - so much for Albert the gentleman - I was glad she'd thrown him over.

Mum soon got ninety pounds for the ring from a jeweller's shop in town. "Just as well," she said, counting the notes yet again. Dad had stopped her allowance - sending just enough for me. "We'll need another lodger."

"As well as Paddy and John? We've got no room."

"We'll have to take the single bed in our room down to the parlour."

"It'll look like a second-hand junk-shop!"

She twisted the gold wedding ring, the one dad had placed there so long ago. It stood out plain again now the diamond was gone. "Oh well, ninety quid's better than a kick up the . . ." she didn't finish.

The news was great - the German army had surrendered at Stalingrad. Everyone was full of it. Mr. Evans told mum the Russians were "wonderful fighting people, brave as tigers - we owe them a great deal". Mum said yes, they were and we all walked about a bit lighter. I kept thinking how happy dad must be. P'raps it would be a good new year after all -

Paddy and John were leaving us. Mum got in a panic. "Just when I was depending on their money."

"It's not their fault they're being moved on." I was quick to defend them - Paddy really - somehow guilty at the way I'd been with him. Now it'd all be finished - yet it hadn't really started - never would now. He didn't know what to say when it was time to part. I held out my hand. "I'll write . . . if you like." He dropped his chin a bit to his chest in a kind of a nod - I could see he didn't think I would.

It was all so quiet once they'd gone. I even missed the smell of their drink about the place. Again the back room was 'spring-cleaned' and that done mum was all set on replacing them as fast as she knew -

A few nights later she poked me hard out of my sleep. "You're home . . . early . . ." I mumbled.

"It's O.K. I've found us someone!"

"What . . .?"

"Told you there was nothing to worry about. Go back to sleep."

So Pat moved in. She was a good bit younger than mum - and she had a dash about her. She wore her skirts very short and straightaway I wished I had legs like hers. Her hair was shingled and she did the same bunch of curls over her forehead mum did except her curls were harder. Her cheekbones were high and eyes set wide apart - they were large and slateyish-blue - doll-like eyes and I gawked a bit so that she smiled at me till I felt caught out and as she smiled a dimple went deep in each cheek. She was indeed a *shikse* my grandfather would have approved of. Her husband was serving overseas and once she'd told us that she passed quickly to other things, like about her job as a conductress and how she was training to be a driver.

We soon learned she had a man-friend. I saw them by chance, in the town - she didn't see me - they were in an alleyway talking up close together and I noticed by the way he held her elbow and her head was leaned in towards him that they were "up to something" as Fay would have said. "He's fat and much older than her!" Mum didn't answer, a lodger was a lodger. With Pat about mum didn't seem so pretty. She was eating lots more - a sure sign she was miserable. She wore her loose smock nearly all the time trying not to look at Pat's long, shapely legs and slim hips. Pat rode a man's cycle to work and when she got in her face was glowing with health like the advertisements said you would if you took Bile

Beans - no sooner would she be in then she'd be off again - lifting her leg right over the cross-bar in an easy, graceful sweep till her skirt went up even shorter. "You notice her fancy-man don't call here for her," mum observed thoughtfully.

Suddenly the forsythia was out in a cheery, yellow mass and the last of the dead leaves blown away leaving space for the Spring narcissus and the same strong daffodils coming up year after year. I went and took deep, big sniffs at them - no wonder that Mr. Wordsworth did a poem about them -

I was fourteen. It didn't feel different from thirteen. Father sent a whole pound note so I knew fourteen must be significant.

"He wants me to go stay with him in the Easter break."

"He's your father. I'm not putting you one way or the other - as long as he don't come here -"

So, I wrote back saying I would. I kept thinking and thinking - if only I could get Anna to meet him - maybe I could slip away from dad and meet her and talk and talk till she came round to seeing just how good they'd get on - if only she'd agree! But already I knew enough of her to realise she had a will strong as an ox -

The girls at school gave each other home-made Easter cards. Mary gave me hers, saying, "Thought you'd like one though I know you don't keep Easter same as we do."

Why'd she have to say "we" like that? Or was I being too sensitive? I thought about the Passover festival, *Pesach*, *our* Easter - memories like bright jewels flashed in the darkness of my head - mother's mother with her quiet, tidy body going from room to room. The children gathered, sons-in-law and their children, eager, bored with grown-up prayers and chanting, for the religious bit was something to be got over quick as possible so's the real bit, the best bit could be got on with. It was the food me and my cousins waited for - the *fress* that grandmother and the daughters had stayed up nights for preparing, shredding, mixing, simmering, tasting and finally laying out on long tables that went right around the walls for the family to gaze at, praise and finally to eat!

"Let's hide under the table!" Sarah, Melanie and Rebecca would pretend innocent - "Why?" But they crept, with me, under the long, white cloth and there we'd wait till no-one was about, above our heads, fish, cakes, biscuits and best, almonds and raisins in glass bowls with fluted tops set along the length of the table. And Oh! The feasting, the munching of white almonds with the light brown skin still on them and the sweetness of the dark sticky raisins from warm, sunny lands - and Oh! The way our heartbeats went in case an aunt returned and we were caught out. Once it was uncle Mark who came in - we were still hiding and him it was who stole the almonds, big handfuls, so that we heard the gnawing of his teeth above our heads and while the others covered their faces to keep the giggles in all I thought of was that my chance to have a go at the almonds had been spoiled.

Afterwards there would be games outside - cobnuts rolled along the pavement, hard, till you saw how many you could hit against the wall and keep for your own. We were rich as princesses with kings for our fathers.

Mum and dad would be 'friends' for *Pesach*, mostly because she was ashamed for the others to see just what a mistake she'd made and he because he loved grandmother better than his own mother. "A fair woman she is, always fair." That's because she never took sides whenever mum went to her with tears and pleas to return home.

So we dressed in our new clothes grandma got us from the workshop and everyone would exchange compliments - "How well you're looking!" and "What a beautiful girl she is *kayn aynhoreh*!" and "He's the image of his father's brother, God rest his soul!" And the fascists holding meetings off the Whitechapel High Street seemed a tiny band of hooligans compared to our great family strength and unity.

"Do you miss *Pesach*?"

"'Course I do." Mum took on a soft, sad remembering look. Would dad be remembering, stuck in London with his sallow-looking sister? And would he think also how well he and mum acted so's they almost really did like each other?

All this I was still thinking of on the train journey to dad. It was very full, mostly servicemen being sent from one place to another, some loudly complaining of it too though where they'd come from or where they were going to we were never allowed to know - Mum got an elderly couple to "give an eye" to me - soon dozing, the pair of them, as the train made its way towards St. Pancras station.

How would dad be when we met - joking like nothing had happened? Full of his talk on how to settle the world's problems? Silly that, him fixing the whole world yet not knowing where to start when it came to his own life.

There he was at the barrier, stretching to see where I was, a bit of panic in his eyes in case I hadn't come after all. "You're looking good!" He kissed me though I couldn't kiss him back.

"So do you. You got a new coat." He should never wear dark navy, it made him seem paler than ever and severe as an undertaker.

The station buffet was crowded like the train and queues soon formed for steaming teas - odd bits of talk cut into dad's chat so that instead of listening to him I looked about. There was the familiar poster, 'CARELESS TALK COSTS LIVES' - p'raps I ought to be listening to the chat around me - just in case. He was poking at me. "Your mother - well is she?" I nodded. "Sorry . . . about Christmas . . ." He looked away, seeming interested in what a couple were whispering at a nearby table - they seemed in love - he watched them for a bit - "I didn't mean to . . ." His voice was trembly - p'raps I should tell him now about Anna - give him something to hope for - "I love you both," he was dabbing at his eyes. "Miss Arnold says I'll be top of the class this year." My voice was too loud. "You were always a sharp one." His was dull.

I didn't like it at my aunt's. She was long with the same severe, dark looks of all their family. I was glad when we left there next morning. "She doesn't like me."

"Your aunt Sarah?"

"She don't like mum. That's why she don't like me." He didn't contradict me but made sure we were out most of the time.

"I've a special treat for us tonight," he said on Saturday. We were in Trafalgar Square. It was a sort of ritual, everyone did it when they came to London, just to see if Nelson was still there, on top of his high column, defiantly daring the Germans to come, one eye and all. "Got two posh tickets in the dress circle of the ADELPHI!" He said the name deliberate the way a circus-master might. I grinned and didn't say a word. I didn't have to - he knew I was thrilled.

That evening at the theatre I had the same feeling I always had

94

when I was at the pictures - that outside wasn't the real world at all, where things didn't come right and people didn't stay loving each other, the real world was here, soft and full of colour and everything working out so's people were happy and getting their proper rewards.

"Mum would've liked it," I told him at the end. "She would," he answered.

He sat quiet on the bus back. I oughtn't to have mentioned mum. Maybe this would be a moment to tell him of Anna - "Dad," I could say, "I've got someone for you, she's just like Rosa Luxemberg, a communist, just the same . . ."

"Albert . . ." he was asking.

"He don't come round no more."

Just before we went to bed that night he said, "Albert's a nice chap." I lay on the bed-settee thinking of that - Miss Arnold would have called it a "charitable attitude" - so too would Mary and her mother - and Ethel - p'raps all gentiles thought that way - p'raps Jesus drummed it into them - anyway I believed dad was being "charitable" because he knew he didn't have nothing to fear any more from Albert.

The week-end was over. He put me on a seat in the train. "Look after yourself won't you?"

"I forgot to tell you - we've got a lady lodger instead of . . ." The train was moving and he rushed to leave. "That's good!" he called from the platform. I went to the carriage window and waved. There was a sweep of steam and for a bit he was lost in it - when it'd cleared he was gone. Then I remembered, mum had said to get round him to send money for her too. I'd forgotten, completely.

CHAPTER THIRTEEN

April - July 1943

One of mum's favourite songs was "Lover Come Back To Me". Lately she was singing it a lot. "You sorry you gave Albert up?" I'd asked it before I thought. "He was good to me - and you need a man to tell you you're lovely - every woman needs that."

95

Pat's husband was always writing to her. He was in the Far East - "running away from the Japs" Pat tried to joke. Sometimes weeks would pass and no letters arrive then a pile would be pushed through the letter-box and mum would stack them on the mantlepiece, waiting to see Pat's expression when she got in but she would just glance at the carefully printed name and address, hurry to wash, eat her meal and be out. "D'you ever worry about him not coming back?" mum asked once. I saw the temper flash up and as quickly the dimples returned. "He's my husband isn't he?" After, mum said, "She's not bothered if he's blown to smithereens!"

It was May, with the air sweet again and the days longer so that the black-out curtains didn't have to be closed so early, shutting us off as though we were in a tomb. The latest war news was good - a funny word that, to describe a lot of killing and women left widows on both sides but if it meant the war ending sooner then I suppose it was 'good'. The Germans were surrendering in large numbers to the British and American troops in north Africa and Mr. Evans repeated the details from the papers to his customers as proudly as if he'd plotted the battles himself, from behind his counter with the marble top and the big bacon-slicing machine.

There were lots more U.S. airmen in the town now. The 384th. Bomber Squadron had arrived at Grafton Underwood and everyone knew it. They flashed about - big-hearted, big-mouthed, bigger even than life itself. Once an open truck full of them passed me and one yelled out, "Hey! Good lookin'!" I held my school satchel tight, pretending I couldn't hear the wolf-whistles, but I couldn't wait to tell Sylvie -

Mum had come from a family of card-players - not gamblers the way Fay's Sid had been till poor Fay didn't know how she'd find money to pay the rent from one week to the next. They played cards 'cause they loved it - the challenge - the outwitting - so it would be rummy, pontoon, whist, week-end after week-end the tribe gathered, voices high, tempers flaring and grandfather, always a bad loser would scream at wife and children for their "cheating and conniviving to make me for a fool!" Once he overturned the oval mahogany table round which they all sat and cards, 'kitty' - the pool of coins in the centre - went spraying over the floor. After every 'hand' there'd be an inquest with all trying to be heard at once - who played what card - who should have and didn't - the cunning, craft, skill, all was discussed, analysed and we children listened and learnt. When they were all hot and dry from so much talking it was our task to hand round mounted dishes of fruit - oranges cut in half, apples peeled and quartered, grapes with the bloom still on them, then they would suck, eat, chew, spit out pips onto small, decorated china plates and refreshed, play on.

Now mother, without husband or lover, took to playing cards again. But instead of the family, it was the Yanks who sat with her around the clean deal table. Like her they were lonely - bomber pilots and gunners who flew their missions by day and if they didn't get shot down, came into town at night for drink, women and excitement. With them mum played for money too but for high stakes and for mum that was excitement also.

That's how I met Rex . . . Mum brought him home from the pub with a couple of his buddies. He was a muscular man, the kind dad would have described as "good build for a boxer" - dad's hobby was studying boxing which I thought was odd for a communist. He kept his hands in a semi-clenched position, just as though he knew how dad would have described him and he had the clean, blonde looks of a German. He stared at me like I was a woman.

"This is Rex, from Ohio, short for Dexter really," mum introduced. "Say hullo."

"Hullo Dexter," I obeyed.

"Hi kid," he said, bearing a bit heavily on "kid" which made me all the surer he didn't think I was.

"She leaves school in a couple of months," mum added, for once missing everything.

"Sorree! Hi, young lady!"

They played till after midnight while the ash-trays got fuller and the gum-chewing harder. Rex was winning and mum getting worried though she wise-cracked away.

"You're sure a game one!" the second lieutenant from New Jersey told her. It was blackjack and now she was playing in her "to hell with everything" way, bidding for higher stakes with a devilish challenge in those eyes so's they didn't know where they were at and all the time the half-smile about her mouth and the cards held to her chest the way women hold a baby. She glanced back at me through the smoke. "I'm O.K." the look said. I sat in the rocking-chair, the sound of their voices with "Gimmee' another"

97

and "Show me what you got", gradually waving over me till I fell asleep where I was.

It was after two. They'd all gone. Mum was still at the table, except now she was eating bread-pudding. "Awake are you? I'm starving. Want some?"

"Well?"

She opened her handbag, shaking it over the table. Coins, notes, cascaded down while she went on chewing and laughing till she almost choked. This was exciting - maybe if she went on like this through the war we'd end up rich! Same as my uncle in Philadelphia!

"Not such a fool am I?" She got up, kicked a leg high in the air, saying, "Sod your father! This'll keep us going!" It'd been a while since I'd seen her so full of herself.

Next morning in bed I felt different - I lay there - trying to work out why - and why I kept hearing that "Sorree! Hi, young lady!"

Card games became a regular thing. So did Rex and Buddy, the pilot from New Jersey. When they were in a reckless mood, throwing notes down like they didn't give a damn whether they won or lost, that was when she came out best. Rex took no notice of me and I found myself greedily watching mum as she sat beside him, her face animated and kidding like some gambling house 'queen' on the westerns. Sometimes Rex was extra quiet, just flipping cards across the table and without him saying we knew there'd been heavy losses on one of the latest daylight raids - maybe him or Buddy would be next -

"What do you do in the planes?" I asked one evening before they got down to the business of cards.

"Turret gunner," Rex answered. "Don't mean nothin' to you, that, huh?"

"Maybe if you explained properly I'd know." Why did he always talk down to me -

"Don't mind him honey," Buddy put in, "we ain't been havin' such a good time of it lately." He always brought Scotch with him. Now he tipped a generous amount in a cup and drank it in one. I didn't ask any more.

Pat was hardly ever around, what with her shifts and her man-friend. Usually she'd get home and in a breathless, excited way dash up to her room and minutes later it'd be downstairs, discarded cami-knickers pushed into the washing basket and I'd play guessing-games as to what colour the fresh ones were. She'd smear blue eye-shadow on her lids with vaseline on top so's her eyes were more doll-like than ever - then it'd be scent around her neck and wrists - a leg cocked over the bike - and away -

Mum and Fay speculated. "Why worry?" Fay said. "He keeps her happy and out your way whoever he is."

"Maybe," mum said, "but I don't want any irate wives bashing my front door in."

The neighbours were talking again - 'specially Mrs. Allen from opposite. I was in Mr. Evans' getting the rations and she said, just loud enough for me to hear about the "innings and outings of the whole Yankee Air Force". I stood at the counter refusing to turn around while Mr. Evans went on busily about us sinking forty-one U-boats in one month - he could see though the same blaze on my face our family were known for -

I tried hard as I knew not to think about Rex. It was end-of-term exams, the last I'd ever be doing - the ones I'd promised myself so many times would be my final chance to "show everyone". All the subjects I was bad at seemed to be first - arithmetic was a shambles, geography a foggy nightmare. Each day I got home fed-up and more disheartened. "How you managing?" I didn't answer mum but took myself out her way. In the bedroom I sat on the chair with the torn rush seat. The sun threw late afternoon light in cheering bands across the flowery wallpaper so that its dead colours came alive and I saw it with the eyes of that first person who pasted it on the walls. So what if you can't tell the latitude of Cape Town, I said to the glum face in the dressing-table mirror, you can wave hair without that can't you? I leaned closer to my reflection - there was no prettiness there, not like Pat's. I saw only father's intensity with the same dark eyes and mouth held firm. Why couldn't I have looked like mum with a face that danced a million expressions and eyes that even women said were "designed to get you in nothing but trouble". She was playing and singing - the "Indian Love Lyrics" - I knew it so well I could almost sing it with her - "When I'm calling you-ou-ou-ou-ou-ou-ou, Will you answer too-oo-oo-oo-oo-oo-oo?" Her voice was so much better than mine, no wonder Albert fell in love with her - anyone would - and who would love me? Rex for sure wouldn't - he was too old for me anyway - and besides, even he was caught in mum's charm wasn't he?

"It's over! Freedom!" Mary danced me around the playground. It was all done with - exams - results - my childhood - our last day at school was here. Some of the girls were crying. "Look at 'em, great booby-babies!"

"I start my apprenticeship next week." I wanted to cry too.

"Will you do mine for free? Fix me up with a peek-a-boo hair-do same as Veronica Lake?" She strutted about like the film star, hand on waist, pulling her hair right over one side of her face.

Miss Arnold asked what I was going to do. "My parents are still undecided," I mumbled. I hadn't let her down completely though, being top in English and History. Maybe I could tell the ladies whose hair I'd be washing about the Battle of Waterloo or recite passages from "As You Like It".

Mum and dad agreed before any premium money was handed over to Maison Andre I would do a month's trial there. My wage would be seven-and-six a week. Dad said he was 'a capitalist opportunist' - I tried to forget it all in the little while left to me. Would Rex see me any different now I wasn't a schoolgirl - ? He and Buddy hadn't been around for a bit - I didn't want to think of them being shot down by German fighter planes yet I longed to talk about him with someone. If only Sylvie could keep more than one secret at a time - Should I write to Anna? What could I say - ?

'Dear Anna,
    It is so important to me, getting your letters. It's like you were my big sister, one I never had - a wise and kind one who I could tell my deepest secrets to - and that's why I'm going to tell you . . .'

I read what I'd put. What was I going to tell her? Was there anything to tell? I was sure Rex really liked me a lot - there was that look about him - only when he talked to me - a cheeky, impudent look, daring, yet trying not to show it too much. But would Anna think that was special? It was - to me - I picked up my pen again.

'. . . my news', I finished. 'Now I'm going to be a hairdresser. Mum thinks it's a good idea but I don't

100

think so. What do you think?'

Rex hadn't been shot down. When he and Buddy came again I nearly hugged him, right in front of mum. As usual they got down to the real business - cards -

"Rex isn't feeling so good, are you?" mum said after a while.

"I'll live through it," he tried to joke but I saw he was flushed - almost feverish. I did them all coffee. Rex took his at one great gulp. Soon he was sweating hard. Mum studied him over the top of her cards. "Better lie down a while in the parlour - Don't argue -" as he tried to protest - " there's summer flu' about." He went, obedient as a dog. Buddy and mum went on playing. "Get him the eiderdown," mum ordered, throwing another half-a-crown into the 'kitty' -

When I took it in to him he was on the settee, arms gripped each side of his ribs, shivering and pathetic. "Lie down," I ordered, in mum's voice. I placed the eiderdown over him. "Thanks . . ." came from beneath the blue silk. I longed to touch him, stroke the damp hair away from his forehead - be a gentle ministering nurse so that he'd realise what a mature person I really was -

"He looks awful," I told mum.

"Wait." She left the table. "Give him this while I do a water bottle." She gave me a Beecham's powder.

"A bottle! He's already sweating like a pig!" She gave me one of her most distasteful looks - one that said, you're the daughter of him alright - of course, it was one of dad's remarks - the workshop guv'nors had him "sweating like a pig" - the nights in front of the cornflakes ovens had had him "sweating like a pig" - the whole capitalist system had dad "sweating like a pig" -

"Open your mouth," I told Rex, tipping the spoon carefully onto his tongue. He let it stay there, pulled a face then suddenly grabbed me and kissed me. I was rigid. Solid and unyielding. The kiss was wet and tasted of Beecham's. He let me go.

"Sorry." He slid down the settee, pulling the eiderdown high.

I crept upstairs. Was this what being adult meant? Was this what mum yearned for and Fay missed? And what Sylvie thought of most of her waking life? I looked in the dressing-table mirror - did I look any different? I did. Around my mouth was a large white ring of Beecham's powder. I looked like a clown! "It's awful! All of it! Awful!'' I wiped it away harshly. If this is what kisses were about they could keep them.

The next day Rex went back to the airfield. He didn't look like he'd die anyway.

CHAPTER FOURTEEN

July - November 1943

The Allied forces had landed in Sicily. Mr. Evans was saying, ''It's the start of the finish, so to speak. Mind, them Italians was never known for stout hearts when it comes to fighting.'' Funny, that's just what dad always said - him and Mr. Evans had lots of ideas the same - though I didn't think Mr. Evans wanted a world revolution.

Mum didn't speak much about after the war - when Fay went on about having no home of her own to go back to, mum just said in a mechanical-sounding way, ''Something'll turn up.''

I hurried to my first morning at Maison Andre's just as a rainstorm started. At quarter-to-nine I stood outside the large windows with the coiffeured heads immaculate and haughty, a contrast to my own wet hair.

''Pleased to note you're a prompt time-keeper,'' little, fat Mr. Andre said with a switch-on smile, unlocking the door. He rolled up the sun-blinds and pointed me to the back room. Rita, the First Assistant was very cool and her eyes squinted narrow as she noted my bedraggled head. She gave me a green overall, too tight across the chest and long, probably one of her cast-offs - She pointed to the implements I was to become very familiar with - not scissors, combs, pins and curlers, but a broom, dust-pan, mop and bucket. ''Sweep the step and pavement, then polish the door-handle and brass trim around the window.'' The rest of the morning went with me washing down the cubicle walls - the same bilious green as the overall - cleaning the wash-basins and sweeping up after the First, Second and Third assistants cut and shaped head after head with such enviable authority.

"It's like being a skivvy!" I complained to mum.

"They didn't say about that," she said but though I was dying for her to say chuck it in, she just walked out the room.

Saturday night at half-past-six I got my seven and sixpence. When I got home, Rex was there.

"How's the working gal?" I saw at once he meant for us to forget what happened that last time. I told him about the job. "Must be plenty beauty parlours around, get yourself fixed up some place else." We were on our own and now he was speaking confidentially and fast. "Guess I owe you ... what I mean to say ..." he pushed his fingers through his hair. ". . . I'm sorry . . ."

You should be, I longed to say back, you were my first kiss - it ought to have been smashing like I'd always thought with tingling to my toes and magical till I felt like all the heroines in all the books mum had ever read -

"Your mom . . . you didn't tell . . .?" I shook my head. "Thanks. I swear it'll never happen again." What was he saying? Was it that disappointing for him too? 'Course, it must have been - but there was time - we could try again - he could teach me - Mum came back and I couldn't say a thing.

I kept remembering Paddy and that time by the fire - what if I hadn't stopped him? Maybe his kiss would have been like they should be - sweet and firm and thrilling - I got the green leather writing-case out - I never had kept my promise to write to him. Now I wrote, not to him but to dad. 'Don't pay the premium to Maison Andre. I'm going to find myself another job.'

Miss Minch seemed nice. I got the feeling that when she said something she'd stick to it. So, even though she couldn't take me on as apprentice she promised if Cynthia, her junior left, I'd be taught in her place. Meanwhile, for thirty shillings a week I would have to serve in the shop and assist her and Cynthia. I was rich! Thirty shillings!

Mum worked it out that she'd have twenty-five and out of what was left I should put something away for savings and the rest do what I liked with. "'Course, you'll still be a bloody skivvy," she added, disappointed her and Mrs. Lee's plans for me weren't what she'd thought.

Dad wrote he wasn't sure what prospects there'd be at Miss

Minch's. 'Once the war's finished we'll sort out something proper for you - p'raps it won't be so long now, mind, the Germans won't give up Italy as easily as the Italians -' It sounded funny that - p'raps the Italians really were more peaceable than I'd thought - 'Why don't you and mummy . . .' - I got suspicious the moment I read 'mummy' - '. . . think about coming back here? There's no problems getting flats now. The raids are finished with, looks like. We could go out together tell her, there's still shows on and I'm working regular. It'd be better than where you are . . .' - I gave the letter to mum. "He can go to Hell!"

While we were waiting for the war to be over I got on working for Miss Minch with as good a will as I could. Then I kept thinking how dad was hoping - waiting for us to come and getting excited about finding a new home - if only Anna - I composed a letter very carefully, just slipping in, was she ever lonely even with her work helping other refugees and right at the last mentioned how dad was looking for a place and how happy he'd be when he found one. It was probably the idea of him always so unhappy had put her off him. I'd have to start presenting him better - tell how funny he could be with his belly-dance and his daring like when in the First War he'd stolen eggs from a French farmer's wife and the way he told it doing "cluck-cluckings" of the hens - then that time he'd been tied to the barrel of a field-gun for sticking up to that officer - Anna would approve of all that -

Most nights I got home worn out from work. Thursday half-days I helped mum with the heaviest housework. She was complaining of her 'inside' again. "Will you always have that?" She just sighed. "Did you ever want . . . another child mum?" She gazed at me like I was mad. "It would have killed me." Like always, I immediately felt guilty about breathing life.

We were seeing little of Buddy and Rex. When they did turn up straightaway all Rex's energies went into the cards, he hardly glanced where I sat, watching all. It was better at school - I always had hope then, p'raps that was the difference about being grown-up - you didn't have hope no more - p'raps that was what mum was looking for in her books and at the films - p'raps she'd given up looking for it in real life - dad hadn't. I knew he wouldn't, not even if mum and me never went back to him - not even if he had no-one and Anna never wanted to meet him - dad would always go on - hoping -

The Rising Sun was mum and Fay's favourite for their week-end outings. It was packed always with servicemen, mostly American. After these outings she'd get back, happy and rosy, a 'celebrity' with her piano-playing and songs. Then I'd hear of the 'pick-ups' and fights between the Yanks and British servicemen. "Jealous they are, poor sods, not that you can blame them with hardly anything in their pockets. The women don't give 'em a second look when the Americans are flashing their money."

Sometimes Fay would come back and they'd stay up talking over the night's events or consoling each other about their Fate and why life had dealt each of them such cruel turns.

One night it was Jim she brought home. "Isn't he beautiful?" she said, her arm through his, drawing him into the kitchen. He smiled wide, not the least awkward at her praise and I watched her as I would a stranger for she was quite new to me and not my mum at all. Without knowing anything about love I knew at once mum was hopelessly, deeply in love with him.

She was right - he was beautiful, with a mix she later told me, of Irish and American Indian that gave him womanish eyes of blue, almost purple, with thick-smudged lashes and an easy walk till I could see his forebears padding soft-footed through the forests. From that night she was a girl, fresh, excited and life was no more a drudge of being unwell and dreaming what might have been - even dad wasn't cursed to hell - he didn't matter - nothing mattered but Jim, her God of Love, her Movie Picture Man, Clark Gable and Rudolph Valentino mixed together and presented to her in one unbelievably gorgeous package.

"Talk some more darling," she'd tell him, just to hear the soft, Louisiana drawl and he'd say, like a talking doll, "What you'all want I should say honey?" That "honey" and that voice were to become part of my life too.

And so her world narrowed - Fay, Pat, father, even me, were shadows. The only thing real to mum was him.

"You're looking grand lately, my duck," Mrs. Lee told her and she'd take the words without surprise for she knew she was looking lovelier. Now there was no need for the excitement of gambling, no need for the money she won - he - Jim, was generous and besides, he didn't want his "woman entertaining any other guys" when he wasn't around.

"I'm so happy," she said, her voice almost shy, one night in bed. "You're happy for me . . .?"

"It's all so . . . quick . . ."

She was breathing short, full breaths, full with the thought of him. He might have been there in bed with us. "He isn't . . . married?"

She was talking fast. "His wife's been unfaithful . . . often . . . he's put in for a divorce."

"D'you believe it?"

One night mum and him came home from The Rising Sun. "Rex was there . . . he sends you his love." It came out casually, easy - I turned my back on her -

Dad wanted to know how I was finding it at Miss Minch's. I wrote back at once, wanting only to keep him away - It was fine . . . interesting . . . I was watching everything, learning, even if I wasn't a proper apprentice -

It was true - I'd never realised how skilful hairdressers were - Miss Minch's movements were quick and nimble and while the customers chatted about how to stretch their clothing coupons or another recipe for disguising dried egg, she trimmed and wound strands of hair smelling of ammonia around long, thin metal perm curlers - all to make them beautiful - keep them lovely - so that when their husbands got leave they would find them as womanly as when they went away - and the ones who weren't being faithful could 'tart themselves up' even more outrageously with halos of bleached hair till they were like angels tipped out of heaven.

Mum was awkward like she always was when she had to ask my help in something. "Would you . . .?" I waited.

"I've asked Pat . . . she don't mind . . ."

"What?"

"You could share in the back with her . . ."

"I don't want . . .!"

She grabbed my arm. "He's what I've needed, all my life . . ."

"Dad . . ."

"You know, more than anyone, what life he's given me . . . you should be happy. . ."

"I . . . am . . ."

I shifted my clothes to the back room. Jim got sleeping-out

passes most nights and they wound words like "sweetheart" and "dearest love" around each other till the house became nectared and sticky with it. At night I'd lay on my own bed, uneasy, thinking on father. When I slept it would be wild dreams - like dad arriving and as a mad dog, throwing words foul and bitter - "Wake up, you're in a nightmare," Pat had called from her own virginal bed. She had gone straight back to sleep - lucky Pat - with a husband far, far away -

"Make an effort to be nice to him," mum pleaded, "ask him about Shreveport, his home town, he's always telling me how lovely it is . . ."

When I did he was ill-at-ease, giving out just a travel summary - sentences, slow-drawling and strange names coming at me that meant nothing - Red River - lumber - roses - the early Captain Shreve who cleared the great logjam that had formed along the river - then of course there was the cotton. I thought of "Uncle Tom's Cabin" but didn't dare say - Jim didn't have time for "niggers".

"Dad'll kill you for sure when he finds out," I let out once after he'd gone. She was calm. "I'll just have to take my chance, won't I?" She couldn't have kept Jim away if the guillotine was over her.

It had been a long Saturday with the hair-dryers blowing hot over the salon till I felt like a towel left in a Turkish bath. I must have shampooed twenty heads of every colour. Miss Minch and Cynthia expected soldier-like response from me - "Pass the pins" and "Rinse off the perm-lotion." "Put my lady under the hair-dryer." "Take my customer out the hair-dryer." I stood by each in turn, watching their precise movements as though we were engaged in the most complicated of surgical operations. At times it was like being in a sorcerer's den with smells acrid and foul and steaming sachets bubbling on wound-up heads or heavy, muddy henna rock-like and sculptured in shapes seen only in nightmares. Then I would wash the mud or perm-lotion away down a constantly-running basin and stand by noting every manoeuvre while sweet-smelling, sticky lotion was poured over frizzed-up hair to make it obedient again to each of their wills. Finally, nets and pins would be removed from baked heads and stiff curls and waves combed through with brilliantine, glossily putting back what the processes had taken away. Never would I have thought my feet, so light and quick at tap-dancing could be as heavy as stones by the end of a day.

Mother's sobs were the first thing I heard as I got in. I ran upstairs, two at a time, like I used to in the buildings. The front bedroom was flung about - drawers jutting - bed-linen and clothes jumbled on bed and floor. There was a space against the large wall.

"Where's the wardrobe?"

"Your father . . ." She couldn't speak more, rubbing her chest so's the pain would go. Now she was pulling at the collar of her dress - I pushed her hands away - were there marks - had it been the old game - of murder, that he always played - ? But her neck was clear and white - without bruises or fingermarks -

"He came . . . and a van . . . took what he wanted. First he was smiles, bastard actor - everything he'd got organised - the flat - thought I'd jump at it - How can he still delude himself? Haven't I told him - haven't you?"

"You must be lucky mum."

"Lucky?"

"Jim. If he'd been here -"

"I wish he had! He'd have done the *meshuganah hunt* in . . ." She went to the mirror. "Look at me . . . bastard that he is . . ."

"You didn't mention Jim?"

"Think I'm mad?" She circled rouge hard on her cheeks, then it was mascara but as she brushed it on her lashes tears came again.

"Mum, do your face."

"What good's my looks ever done me?"

I took her handkerchief and wiped the black streaks away then I unscrewed the tiny silver top off the scent bottle. She tipped some behind each ear lobe then a bit in the place where her full breasts met. Inside me I gave a thank you to the Fates or whoever it was had kept Jim busy at the base that Saturday -

Most of Sunday went packing our 'homeless' clothes into boxes. "You'll manage," Pat said, helping push them under the bed. She'd got back in the middle of dad flinging everything about. "Excitable, isn't he?"

"What do you think?" I don't know what I expected her to answer. I needed someone to tell me it would all work out - even

108

that none of it was happening, just my strong imagination thinking it all up in colours wilder than in real life -

She tilted her head and gave me a wink. "Here . . ." She stuck a bag of pear-drops in front of me. They were large and strong-smelling. I put one in my mouth. She took one, placed it between her teeth, holding it there a moment, then slid it to a side where it bulged her cheek. "Lovely," she said, rolling it in her mouth with a slopping sound. I hadn't realised she could be so nice.

Jim was like honey on a wound to mum - soon she was cooing again while he gave long, adoring looks into her upturned face. Even with me around he kissed her long, passionate kisses and she'd cling to his big, easy body till she seemed part of him, like the stamens in the head of a flower.

"It won't be long now baby," he'd tell her and once he'd gone she'd spill it all out - "The divorce's going through . . . he'll soon be free. Imagine any woman looking at another man with a husband like Jim?" Then there'd be a vibrant sigh of gratitude to this woman across the sea, this unfaithful first wife who was now making it possible for her to be happy for ever and ever. "If only it was mine."

"What?"

"The divorce." The sigh now was of regret. "I could have got one eventually, on mental cruelty." I waited for her to tell it again, that I was the cause of her years of bondage. "How many times did he threaten to take you from me if I went through with it . . . imagine . . . never to see your child again . . ."

"He couldn't have, could he?"

"He made it clear, oh yes, if I didn't want him to defend the action I'd have to agree beforehand to give you up . . ." The sweetness of Jim had gone from the room - now the old sour smell of dad was there.

"What's the good then of Jim being free?" I knew that would hurt her and at that moment it was exactly what I wanted - she showed the hurt and briefly, surprise.

"He's being straight with me - I'm grateful."

I knew why - already there were a number of 'broken-hearted' girls left by those Yanks moved on, some of them pregnant too.

"You like him . . . a bit . . . don't you?"

We were sitting outside the back door, the sound of bees working in the depths of a blackberry bush. "Yes," I finally got out.

"Sure?"

"He's O.K. You love him."

"He's under terrible strain - if you heard the things he tells me - what he sees when they get back from the bombing raids." And now she was feeling the pain of war, through him, more than she'd felt it yet. "They're so young, most of 'em - a wicked waste -"

There had been that night I'd heard Jim calling out - "Watch yourself kid . . . don't let the bastards . . ." and then he'd sobbed while mum tried to quieten him. She told me later that a boy, also from Shreveport, had had to be cut free from the top turret when the plane returned badly damaged. Soon after he'd died. She shivered now though it wasn't cold. "Autumn nearly again. I wonder how long it'll be."

"What?"

"Till Jim's moved on." She went back indoors. I sat a bit, listening to the bees.

The Yanks had reached Salerno and all of a sudden I knew that Salerno was on the west side of Italy, half-way up the 'boot'. While mum was now caught up in the progress of the advancing forces in the Italian campaign, dad was still following events on the eastern Russian front and sending me excited notes with, 'They've taken Smolensk - like I said -' and 'Kiev back in Russian hands' - He never wrote about the visit when he'd come with the van but that was his way - doing what he thought was right - taking what he could - by right -

"His flat's nice he says." I'd just read the latest letter.

"Oh?"

I handed it to her. She glanced at it - it might have had his face printed on it the way she threw it on the table. I picked it up. 'I'm not far from Old Street', I read out. She lifted a Netta Muskett novel from a pile on the floor. 'It's handy for the West End so's next time you're here we can have ourselves a smashing time'. She turned a page, saying nothing. "He says he'll buy me some new clothes."

She didn't look up. "May as well get what you can while the going's good." Then she added. "He's your father when all's said and done."

"I don't suppose I'll go."

"Oh?"

Now it was me couldn't look at her. How could I tell her I wasn't able to face him because I was a part of what was happening here - part of a betrayal - of a "life of immorality" like it says in the Sunday papers - and the strange thing was I didn't much care. So what if I didn't much like Jim - mum was happy, for the first time that I could remember. I wrote back. 'Don't know when I could get a Saturday off, it's our busiest day.' But it would have been nice to have had something different to wear.

I managed to find some black-out material and later that week cut myself out a very full circular skirt - a real war-time luxury. Mum watched me stitching it carefully.

"Gonna' take you to the end of the war to get that done." I bent lower, stitching faster, pricking my finger. I sucked at it. "Put that down. Come on."

"Where?"

"To Mrs. Lee. Time you had a new dress."

CHAPTER FIFTEEN

November - Christmas 1943

Miss Minch's was near the public library. Often I'd see people going in and out, books held tight to them in the damp November days, then I'd long to run across the wide road and up the stone steps, saying, "Make way, I've got some proper learning to get on with!" Sometimes in dinner-break I would go, wandering from sections of history books - why did we spend so much time reading of wars - ? p'raps that's why we were always getting into them - to shelves on Politics and Economics and lots of these would be out on loan like suddenly everybody wanted to know what had been happening to them all their lives. Here for the first time I discovered American writers, reading of a world much different from what I'd seen at the pictures. I'd borrow as many as I was allowed and after work rush home with stories by Jack London and John Steinbeck

111

and when Pat was out and mum and Jim fixed with their eyes on each other I'd lose the hours and with them my childhood.

"What d'you do up there all that time?" mum asked once as I came down to warm my cold hands at the fire.

"Read."

Jim was pouring himself yet more coffee. "Reading ain't going to teach you about life. Ain't nothin' gonna' do that 'cept livin' it."

"That's not true!" They both were surprised at my sharpness. "You can get everything from books!"

"You goddam talking shit!" His temper from his Irish half was up - "You wanna' come along with me sometime kid, yeh, to the airstrip when they get back shot-up - see 'em - hear 'em crying out - you'll see life alright - you won't see no goddam books around though!"

"What d'you know about your own people eh?" Now I was angry. Who was he, this fool from Louisiana who manipulated my mother till she'd have kissed the ground he stood on - "I never hear you say anything intelligent - or anything I can learn about" -

"You wanna' hear fancy talkin' huh? I ain't no person for that - I ain't no high-flyin' talkin' man - I just a simple man, over here doin' what I gotta' do. If that don't suit you there ain't a goddam thing I can do - an' I tell you somethin' else - I don't give a shit what you think!"

"She don't mean what she's sayin' honey." Mum was picking at his shirt with hands anxious as her eyes. "Tell him, tell him you're sorry you upset him." I stayed rigid. "You should be ashamed, I thought you had more sense."

I left the pair of them - my cheeks like hot coals - I knew she'd side with him - her God - Is this what love did - blind you to the weak and wrong things in the object of your love? If that's how it was I'd keep to myself - It started to rain, unexpectedly, hailstones hit the window-panes like small angry bullets. How could she love him? I thought about whenever he'd had too much to drink and start on about "those goddam niggers messin' aroun' white women" and what they'd do to them "back home when this show's all through and done". I asked why she didn't stop him talking that way. "He's from the south," she apologised for him, "brought up to think like that, can't really blame him . . ."

112

"They're in the war too. If the girls want to go with them it's their business."

"Don't ever dare speak this way when he's here -"

And again I compared Jim with dad - if only a miracle would happen and mum would fall out of love with Jim and in love with dad -

I heard him leave much later. She sat in the kitchen, her head bent over a soft, white bundle of finest parachute silk. "Look how lovely it is." She held up a piece. It was - fine and delicate, how could such a thing save a man's life - ? "I'm making a nightdress from it."

"That'll be nice."

"You won't ever talk that way to him again? Promise? For my sake?"

I promised but would I be able to keep it - ?

Like all the Yanks Jim was generous with money. He liked her to look good and Mrs. Lee was all too ready to oblige if the cash was there - with or without coupons. "Does this make me look slimmer?" mum would ask anxiously whenever she returned with something fresh. Her favourite was a "jigger" coat - a short, loose jacket without lapels and a small stand-up collar. She'd wear it over most of her frocks, 'specially if she imagined they were a bit on the tight side. "His wife was beautiful, I've seen pictures - young and slim -" Poor mum, trying so hard to equal that other wife. "It's the children as well," she added, "breaks his heart over them, says he'll never see them again." She seemed frightened then, more that she might lose him over them than over the wife -

I needed to see Sylvie - After work I stood outside Woolworth's - a long, cold wait. At last she was hurrying towards the glass doors, trying to button a too-tight coat - her stomach was fat. Just her stomach. She was awkward with me so that we greeted each other politely - "How are you?" and "Nice to see you". We didn't link arms like always, just walked, a bit apart. P'raps I shouldn't have come -

"Got something to tell you!" She stopped suddenly so that a woman walking behind nearly bumped into her. "Look!" She stuck her hand out, the left one and wiggled the third finger so that tiny diamonds around a small opal flashed as the light caught them. "I'm engaged!"

113

"Sylvie!"

"Like it?"

Her finger-nails were untidy as always and I wanted to tell her such a ring deserved a well-cared for hand. "Well?" she asked, a bit impatient.

"Smashing." I'd heard opals were unlucky but didn't want to make her happiness grey. "You're young . . ." Now she put her arm through mine and led me on like she had a full right to be in charge. When we parted I hadn't said a word about my own worries.

"Why didn't Fay tell me?" Mum was indignant at being left out. "The girl's much too young to be thinking of marrying . . . engaged . . . it's ridiculous!" I hadn't dared mention the fat stomach -

Now another part of my life was over - Sylvie a mother - the poor baby born a bastard. P'raps she might be lucky and Harvey marry her, after all, wasn't that what she always wanted -

It was mad at work - it seemed everyone wanted a "perm for Christmas" - By Saturday night I was worn out as a horse after a milk round. Miss Minch was beaming, her takings up and even Cynthia had a good word to sling at me. The shop would stay shut a whole week. All that time off and with pay!

"What you going to do Christmas?" Pat was making herself glamorous for a party at the garage.

"Stay in bed and read and read!"

"You should get out - enjoy yourself. What about your friend?" I couldn't look at her - somehow I felt guilty like it was me in 'trouble'. She was concentrating on her hair with fingers almost as nimble as Miss Minch's - she knew exactly where each curl ought to be placed. There was a bluish tinge about her body as the light caught the imitation silk cami-knickers. She leaned to suspender her stocking and yet again I envied those legs, so different from my short, plump ones - the same as mum's. There were freckles on her back, dark gold and her face was golden too. Downstairs mum was singing.

" Yours till the stars lose their glory,
Yours till the birds fail to sing,

114

Yours till the end of life's story,
This pledge to you dear I bring,''

"Likes that don't she?" She stretched forward, better to see her face. Her doll's eyes reflected in the mirror but I couldn't read them and I knew I could never keep my eyes so safe from the world.

"Does it suit me?" Mum also was getting ready to go out. She had on a two-piece in dark, plum-coloured rayon crêpe. "Not too snug a fit is it?"

"You look beautiful, 'specially the posy." She liked small bunches of artificial flowers, pinning them high on a collar or at the "V" where the neckline ended. "You worry too much about being plump."

"Every woman does!" she defended.

Yes, I thought, but not so much they made themselves sick after meals sticking a finger down their throats. She didn't think I knew why - I didn't believe that story of her gall-bladder playing her up - no, it was him, Jim, she did it for.

She waited for him, the pulse throbbing in her neck like her body was counting the seconds till he arrived - how could he have wound himself into her as quickly as this? Constantly she told me she was happy - yet now she was fearful, glancing frequently at the clock - the mirror - assuring herself that she was indeed lovely, with eyes no man could resist. Hadn't Albert told her? Hadn't the lodger from years ago told her? And dad - even he had told her - and unexpectedly I felt frightened. She saw it and drew me to her. "What's the matter?" I couldn't say - just shook my head as a backward child. Now I rested against her and the smell of her scent I knew so well came over me. I breathed deep its cheap sweetness - if only I could have captured it so that no-one knew it but me - I held on, not wanting her to go out, to stay with me, her child, her baby who needed her love more than any man.

She started at his key in the door. There were the usual tight embraces and long kisses. I went upstairs. Pat had gone and the glass tray on the dressing table showed traces of her face powder. Soon the house was quiet and just mine. Downstairs the fire was low. I put small lumps of coal on. Now I would read - look in my books and see what the people who were part of another's imagination

115

did on the pages.

I'd forgotten them all - mum, Jim, dad, the war - minutes had slipped into hours and words, like a sorcerer's brew had taken me over so's I was safe and secure in this other knowledge - Now I could try out loud names like Clytemnestra with no-one to look twice at me - it was a luxury and I spoiled myself, going over and over it, saying *Cly*temnestra and then Clytem*nes*tra and it didn't matter if I was getting it right and I saw Miss Arnold before me and her way of looking if things weren't as they ought to be and I wanted to tell her, it's all your doing Miss, you shouldn't have let me loose in your library for once I'd got a taste of such beauties you can't blame me for having a go myself even if I don't know how to say the names -

They were back - at once I knew something was wrong. Mum was by me, untidy, flushed, talking quickly and out of order - "Kettle . . . come here . . ." Jim staggered after her, blood on his forehead. He held to a chair -

"What's happened?"

She stroked his head, mouthing jumbled sentences - ". . . shouldn't have got . . ." - ". . . might have been . . ." - ". . . the iodine . . . where . . .?" He was easing himself from his torn, stained jacket. "Fuckin' nigger-lovers," he slurred out, then louder, banging the table so's the iodine bottle I stood there tipped and made brownish uneven rivers on the American cloth. Mum dabbed her hankie in it, then on his forehead.

"Ouch!" He pushed her hand off. "Fuckin' nigger-lovers!" he repeated. "They'd all be strung up back home, messin' aroun' white women . . ."

"It was terrible," mum began, "a *broche* on those that started it . . ."

"Coffee . . ." Jim demanded. "What if he dies?" mum's voice was high again.

"Who?"

She didn't answer me, blowing her nose and crying now. Jim touched the gash, examined the blood on his hand and yet again let out an oath of hate. "Harvey," mum said at last.

"Harvey? Did Jim and Harvey fight? Why?"

"Not Jim and Harvey!"

116

"Who then?"

In jerks she gave out the story. "Girls . . . black G.Is. Sylvie was there, with Harvey . . ." All I could think was she's too young to be in pubs - "Jim said something to one of the negro soldiers . . . there was a fight . . . bottles . . . tables tipped over . . . Harvey helped him and gets his head bashed in . . . with a chair . . ."

"Oh no! And Sylvie?"

"Went to hospital with him, in the ambulance."

Someone passed outside, trying to sing. They were always out-of-tune when they'd had too much to drink - p'raps the ambulance had passed him, blocking out the sound with its clanging bell - Jim's eyes were bloodshot and resentful. What did he have to come into our lives for, bringing his nigger-hate from a place we'd never known - and what was so different about his hate of black skins and Hitler's hate of Jews? Maybe Jim was in the wrong uniform - maybe he should be wearing high black boots and a swastika armband.

"Why you starin' at me that way?" I looked away. He pulled himself up, went to the mirror and carefully looked at the cut on his head. "Ain't nothin' to get all worried about . . . nigger-lovin' whores . . ."

"I'll go tell her you're here." Fay didn't seem to want to speak. I waited down in the hall for Sylvie - the floor was done like in museums with white and blue tiles and a fancy green edging. A cream-coloured runner lay at the far end - it seemed such an extravagance - I hoped they always remembered to wipe their dirty feet.

"Well?" Sylvie said, close to me. All the words I'd worked out went away and I stood dumb. Then I put my arms round her and shut my eyes so's I didn't have to see how suddenly she'd grown up. "It's finished," she said in the voice of an old lady. Then her cheek was against mine and I tasted her salt tears. We stayed together and soon my tears went in with hers. I didn't dare ask about Harvey - She pulled away and sat on the second step of the stairs. I sat below her. "He'll be like a baby . . . all his sense gone . . . bashed out of him." She was telling it straight - with no feeling - like the man did on the wireless with the news -

"What d'you mean?"

117

"I said, didn't you hear? He'll be finished, like grandma says -
meshugge -"

It was a relief to leave - I wished it wasn't but it was -

Soon after, Harvey was sent back to America, for good. And
Sylvie now was going around with a nice flat tummy. "Mum fixed
it all up," she told me, quite openly now it didn't matter. I wanted
to know the details. "D'you mind if I don't say . . .?" She didn't
seem to want me - even though now I thought she would - more
than ever. It'd never be the same with us again - I hadn't changed -
I never would - even if I fell in love as mad as mum was - I'd
always keep space for Sylvie - maybe I got that side of me from
dad - p'raps me and him were more alike than I'd ever realised -
p'raps he was the only one who really understood me - and p'raps
this was time for me to go and stay with him - make a break - mum
had Jim now - dad had no-one - all my tries with Anna hadn't
worked -

'Dear Dad,
    It'll soon be the Christmas holiday. Would you still
want me to come and live with you? If you do write to
me at work. I'll explain why another time.
From your loving daughter.'

I stuck the envelope down hard - yes, it was something I ought
to have done long ago.

"You can't hold it against him for ever you know."

"What?" But I knew what mum meant - since that night with
the fight I'd hardly been able to look at Jim. When he arrived I'd
leave the room - upstairs with a book or in the parlour - I couldn't
bear the sound of his Louisiana drawl and even his way of chewing
gum irritated me.

"I love him. He's got faults I know, but I can't live without
him."

"I know you can't."

"Be nice . . . for me . . ." she pleaded, with a deep sigh.

Dad soon answered, sending the letter not as I'd asked, to Miss
Minch's, but to home.

"Now what does he want?" mum asked curiously. I started to
read it. "Well . . .?" I shoved the letter in my pocket and left her.

118

"You're in a bad mood!"

I slung myself on the bed, pulling the letter out again. '. . . and while the Russians are spilling blood and our boys are getting killed in Italy, what do we do - release the bastard Mosley!' It was full of it - no mention of my coming to stay - no eager telling me yes, it would be wonderful having you with me, someone of my own, someone who cares - just ranting on of '. . . the ruling classes here, hand in glove with the fascists same as it's always been . . .' I didn't understand - for a crazy moment I thought of getting the first train to London - not to dad but to Anna - ask her, what did it mean - what did the 'ruling classes' get up to, not only here but everywhere - ? Maybe when I was really grown-up I'd understand it all but now I just wanted dad to want me - maybe he hadn't got my letter at all - yes, that was it - I pulled my case from under the bed and unpacked my things.

Mum had a glum face. Jim wasn't getting off the base over Christmas. "What a miserable, bloody business. They're probably still holding it against him over the trouble."

Jim had had a rough time of it at the Service enquiry over Harvey and lost his corporal's stripes. It just made mum love him more than ever.

On Christmas Eve two letters arrived. I got to them first - in case dad had finally got mine and was saying come but they were for Pat, from her faithful husband who wrote to her under heat and gunfire, probably telling himself how lucky he was to have a wife of such beauty and patriotism, working away on the buses, helping to bring the war that much nearer ending. As always, she only glanced at them propped against the clock and they sat on, like awkward, unwelcome visitors. Mum was dreary again, thinking of Jim unable to come - she'd been picking on me - now Pat was home. She took the letters and set them deliberately beside Pat's plate. I watched, to see if this time Pat would allow the mask she wore to slip - just a bit. She didn't look up and with the tip of her forefinger tapped the letters beside her on the cloth. Mum watched. Neither of them spoke.

Christmas day the three of us ate our dinner in silence. "We knew nothing of Christmas before we came here," mum said later, "so why worry now?" Then she went to phone Jim. I could almost hear all the "sweethearts" and "dearests" they were passing to each other and when she got back although her eyes were red-rimmed she seemed easier. Pat had gone off on her bike. "God only knows where she meets her fancy-man," mum said. Strange the way mum was so moral when it came to someone else.

CHAPTER SIXTEEN

February - November 1944

Jim was getting less and less time to spend with mum. When he did he drank hard and talked harder of what it was like - his part of the war, as one of the ground-crew getting the B-17s to Germany - their objective, to destroy as many fighter planes as they could. Some of what he told I didn't understand but I wouldn't ask him to explain - right now he was strung-up as an overtuned piano, but it gave me a deeper look at why they were over here and why so many were getting killed. The end of February had been "Big Week" for them with thousands of tons of bombs blasting German aircraft factories. As he told about it he looked anything but the slow-speaking, charming stranger who'd stepped straight from "Gone With The Wind". Now there was a flabbiness in his neck and his face seemed veiled making him look much older - until he'd got several glasses of Scotch in him he'd be bad-tempered and mum would wait, patient, frightened, for now she was seeing the whole of her hero. Both of us got used to his nightmare screams and it told plenty of how he helped drag from shot-up planes pilots, navigators, some of them his buddies - dead men whose luck had run out.

It was 1944. Almost four years since we'd come here, frightened strangers. Now I was fifteen and we'd lived in the same house longer than we'd lived anywhere. Dad was still 'faithful' to London and although write me he was lonely, would never leave the 'big city' again. Sometimes I would want him with me and start off a sprawling letter but I never sent them, knowing in my deepest self that no matter what, my place would always be with mum. Once I dreamt of him with Anna - they had both been marching at the head of a demonstration, Anna holding the flag in red, on it the hammer and sickle. Dad had his arm through her free one and she looked up at him, admiration and respect clear on her face. Never had I seen him so at one, so wholly complete in a sure, happy way. If only I might see him that way in my daytime waking world - just once -

Mum filled the hours when Jim wasn't there playing the old pieces. One, "Humoresque" by Dvořák I thought the whole street must know its every note - on lighter days she'd whistle the melody too, then she was as a person without a single thing to burden her so sure of itself was the sound she gave out. I liked that piece also - because it brought back old pictures of the two street musicians who stood on the Mile End Waste, one with a fiddle, the other an accordion, playing to passing people who might stop to listen or just gossip but all the while they played till you wondered if they ever went home or to bed -

Everyone was speaking of our likely invasion of France. Mr. Evans grew redder and his voice lilted up and down with eagerness till you'd think he was organising the whole operation himself. Then there was the fear in the faces of the women - whose husband, son or brother would be among the first to land on French soil?

"What'll we do when it's all over?" Mum didn't answer. "We ought to think about . . ."

"Time enough when it's here!" she snapped. Then quietly she added. "I'm going to make every day left to me mean something d'you know?"

I did. And I knew also that it made me scared.

I was on a merry-go-round at Miss Minch's, my days pressed into running after her and Cynthia, sweeping, cleaning, shampooing, never getting anywhere. What would Miss Arnold think? How pleased she'd been when I'd reached top in English. Would I end up like Sylvie dreaming of filling my life with babies and cooking? Now when we met there was awkwardness between us for wasn't it Jim, the man my mum worshipped, who'd brought about the loss of her cowboy? Fay must have thought so also for she hardly spoke when she and mum came upon each other at the Saturday market.

"You're a good worker," Miss Minch would say each week as she handed me my wage envelope. She'd wait for me to give back thanks but all I could feel was how and when am I going to get out of this? All mum would say was, "You ought to have listened - I said you was made for the stage - a gift you had, a *mitzvah*, what d'you do with it?" Seems she'd forgotten the whole hairdressing thing had been her idea. "Why don't I just leave?" I tried once. "And what d'you suppose you could do?" She looked up at the ceiling - maybe she was hoping God would drop down the answer - then she sighed. "You've lost the opportunity, one doesn't get many in this life."

Wasn't that what dad said? Seemed like you had to be looking out all the while for these 'chances' which were hovering somewhere, waiting to slip from some golden-lined cloud for "sure as hell", as Jim'd say, if you didn't you were doomed, to be a nothing, a servant forever to someone else.

We were going to pictures a lot again - like when I was small, except now mum waited for me outside Miss Minch's. Most of the films were war ones and I really got to hate Conrad Veidt who nearly always played a German or a foreign spy. Mum still preferred love stories and Joan Crawford and Ingrid Bergman were her favourites. When the newsreels came on she watched with a new intensity and I could feel her next to me in the dark, taut, taking in every word the announcer was giving out.

Once we got back to find Jim there. "Where you'all been to?" His voice was surly as his face.

"Just me and her went to the films honey . . ." In a lower voice and going close, "You don't mind . . . I miss you . . ." He moved from her. "Shall I do you some food?"

"Don't want nothin' - did I leave any Scotch aroun'?" Her eyes flashed a warning and as quick she put it out. A bottle appeared from the larder and she poured him a drink, then stood by him, waiting. He swallowed it. Still she stood there. She placed her hand on his shoulder and he took it and put it to his mouth - she closed her eyes and he kissed it then he pulled her head down to meet his own and kissed her mouth so that she had no resistance and wanted none and eased her body till she was across his lap, her arms tight about his neck. I went into the parlour. I heard them going upstairs to the bedroom.

I sat at the piano. I wished yet again I could play like mum did. With one finger I tapped out an old, old tune and half-speaking, half-singing, I repeated,

> " Oh will you wash my father's shirt
> Oh will you wash it clean,
> Oh will you wash my father's shirt
> Oh will you wash it clean''.

Now the sound of bed-springs above me moving in a set pattern merged in with my repeated tune -

> " Oh yes I'll wash your father's shirt
> Oh yes I'll wash it clean,
> Oh yes I'll wash your father's shirt
> Oh yes I'll wash it clean''.

Jim was gone early next morning. Mum sat quiet, her hands around her cup, staring into it so that she seemed a fortune-teller. "They're losing boys like bloody flies at the minute." I waited, knowing she'd have to go on. ". . . God knows how much longer . . ." A sudden quick gust of early March wind lifted a pile of curled leaves, charging them about the back garden noisily. Maybe that's how the planes were tossed out of the sky when they were hit and what did it feel like, going down fast in a plane, knowing when it hit the ground you'd be finished with - done and done with - deader than the withered leaves still protesting up and down the path -

Sparrows were quarrelsome - and fighters too. I threw the crusts of my lunch-time sandwich to a timid one watching at the side of the seat. He waited till the rest had undone themselves from their frantic squabble, then picked at the bread, his head swivelling this way, that, hopping, turning, picking, always ready to move off fast. It felt good sitting here on this warmer April day, in my break on the bench-seat outside the library. If only I didn't have to go back -
"You come here a lot." A young man was close-by. He was smiling at me with very white, strong teeth and the whole manner of him was wholesome as fresh-baked bread. Unexpectedly shy, I looked down - his shoes were as wholesome as the rest - brogues, with punched holes in a waving design. "D'you like books then?" I let my inspection work upwards - a tweed jacket - leather patches

on the elbows - a clean, almost choir-boy face - "Silly question that, you must, seeing as you're always in there." He'd noticed me - I hadn't noticed him. "I'm Malcolm." He sat down beside me. His talk was easy and the accent was unlike most of those this way except sometimes he said "shent" instead of "shan't" - his was the tell-tale speech of the 'educated' and though it was nice to hear it made me feel uneasy and at a disadvantage. "I work half-a-dozen doors from you, did you know?" Then he went on about his uncle owning Jessup's the ironmongers and how he'd be in the R.A.F. soon as he was eighteen. The more he talked the wider seemed the difference between us, yet I liked him, he was easy and polite, asking me about myself yet not in a 'pushy' way, more like he really wanted to know. The church clock beside the library let out two booms for half-past one. I darted off, late.

"Tomorrow? Here? Same time?" he called.

He started bringing sandwiches except his were in quarters like in posh tea-shops - and as we sat, chatting, throwing crumbs, the meaningless days at Miss Minch's didn't seem so long - Malcolm was close-by working at his uncle's and the mornings soon went and dinner-hours came and weeks passed with days lighter and warmer and life was altogether better than I'd got to thinking it could be.

Sunday afternoons was when the spinsters next door did their garden. The two of them were working together, quietly, efficiently, touching each other as they passed a fork or trowel, sometimes a joke, private, was shared and it seemed to me if they were lesbians it couldn't be so bad if they were that happy. Mum tapped on the window for me to come in.

"I've something to say." She seemed unusually serious.

"It's Sunday and I don't want no lectures," I said, trying to keep my happy feeling going.

"Sit down." She sounded like a headmistress in school assembly. I said so.

"This is no lesson - not from a mother anyhow. The thing is . . ." She turned away. "I'm going to have a child."

"What?" She said it again. "You can't . . ." She'll die - didn't she always tell me that -

"I want this."

I went to the window - next door were still working away. The

124

sun lit the outhouse at one side. "When?"

"Early next year."

"The war could be over." She knew what I was thinking - Jim might be back in his own land and mum, like the others, left with a child. The sun caught at the yellow vase which had belonged to Mr. Parmer's mother, making it bright gold and the room also was full of unexpected light and I wanted to lift with it, so welcome was it but all I could feel was fear - a cloud took over then so that the sun was hidden and the vase went back to being just yellow.

"Where you going?"

I was out of the door - the house - and now it was chill with more clouds moving in, thick and like dragon's breath and I'd no coat. Children were skipping at the corner - "I call Betty in," one sang out as she jumped lightly up and down. We played that before the war - and ball-up-the-wall and spinning tops where you'd whip and whip to keep the top spinning around in a mad competition between you and it. I wanted to sing out too - "Eenah-deenah, abba-dasha, rer-rye, dommanasha -" sing it out louder than I ever did, louder than the skipping girl, loud enough to forget mum and Jim and dad and my job and remember only the fun and friends there used to be.

My face was wet. It was showering small, quick raindrops. I ran past the alike houses, past an open window where the lace curtain was pulled in and then out by the wet sucking wind and I thought if mum dies I'll have to go to dad - that'll settle it - I was cold - the idea of mum dying was all I could think of - how dare she - risk her life and not care, not care if I was left without her - so much for her love.

She never looked prettier. "Keeping well are you then?" Mr. Evans asked, while the neighbours passed our front door with meaningful half-glances and I walked out without looking anyone in the face, telling myself it would be nice having a little brother or sister and wasn't I always complaining about being an only child? Jim came whenever he could, then he'd fuss mum and walk her up the street, his arm protectively round her. Once, when he saw a curtain pulled aside he stopped and kissed her full on the mouth, a lingering, passionate kiss it was, mum said with a smile and then he turned and saluted the window where the unseen face was while he and mum went on, giggling like kids.

"She might die," I confided to Pat. She reassured me with the same dimpled smile but next time I caught her watching mum it was with an oddly unbelieving look to her.

"You'all be sure an' watch her good when I'm not aroun'," Jim instructed and I promised I would, longing to say, who d'you think you are, telling me that, when it's you who's got her into this - He brought extra tins of ham and chicken and fruit from the base till there was nowhere left to store it all and mum got scared in case the M.Ps. raided us, so we took the front off the bottom of the piano and stacked the tins in and I told mum remember not to press the pedals next time she played so that set us off laughing and it was good to laugh again and p'raps a baby coming wasn't such a terrible thing after all -

I tried to push dad from my thoughts 'cause if I didn't a sickness started in the bottom of my stomach going right into my chest till I was certain I'd vomit.

"D'you think about dad?"

"Yeh," she answered, straight out, "think of him a lot." I waited for the curses on his head but she kept quiet as though there were no more left in her.

I fussed and watched after her like Jim said to and we waited for the life growing inside her and meanwhile on the beaches of Normandy in the June sunshine, thousands of men, young and not so young were being killed in the '44 Allied landings.

There'd been rumours around of the Jerry's new secret weapon. Mr. Evans said it was "just more of the Nazi propaganda machine trying to get us down . . ." He seemed to know what he was on about and dad wasn't here to ask so I put it out my mind - better to listen to the wireless telling of "our lads crashing on through France" -

"I thought you'd taken offence." Malcolm sat down by me and lifted his foot with the heavy brogue till it lay across his lap, easy like the rest of Malcolm. I said my dinner-times were changed - how could I tell him I was ashamed to see him - afraid he'd find out about mum - he'd never understand - "So, that's all!" He seemed relieved and I was glad he was, I'd missed him too and when passing Jessup's had had to hold back from running in to see

him. He talked, on and on, using words all in their proper place -
"S'pose all your family are great readers, same as you?" he was
asking.

"My dad reads a lot - mainly political ones -" He was impressed
I saw but I didn't add they were communist books for I could see
by Malcolm's manner and his brogues that he'd be anything but a
supporter of Marx and Engels. What would dad think if he knew I
was with someone like Malcolm? Not that I was 'with' him - not
in the real sense - he'd never even asked me out and what would I
say if he did?

"Would you like that?" I felt like a baby - Malcolm *was*
asking. "Saturday?" I couldn't finish the rest of my lunch -

It was a long week. Nights in bed I was sure Pat could hear the
secret thoughts charging about my head. What did I know of
Malcolm really? What did I know about boys - grown-up ones?
What if he kissed me? Would it be wet as well and were adult
kisses all like that? What if it was lovely and I liked it - I'd have to
be ever so careful - looked what happened to Sylvie - but I wasn't
like her - desperate - yet - what if I fell in love with him - the way
mum loved Jim? Or even the way dad loved mum. There must be
something about the way Jews loved - all passionate and total so's
it made them act *meshugee*. That was something I'd have to be on
my guard against - falling in love too much -

"Is that lipstick you've got on?" I thought mum'd spot it
before I managed to get out the door Saturday.

"Only a bit."

"Wash it off. You're too young."

"But . . ."

She got out the rocking-chair, her hands splayed on her stomach.
Taking a handkerchief she wiped hard at my mouth. "Where you
off to anyway?"

"Pictures, with Sylvie," I lied. P'raps I should tell her about
Malcolm but what if she asked me to bring him home?

I stood in the queue with him, thinking I mustn't lick my lips
too often so's the lipstick I'd put on again behind mum's back
would last all night. When he paid for my ticket I almost stopped
him - it didn't seem right in a way - I was grateful of the dark
inside for I knew my face was burning and when the soldier in
front put his arm round his girl my heart beat madly in case Malcolm

127

copied. When it was ended he saw me to the corner of my street - I wouldn't let him come further. It was a still, warm night and neither of us wanted it to end. He chattered on, about his plans - "What I'm going to do is go to college, after I've been in the R.A.F. - that's if the war isn't done before then - want to make something of myself . . ." It seemed quite natural and proper that Malcolm should make something of himself.

"Does it cost lots, going to college?"

"Mum's dad'll foot the bill. He's not short. Wealthy, I s'pose you'd say, been in the clothing trade all his life - all the family has." He paused. "What do your folks do?"

"My father's a clothing manufacturer too - a designer also. He was badly wounded in the First War but manages to run the business still - in London - stays there most of the time."

"What a coincidence, both our families in the same line."

"Yes. I better go now . . . My mum's very strict."

"D'you enjoy tonight? I did. Immensely." He gave my hand a squeeze. I was dying for him to kiss me - "Shall we do this again? I'd like to."

In the night I heard next-door's clock chime two, then three-o-clock. Why did I keep thinking of my horrible cousin Nigel? Then Paddy - and Rex - this wouldn't go any better I was sure - and all my lies about dad - it was no good - I'd be a failure at relationships same as him - why did I ever agree to go out with Malcolm -

He took to waiting for me after work and couldn't understand why I wouldn't let him visit me at home. "You ashamed of me then?" He flipped it out lightly.

"It's my family . . . my mother actually. You see, we're very . . ." It was difficult making up stories with his frank eyes looking straight into my own. "I'm . . . Jewish!"

"And they don't want you to have contact with a gentile, is that it?"

No Malcolm, that was not it at all and I was telling him, "I'm sorry, there's nothing I can do about it."

He had a stubborn edge to him. He argued, from a position of someone who knew exactly how to get his view over yours and in doing so flattened your arguments into a pitiful mumbling of words which might have been blown like dandelion heads, into the wind. "What we're fighting for isn't it?"

"Yes," I mumbled back. He walked off, victorious, but once we'd parted I got my thoughts into order again and none of them included Malcolm. I asked Sylvie what I ought to do.

"I'm a fine one to tell anybody."

She was so miserable - so unlike the easy-going girl I'd come to rely on. "It's not your fault what happened Sylvie."

"Sometimes I'm certain God's punished me for what I did."

"That's old-fashioned talk - I'm not listening."

"It's true! I should have done like grandma said - wait till after the war and when we go back try and find a Jewish boy."

"That's old women's talk!"

"Stop saying that! And if you want to know what I think, I think you should forget all about this Malcolm 'cause if you don't you could finish up same as me!"

So I got Miss Minch to let me off earlier each night by having less lunch-time and that way I was on my way home before Malcolm could catch me. I ate my sandwiches in the stuffy, upstairs kitchen where the towels were always soaking in the white Butler sink ready for me to wash and the fumes from the perming ammonia crept out their corked-up bottles and all the while I was miserable, wishing I was someone with a proper family and if only Jim would disappear back into Louisiana - and all the while I was wishing it I knew it could never be.

There were new evacuees in the town - skinny, scared-looking - this lot running from the buzz-bombs, the latest and to many most frightening of all Jerry's weapons. Mr. Evans said they were "trying their damn'dest to break our spirit - a sign for certain we've got them on the defensive . . ."

Mrs. Allen opposite was asked to take in a mother and son but just as they were to be billeted on her she dug up an "ailing mother needing attention and a room to herself" - Mum said, "she thinks all us Londoners have horns". I kept thinking, what if dad was caught by a doodlebug - dad who always bragged he'd "live to a hundred and see the Red Flag flying world-wide!" Mum would be free then - she'd have something to thank the Germans for then.

I turned up the wireless - Paris had just been liberated. The B.B.C. man was there, trying to yell over the shouting and clapping and people singing the Marseillaise. It must be wonderful there - dancing with strangers - kissing each other with wine on their lips -

129

one day I would go to Paris - would I go alone - or with a man?

Mum called down. She needed a fresh hot-water bottle. Her back was aching, the way it always was lately. I told her the news. "Good, I'm glad," she said and put the bottle to her back. Jim saw none of this. When he came it was on with the make-up - never did she let on what she was going through and more important, the risk she was taking with this baby.

"You ought to tell him."

"About a silly backache?"

"You know what I mean." She closed her eyes. "Why won't you let him know? He loves you."

"Yes!" Now she was all alert. "That's just why I'm having his child."

"But what if . . ."

"I kick the bucket? I've too much to live for." She put her hand over mine, picking at the blanket edge. "God, you look solemn. Just like your father, as though the whole world was ganged up against you."

"Why don't you tell Jim how old you really are?"

"It won't make no difference - and why worry him with all that?" She squeezed my hand. "You won't let on?" She said it lightly but I saw she was bothered. "Anyway, I don't look forty-three do I?"

"No, you don't." Poor mum, always lucky at cards and now each year was like a card in a game where the odds were against her.

Jim changed the front-door lock in case dad did a surprise swoop. I thought a lot how it might be if the two of them met - would they fight like knights of old or would Jim feel sorry for dad when he started weeping?

After a long while Sylvie brought a letter from Anna. She was surviving the doodlebugs - still, she was a survivor wasn't she - Sylvie couldn't hide her curiosity as I read on in silence.

"Oh, no!" I dropped the page of neatly printed words.

"What's the matter?"

"She's . . . she's . . ."

"She? What she?"

"Getting married . . . again . . ." I laughed - "It's a joke isn't it? Isn't it a big joke?"

"Will you talk so's I can understand!" Sylvie didn't often shout.

"Anna. Anna's getting married. What about dad?" And I told her, after all the months of secrecy, my hopes for her and dad - now it was all done with.

"Funny isn't it?" she said. "I been thinking all this while you had a secret admirer."

"Me? That's what you really thought? Oh, Sylvie, it's all such a shame."

"Not really," she said, wiser than me, "he loves your mum. He won't ever love anyone but her will he?"

"No," I answered, "I don't suppose he will."

CHAPTER SEVENTEEN

Christmas 1944 - January 1945

This time I cooked the Christmas dinner with mum instructing, her stomach now high, her face strained with waiting. Jim was here, obviously fussing her - both of them waiting for their child.

After the meal mum went up to rest, Jim following, bottle of Scotch held almost dangerously between first and second fingers as though held casually it was only an afterthought with no real need for it at all.

"Anything but exciting," Pat observed as we cleared away. "Time you had a bit of life as well. When you gonna' find yourself a boy?" She stressed "yourself" as if to say I had as much if not more right to one than mum did. I almost said straight back I've got one - but then I didn't have - now - Malcolm was probably sitting around his own table with the good starched cloth and silver cutlery, same as mum's rich sister, his Captain father home on leave, carving turkey or goose or whatever well-brought-up gentiles with no shortage of cash eat at Christmas, even war-time ones.

"Fancy a game of ludo?" I asked, wanting to change the subject.

Mum seemed easier when she came down, even squeezing herself between the chair and piano keys. She did the old "Suzette" song but without the cheeky wink at the end like she didn't think it proper for a woman in her condition. Then came "Yours", while Jim listened, a melancholy sheen filming his eyes so's I wasn't sure if it was the words of the song or him still pining for the children left at home.

The smell of our meal lingered in the house and I knew we were lucky to have it and luckier still to have each other even though mum and dad didn't have each other in the proper sense but at least they were alive and free and what would it have been like if my grandparents had never run away from Russia?

A double knock sounded on the front door - it was a firm knock - a sure of itself knock - there was only one person who would knock that way - dad. Jim went to open it. I couldn't get my legs to take me into the hall and stood behind the parlour door, waiting, listening -

"You'all better come on in," Jim was saying - then mum was calling out, "Who's that honey?" I held tighter to the door - I knew that careful, well-brought up, "Thanks very much -" Malcolm! "This here young man says he's a friend of yours -" How had he got my address? What was he doing, calling like this? He stood before us, smiling that clean, open smile. Mum said, "Aren't you going to introduce him?" I blustered out everyone's name, not daring to look straight at Malcolm. Not once did he look at mum's stomach - yet he couldn't have missed it - no-one could - this was the worst thing that could happen to anyone, Jew or gentile, Christmas or no Christmas -

Now Malcolm was politely answering mum's barricade of questions - Where had we met - what did he work at - what did his family do - I watched a tightening of his mouth - a bit too much of a kick of his crossed leg as it beat a regular to and fro into the empty air from his hard parlour chair. "Have another mince-pie," mum pushed, while Jim with an unexpected flourish of old-world southern hospitality, stuck a small cigar in his hand and poured him a large drink.

Still I couldn't look at him full on. The set smile on my mouth seemed to be carved that way. Him turning up like this was a nightmare - my lies about dad the designer were now clear as spring water - I joined weakly in the general talk, listening with more and more horror as Jim put his arm around mum, "sweethearting" her and she "darling'd" him back.

"He seems a nice boy," she said, as we made a big pot of tea on our own. "Why'd you keep him so secret?"

". . . thought you'd make a fuss . . ."

"So long as you behave yourself. Don't want you following Sylvie's example."

"She's miserable!" I whipped it out, still resentful at mum's part in Sylvie's misery.

"'Spect she is . . . it'll be a long time . . ."

I went back in the parlour. Malcolm was struggling to get the last of his whisky down. We were alone. "I've brought you a present . . . here . . ." I stared at the fat, red robins hopping over the wrapping paper and pulled at the gold-threaded ribbon - where'd he get such luxuries?

"You shouldn't have . . ." He became suddenly interested in the picture of a stag that Mr. Parmer had left. "Oh, Malcolm, it's . . ." I needed words that were fine and gracious and right, for in my hands were the sonnets of Shakespeare. "I didn't think you knew about these . . ." I was saying all the wrong things - ". . . what I mean is . . ." But all I could think was, he loves me - after all - he loves me and this is his way of telling me - "Malcolm?" Still he gazed at the noble stag, entranced it seemed by the bold, wide-set eyes and the spread of antlers. He coughed a bit from the cigar smoke and before he could speak, mum was there joining in.

"You've made her day. She loves books." She was asking what the title was but I stuck the robin paper back on fast, turning to Malcolm with, "Will you help me fetch in the water?"

It was cold in the outhouse. Usually I was scared there in the dark alone, always waiting for a long-legged spider to fall from the wood-wormed rafters down my neck or a mouse to dart from behind the old wash-boiler. "The 'Sonnets', Malcolm, I couldn't think of a more smashing present." I heard his breaths, fast in the blackness. "Malcolm . . ." I put my hand on him. "It's freezing . . ." He put both his hands over mine so's I felt like a small bird and again I was like a bird fluttering and beating for Malcolm had leaned to kiss me, straight on the mouth. It was exactly how I'd imagined a proper kiss would be. "Thanks," I told him. We stood there, listening to the water rushing to the top of the bucket and I knew

133

that Malcolm had understood all and that nothing mattered - nothing would affect the way he felt for me.

I went back to work not caring how many towels had to be washed or how much hair swept up and when I shampooed my thirtieth lady that first Saturday after Christmas, it didn't matter that my hands were chapped and nails broken because Malcolm loved me - just as I was. I understood now why Cynthia was bad-tempered - she hadn't got anyone to love her. Most of all I knew how mum felt and why love was so important to her. And dad, I even knew why he was as he was, tormented and miserable, loving mum in his own mad way yet realising she'd never be able to return the feelings he felt were his right.

Mum's suitcase was packed and she waited, eager and afraid though she wouldn't admit it. I'd been instructed over and again to "run to Mr. Evans and phone for an ambulance" when her time came. "I'll be fine, you'll see," she told me and I longed to tell her she wouldn't - but now the panic wasn't so screwed-up in me - now Malcolm was there and he would be strong and a support no matter what - kind, generous Malcolm who had proved himself mature and wise beyond his years.

Like we'd arranged I waited for Malcolm after work - each bitter cold January evening I waited, outside Miss Minch's till fourteen long days and longer nights had passed since Christmas, since my first real kiss. But he was never there -

I considered a million possibilities - he was ill, he had family problems - what problems did people like them have - ? Maybe his father had been killed - but then he was only in charge of an army supplies depot just outside Kettering - P'raps he just didn't care for Jews after all, even though he'd acted, eating mum's mince-pies, seeming conscious of the fact that there we were, mum and me, keeping the great *goyim* celebration, really he had no time for us, same as most of them be they English, German, French, Russian - who really likes the Jews? P'raps God knew best after all and like Sylvie said, threw down punishments on any of us who transgressed outside of our own faith -

It was hard to keep my sorrow to myself. Mum must not be worried and yet surely she guessed - what I'd eventually come to see - that Malcolm, polite and diplomatic though he was, had just been disgusted by what he'd seen of our life. I don't suppose his mother had ever glanced sideways at anyone but her Captain husband - and for all that he'd joined in, trying to be a man, drinking Scotch and smoking cigars, underneath he was still a kid without understanding of life - no, sonnets or not, Malcolm understood nothing.

"Fancy coming to The George Saturday?" Sylvie asked me. I told her yes. Later I considered whether I hadn't agreed too hastily. I wasn't a ballroom dancer and worse, I hated standing around waiting for someone to ask me on to the floor. Seemed to me something like the local cattle-market - the men eyeing you over till one of them fancied what he saw enough to ask you for a dance.

Saturday dinner-time I gave up my break and Miss Minch let me do my hair. I prayed mum wouldn't start the baby this night but now on Saturdays Jim was always there and I desperately needed to get out - all I'd been doing lately was thinking of Malcolm.

"Your hair looks nice," mum said when I got home.

"How you feeling?"

"Tired." Then she added, "Nothing to worry about."

"Jim is coming?"

"You know he is."

"Can I . . .? Would it be . . . alright . . . if I go dancing with Sylvie?"

"Dancing?" With an effort she leaned to poke the fire. "Not been much life for you lately has it?"

"I won't be late," I got in before she could start her warnings. But she was too weary even for that.

Upstairs I lay out on the bed my one 'best' dress, red taffeta with a full skirt which 'swished' as I moved so that I felt excited and aware of myself. After washing and lavishing myself with carnation-smelling talcum I did my face with pan-cake make-up till it was immaculate as a marble statue. Next I mascara'd my lashes till they were like spider's legs, same as mum's. I pulled on the flesh-coloured nylons Jim had given mum - then the dress and finally stuck my feet into the double-wedge-heeled shoes which made me three inches taller and with difficulty made my way down the shallow stairs.

"What d'you think?" I swirled to show mum how full the dress swung out.

"Better not do that too often. Can see your knickers."

Sylvie was shivering outside The George Hotel. We queued with the others - done-up girls, Yanks braving the cold in newly-pressed uniforms without overcoats spoiling their dash, sailors in wide-legged dark blue trousers and white-topped saucer hats tilted back on their heads so's you'd swear they were stuck on.

Inside was warm and smoky and couples already dancing to the regular Victor Sylvester rhythms of a quick-step. It all seemed so smooth and easy.

"Want a drink?" Sylvie looked as nervous as me.

"What sort?"

"I'll get us two shandys eh?"

I stood alone, an obvious, red-taffettad, wobbly-wedged girl with a blank-paper face. The band changed to a hit number, Glenn Miller's "In the Mood" - this was where the experts sparkled and eager couples, sure of themselves and their footwork were making for their own patch of floor-space. I waited alone - I might have been in a synagogue on Easter Sunday. Right in front of me an American sergeant and a girl with a 'busty' figure and hair in a snood were jitterbugging. They were quick and slick with the dash and cheek of a couple of truanting school-kids. She seemed to see into his mind for wherever he put out his hand she'd be there, waiting to be tossed to his right side, then his left and with more and more abandon he sat her on his knee then as quickly took her off again and flipped her around his back. God, I thought, if anyone tries that with me I'll die on the spot, yet anything was better than just standing there.

"Wanna' try this one?" He was freckle-faced and grinning and his accent was like one of the Dead End Kids, nasal and out of the side of his lips. Before I could answer he'd pulled me forward and at once his feet started to shuffle in a native-type movement with the heel of one rising ever so slightly, the other pulled back quick and tipped behind while at the same time his right arm pushed, then pulled me to him and I was jerked this way, then that, all the while his eyes staying almost closed so that it was as though he was sleepwalking a fast and furious dream. The music grew more insistent, the drummer more enthusiastic and my partner, although he wasn't really that - more he was dancing alone and me just an extension of him - he was away in his own state of bliss while I had to use every bit of wit and skill I had to stop from falling over his ridiculously fast feet.

From the middle of a spin I saw Sylvie, two glasses of flat shandy in her hands, watching with amazement. At last, one cascade from the drummer, a rising crescendo from the brass and it was done. I pulled my hand from his sweaty grip and limped across to my friend.

"You were fantastic!"

I drank my drink in one gulp, Sylvie still gazing at me in disbelief. A soldier in the uncomfortably hot uniform of the British army mumbled in Sylvie's direction. He pulled hard at the battledress jacket, trying somehow to smarten it up so that he wasn't inferior to "the bloody Yanks". I stood by myself again. A foxtrot was being played and I knew if anyone did ask "for the pleasure" I'd have to refuse. More and more pairs took to the floor, looking frighteningly expert, gliding easily, all knowing where and when to place a foot. If only I'd stayed home - with mum - a guilty panic took me over - what about mum - at this moment she might be having the baby and facing death -

"Where you hurrying off to?" His hand on my arm was assured and his voice was like Mr. Evans' with the same up and down lilt. "D'you want a try?" Before I could say, his arm was about my waist and he drew me to the centre of the dancers. He had on a light grey suit and was older than most of the men there. There was a sadness about him which made me at once sorry for him but also ill-at-ease for I didn't want that sort of responsibility this night. "Not so bad is it?" He must have felt my awkwardness, my stiff body, which to my surprise followed his movements. Over his shoulder I got a quick sight of Sylvie being pulled in and out, her soldier, his left arm stuck awkwardly angled in the air, clutching her hand, a weak prisoner. "I'm Brian. What's your name?" I told him. "I'm glad you're here," he said and I knew I couldn't go, not yet anyway.

He wanted to know "everything about you" and for some reason I couldn't have explained I was telling him.

It was the last waltz. Sylvie pulled a secret face as her 'Limey' dreamily guided her through it. Above us all a glass ball revolved, slowly sending out sparkles of coloured lights and seeming controlled

137

by a God of Love set on weaving us all into a spell of romance. Brian held me close, his chin just touching my forehead. I could smell my carnation talcum - p'raps he could too - "Nice, isn't it?" he murmured. But now I was regretting it was him I was with, wishing madly it was Malcolm and I didn't even know if Malcolm could dance and it didn't matter if he couldn't and why did I have to tell this stranger all those secret things? He pressed my fingers and to my surprise sharp little darts went up my arm and down the rest of me. "I'm taking you home," he said, sure of himself and I wanted to say who did he think he was but he leaned nearer and the furrows in the side of his face reminded me of dad and even his complexion was the same dad's had been when he was on nights and later when he told me he'd tried it down the mines but wasn't "tough enough with the one kidney I've got" I felt the same pity for him that I used to feel for the old lady who wheeled the broken pram selling 'bagels' in the courtyard of the buildings.

We walked out into the night. It was bright, the snow falling in a clean white shower. He spoke now, as though away from the dance-hall he was free to tell me his personal things. He worked at the steel works in Corby. "Doin' my bit so you see." He said it mockingly so's I didn't know whether he was glad to be or not. He came from the south of Wales, his family always "in the mines" - "The women too?" I joked. "You're a saucy young thing," he said back in a familiar way and I knew I ought to be more distant with him. He asked my age. "Eighteen." It came out before I knew it. "Sure?" He stopped and half-turned to look at me. "I'll show you my identity card if you like." He paused. "And why aren't you in the forces?" I thought hard. "Domestic reasons."

A stroppy wind lifted a bale of snowflakes, throwing them in our faces. We hurried to the shelter of a doorway and it was natural that he should hold me against him. It was light with the moon and the snow and I looked up, now very close to his face. His eyes were intense, darkly so and I became aware of his moustache and considered whether or not you would feel the bristle of the hairs when he kissed you - for I knew that he would. He took a packet of cigarettes from his pocket, a thin, little Woodbine pack which seemed such a poor relation to the fat Lucky Strike's I'd become used to with Jim around. As he struck a match it threw shadows on him. "You've had a hard life," I nearly said right out. He blew

138

out the match before lighting the cigarette, then he kissed me. It wasn't like Malcolm's kiss. It was passionate and interesting and full of change the way his voice was. I liked it, it was challenging and I responded, strong as a man and eager.

"Yes, yes," he was saying, "I knew you had a bit of fire inside yourself." He kissed me again and now his tongue was pushing inside my lips and I didn't stop him even though I thought of the times me and Sylvie had sworn we'd never let a man do that. If only Malcolm would walk past now, him with the stuck-up family and coxcomb of hair that wouldn't stay down at the back of his head and wouldn't that be one in the eye for him, letting me slip, the fool that he was - Brian was opening my coat collar and the buttons at the top of my red, taffeta dress were being pulled apart and then he was cupping my breast and stroking at it and I thought oh, no, you mustn't do that except that the feeling was so pleasurable and new I couldn't make myself stop him. We stood there, in our own set scene, just like in one of those glass balls which you shake and send the snow all flying about. "You're a lovely, little thing, d'you know that?" he said. "Yes, yes, I am . . ." and wasn't Malcolm the loser, the *shlemiel* not to have realised what he had had? And I was glad to be here with Brian, safe in the doorway with him big and strong even with his one kidney and it was good with his arm tight about me and what matter that his hand was now up inside my taffeta skirt and exploring around the waist where my knicker elastic was and for all that I knew I ought to be telling him no, my voice was a weak thing without any will to it. A couple of A.T.S. girls passed and I saw them just over the top of Brian's shoulder and they looked happy and right and there was no man with them and as they walked on they set up singing and the song was the one mum always sang -

"I'll never love anyone the way I love you,
How could I? When I was born to be just yours."

And I saw mum as I'd left her that evening with the fear in her eyes that she couldn't hide because I knew her too well and I didn't know what I was doing here in a darkened doorway with an old man with one kidney and a moustache 'cause I didn't like moustaches anyway - "No!" I shouted and pushed his arm away. "Don't!"

139

And again I pushed at him so hard he almost fell and then I was running and slipping on the snow where it was freezing and trying to pull my knickers up from over my ankles and telling myself that never again would I go out in those stupid double-wedged shoes.

CHAPTER EIGHTEEN

January - February 1945

Jim was alone when I got in, his large body squeezed into the bounds of the rocking-chair.

"Mum?"

"In hospital. Jus' a while after you went out." His voice was accusing.

"Will she be . . ." I couldn't say "all right" - not when I knew she was going to die. He didn't know though did he, him with the mouth sullen and every part of his big self like a baby whose mum had left it alone in the dark. "It's all your fault!" I longed to shout out. "You got her into this . . . when she dies it'll be you who killed her!"

I heard him up most of the night, coughing from his continual smoking, walking in and out of the kitchen, the front room, and the more his fear grew the more my own did till I got out the bed and pulled at Pat, content and apart in her own world.

"Can I . . ."

"Can you . . . what . . .?" she answered sleepily.

"Come in your bed?"

She held open the covers and I squeezed in beside her. She put her arm around me. "It'll be O.K. you'll see." She went back to sleep. I lay against her, smelling her clean smell, wishing in a crazy way mum was more like her, in charge of herself, not letting anyone get really close to her. I should try and be like that - yes - her way was best - her way you didn't risk anything -

Jim had left early. There was a torn bit of paper on the mantle-piece. 'I'm at the hospital, to wait'. It was a long Sunday. Pat was at work and the place was quiet, quiet as death. What did I know about death - how would I deal with it? It was something unreal - something people said in words but the words didn't mean anything in a way I could understand. Life I knew about - life was mine, what I was doing here - feeling, thinking, scared like I was at this moment but death - it didn't make sense to me - if God or whoever, meant for us to die I don't know why he stuck us here in the first place. If only someone was in the house with me - dad - why couldn't he be here? Dad - he didn't even know what was happening -

I put my thick cardigan on and struggled with my rain-boots. Mum usually helped me with them, I thought of the last time she'd tried to get them up my legs, her pulling and ordering me to "push, hard on the floor, with your foot still!" We'd laughed like two schoolgirls, just me and her, on our own. I'd go round Sylvie's - she'd understand - she was always a good listener -

"What happened to you then?" She waited expectantly, for my tale of Brian - Brian - I'd forgotten everything about him.

"Sylvie . . . it's my mum . . ." I was crying, which I hadn't meant to and suddenly was sobbing with fear.

"She'll be fine, you'll see." She was trying hard as always, to make her mouth pull into a full convincing smile. "She had you didn't she?"

"She nearly died then." And I retold mum's morbid tale of my birth - forceps, stitches and all just the way I'd always heard it, leaving out no details - adding to them in full technicolour as though recounting the latest horror film. Sylvie looked petrified. I realised how selfish I was being. "Sorry, didn't mean to push all this on you." But now she was singed with the same dark thoughts as me. "If anything happens, will you have to sit *Chivah*?"

"Sylvie!" I hadn't thought of that - what a terrible idea - and I could see clearly, the way it was when grandma died and the aunts all sitting on low stools in the proper way, wearing black overalls over the dresses, and mirrors covered so's they couldn't look at themselves and food brought in to them 'cause they mustn't prepare it themselves - and I thought, who would bring the food in to me - and who would there be to say the prayers?

It was dark when Jim got back. He looked faded as an old photograph. "They say it'll be a while yet." She was still alive then - I made us both strong coffee. Then I went to bed.

Next day, a cold February day, the baby was born, a girl. "I'll tell your mom you were asking for her," Jim said as he went off that evening. I didn't see why just fathers were allowed to visit - The ten days till she would be home again seemed like ten years - I filled the evenings after work cleaning till everywhere was sparkling like mum liked - and it seemed proper that the baby Sharon should start off with everything as it should be, at least, as right as I could make it.

I heard the taxi-door bang shut. I ran to the front door. "Mum!"

She walked in slow, the way an old lady does. Jim followed, with a small, tight bundle. She sat and he placed it in her open arms. "Come see your sister then." It sounded strange - "sister" - There, tight against her was a red-faced, sleeping baby looking more like a doll, so still was it. "Want to hold her?" Gently, I lifted it, she whimpered and I rocked her till she was once more as a doll. "Got the knack haven't you?"

"What happened to your mouth?" Soon as she'd walked in I'd noticed the red rim of damaged skin above her upper lip.

"Nothing," she said. I knew though - it was the mark made by her lower teeth where she'd bitten hard.

I told Miss Minch mum was ill and had the week off without pay. Mum had been wistful after Jim left, telling me, "Be sure an' take real good care of 'em for me". I did, and I liked it, except for when I had to pour the Dettol water from a jug carefully over mum's private parts while she lay on the bed, her legs spread open. Seeing after Sharon was best - even changing her napkins - soon I'd learned how to bring up her wind and to handle her gently after mum fed her so's not to make her sick. Mum was too weak to come downstairs till the afternoons so every drop of washing water for her and the baby had to be carried up, then down and emptied and never had the walk to the outhouse seemed so long. Even the coal bucket seemed heavier, trying to balance it brim full along the icy path.

"Having a hard time of it?" Pat and me were eating our meal alone - "I don't mind." I played with the food, too exhausted to eat. She cut her food, neatly and chewed neatly too - "Wouldn't you like a child?" I asked suddenly. She reddened quickly. "What time would I have for babies?" She set the knife and fork tidy on her plate and began clearing away.

142

* * *

"Did you save the newspapers for me like I said?" Mum was down all day now, rouged and her lashes black and spiky.

"Glad you're feeling more yourself mum." But she wasn't listening - instead reading the events of the war with the same intensity I used to see in dad - she though, didn't fold them carefully afterwards but threw them in a billowing heap on the floor.

"Making good progress aren't we?" she said finally, then in a 'stagey' voice and with a flourish of gestures she recited aloud various of the headlines, picking them from the untidy pile as though each was a viper. 'ORGANISED FIGHTING IN ATHENS CEASES', 'WARSAW CAPTURED BY THE RUSSIANS', 'BURMA ROAD TO CHINA REOPENED'.

"Yes, it is good," I said, knowing that was the last thing in the world she wanted to hear right now.

"Bloody good," she repeated. And then as though suddenly aware of what it really meant added, "S'pose it'll save a lot more misery for a lot of people."

Yes, I thought, but not for you.

Jim and her went together to register the birth. "I'm proud sweetheart and I want the whole goddam world to know it!" She smiled at him, all she'd gone through so recently, forgotten - she'd proved herself - now maybe he wouldn't grieve for those other children away in Louisiana, those children of the younger, slim wife that Jim had loved - maybe like he loved mum now -

Outside was cushion-soft and quiet the way it is when snow has fallen heavily. Sharon's sleeping breaths came from her small pram in the corner of the room - mum, with a book on her lap was staring into the fire.

"What you thinking?"

She got up - the book fell - she left it on the floor. "Your father . . . I know what would move him." She took a deep breath the way she did when she was in the middle of one of her songs and was about to tackle a high note. "You."

"Me?"

She went to see that Sharon was still covered. "How can we let anyone call her a bastard? How can we?" She came to me now, placing her hands either side of my face. "He'll do anything for you . . . ask him . . . for Sharon . . ." She spoke quickly, leaving

143

no gap for me to interrupt. "Ask him, tell him if he don't give me a divorce you'll never see him, never call him father again." I turned, so's she wouldn't see my anger. "Look at me." Still I kept my reflection from her. Thoughts tumbled about my mind - dad, whenever I was scared of the dark - dad, when he'd made me laugh with his belly-dance - dad, with his eyes bright when he was talking politics - "Why don't you say something?"

"Don't want to -"

"Don't want to what? Don't want to speak or don't want to ask him?"

"He's my dad. Jim isn't."

"What do you know! You know nothing!" She lifted the baby, waking her so that she began a fretful crying. "There . . . see what you've done . . . it's all right . . . there . . . there . . ."

She stayed rocking Sharon, little Sharon I already loved so much, little Sharon, innocent of all, who would be called a bastard if I didn't ask dad what mum wanted. "Yes," I told her.

"Yes what?" mum asked nervously.

"I'll write."

So she dictated and I put down on paper all she wanted. When I went into the white night to post it I thought what would I do if he didn't give way - I would have lost a father.

It was a long misty Sunday. More than ten days and still no reply from dad. "P'raps you'd take Sharon a walk - I'm tired." She looked it - but more than tired there was fear and doubt marking her.

The sun was out, nearly a white one, enormous, daring us not to notice it, February or not - I pushed the small, green pram with Sharon well-wrapped past the neighbours tucked in their sabbath-day houses, holding their papers high, reading the war news, wondering, some of them, how soon till a person they cared about was back, safe. The air was sharply fresh, the baby's small face pink now and I poked at the blankets around her. What would dad do - what would he feel when he read my blackmailing letter - the one I'd never wanted to send - ?

"Miss Arnold!" She wobbled towards me, same as always, pulling along a tall, robust woman in a woolly hat. The wide smile I knew was full on her face.

"Hullo. How are you? How nice," she said one after the other.

144

Her 'poppy' eyes were kind and I found myself wishing she didn't have a goitre and would it ever kill her off? "What are you doing now? Still love to read - oh, how rude of me - this is . . ." she introduced her companion, all proper, the way she did everything. "And who's baby is this?" She pulled the covers from Sharon just a little.

"She's . . ." There were no words coming from my mouth - Sharon sucked at her tiny thumb - I wouldn't tell her - I didn't want her to know - besides, it was our business - just ours. The rosy-faced friend was stamping her feet and clapping her cold hands together. Miss Arnold stood, still, looking at me.

"We'll be late," the friend said and Miss Arnold seemed suddenly sad as she put her arm through her friend's. They turned, then she stretched out a hand, squeezed my arm and they hurried away. I gripped the handle of the pram, watching them go. At the corner she turned - I waved weakly - she waved back but it was a gesture only - she probably thought Sharon was mine -

"I've told him - everything -" Mum had been busy while I was out. "Here, read it." She flourished the pages, daring me to tell her she'd done wrong. It was well-written - all the facts set out - the love she'd never had for him, the fights all through their married life, all was remembered and used with no attempt to soften what was to come - 'I have a love now and I have the child of the man I love. What point is there, you hanging on to me - I've nothing to give you . . .' "What d'you think, will he take notice?" she asked suddenly.

"I don't know."

Now the nights seemed longer than I'd ever known - days were easier, dashing after Cynthia and Miss Minch but night-time, dad crept into the bedroom - no matter Pat was there, dad the intruder stood at the bottom of my bed, stood there in the navy suit, with his undertaker's face, solemn, misery weighting his shoulders. Once, to escape him I went downstairs and tried to read but the words on the pages weren't meaningful now, not real like dad was - not real like all of us were. Back upstairs Pat had asked, "Don't you feel so well?" I hadn't answered. "You don't have to tell me," she'd said, "whatever it is, you'll get over it." She probably thought I was pining after Malcolm or some other secret love - an adolescent passion I ought to be going through - not mum -

"You going out?" Mum seemed apprehensive. I was brushing my hair into a 'sweep' same as Miss Minch did to the customers.

"Me and Sylvie's going to pictures."

"Oh . . . I thought . . ."

"I haven't been for ages . . ."

"It's just that . . . Jim can't get away this week-end again . . ."

"You want me to stay in with you." I couldn't hide the resentment I felt.

"No . . . what I wondered . . . when you've had supper . . . I was going to the base . . . with Sharon, in the pram, walk . . ."

"Walk? To the base?"

"It's only three miles."

"Four." I pushed hard at the hair-grip, securing the 'sweep' as though it should stay that way for ever.

"I'll go on my own then." Now she was beside me, edging me from the mirror.

"How can you - walk there and back! - With the baby! It'll be dark . . . you know you're not good at walking far!" She went on preparing herself - the same old routine - if I counted the times I'd watched her would it add up to a thousand or a million - ? Next, she dressed Sharon carefully, wrapping her finally in a large woollen shawl.

"Put your thick coat on." She did as I told her. "And a scarf." I watched her. Then I got my own coat.

It was that in-between time when people are home from work, washing, eating, preparing for their Saturday night out, the one night that made all the others tolerable. Mum pushed the pram onward, chatting lightly so's I'd believe this was nothing for her - this marathon, for the woman from the big city who'd never walk if she could ride a bus, who was "too weak" to attempt more than a hundred yards or so at one time. I kept silent. "Dead, isn't it?"

It was. The shops shut with no lights to show off the goods - the wax models who'd have to stay shrouded till Monday morning. "You got a lot to say - a great journey this is going to be, like a bloody nun who's taken a vow of silence."

"There might have been a bus. You ought to have found out."

"One every two hours and it's just gone." She pushed harder against the pram.

"What if Jim's on duty? Did you think of that? We might be

traipsing all this way for nothing.''

"Don't come then! I'll go alone!'' She bit on her lip.

"Mum, be sensible. You're not up to it. You know you're not.'' I put my hand on hers clenching the pram handle.

"Who says so?'' She tossed my hand off like it was an angry wasp. I stood still while she marched on, ready to take on anything.

"Mum!'' She didn't turn. "Mum! I'm tired. I'm going . . .''
She kept walking as though she couldn't hear a thing. I stood watching a while, then walked in a different direction - Sylvie's - there might still be time to get to the pictures.

She was already home when I got back - sitting at the table, her face swollen with crying, her whole body working the way it did after the worst of the fights with dad. "Bastard that he is!'' She banged her small hand down. "Bastard! That's something I didn't expect - I'll never be able to step out the house again -''

"Mum?'' I didn't dare ask - had Jim told her he didn't want her any more - ? She started cursing - suddenly an old crone - mouthing them with the spittle almost spilling from her lips - "Came here, like a rat in the night - hiding, waiting for me, like the cowardly rat he is - like he learnt in the trenches -''

"Dad? Dad came here?''

"Yes, your dear father, who should have been blown to bits by a German shell before he could live to persecute me to my dying day.''

And she told it - how he'd come here, stayed at The George - "Him . . . the millionaire . . . at The George . . . some bloody communist eh?'' Wavering back and forwards she told it so's one moment I was with it, seeing and hearing father as he confronted her, suddenly in the street, before passers-by and the next moment both of us back here both going through the shame of it all -

"Why did he come?''

"Do I know? Does anyone in their right mind know how he thinks? He said something about wanting to see for himself . . . me and . . . Sharon . . . Oh, my God, may my poor mother rest in her grave - the names he shouted at me - thank God my baby couldn't know what was happening - You remember I wrote openly to him, telling him everything - even how Jim came from the south - you know what he does - screams out for all to hear, my baby is a

147

Mexican bastard!'' She laughed out - "Mexican! A Mexican bastard! I tried to run away, with the pram, he kept after me - a soldier and his girl tried to stop it all, he tells them his sorry tale, cries to them, the girl pulls the feller away, people won't get involved will they? Still I'm running like a *meshuggenah*, another man stops, an older man - 'Shall I fetch the law?' he asks, 'Yes,' I tell him, 'for God's sake fetch someone!' '' She paused, her head turning suddenly about the room - searching the floor, the walls, expecting father to be there, to appear and continue the abuse -

"Then what happened?''

"He came - a policeman. Your father starts his story, actor that he is, calling the copper 'sir' - you know how he is when he wants to make an impression - tells his story - how wronged he is -''

"What did the policeman say?''

"Says to him go see a solicitor. Says he can't cause an affray on the public highway . . .'' Again she laughed - "d'you ever hear anything so bloody ridiculous?''

"I should have been with you.''

It all sounded so unreal - as unreal as the Jewish melodramas mum used to take me to see at the Yiddish Theatre just off the Commercial Road -

"Wait till I tell Jim - he'll go to London and do the lunatic in once and for all!''

"Yes,'' I agreed, trying to comfort her but all the while I knew I'd have to get to dad first.

CHAPTER NINETEEN

April - July 1945

"It's all right. He's agreed to divorce you.''

She didn't speak, just stood there, her lips slightly parted. Then she squeezed my arm till I told her stop. "Yes, you said? You did it? Got him to agree?'' She clutched me, kissing my face - head - all the while thanking me and laughing. "I must tell Jim! Straight away! I'll go now - phone - tell him - Oh, he'll be so happy!'' She

148

was gone, running to Mr. Evans to use the phone while I tried to calm the baby crying with fright at mum's shouting for joy.

It had been the usual stop-start journey back from London - me full with the thought of my part in dad's misery - so much so that when the fat man sitting opposite waved his Daily Express at the other passengers showing the photo of Mussolini and his mistress spread on the ground, surrounded by the Italian Partisans who'd shot them I couldn't become as excited as they were. Talk of "his dues" and "So much for the Duce!" merged with the turning train wheels while I considered what would they have thought about mum - the 'mistress' of Jim -

All I wanted now was bed and sleep and to put away all thought of the last two days. But I knew I wouldn't rest - I would keep hearing that last question - "You do love me?" And again - "I'm your father". His goodbye kiss had been that of a boy with his first girl - unsure - and that final "You do love me?" wove itself into my head till it felt like it had been there from the beginning and would stay there till the end.

It was a while till I could tell Sylvie. "That's awful . . . your dad." Then she said, "Maybe it's gonna' be for the best." But it didn't sound as though she believed it.

I still didn't know how I'd be able to do it - go to the Law Courts like the solicitors would get all organised - stand straight in the witness box and say out loud what I'd seen - say out loud and clear that yes, I'd seem mum and Jim in bed together, say it loud and distinct the way mum said she didn't mind me doing, the way she said it'd be easier that way, me just saying I'd seen my mum in bed with a member of the United States Army Air Force. Mum seemed happier than she'd been in ages.

"Guess what?"

"I don't know, what?"

"Everyone forgot my birthday," I told her.

"Me as well." Sylvie plonked a kiss on me. "Happy sixteenth anyway."

Now everyone was happy. It was V.E. Day - May 8th. 1945 and the end of World War Two against Germany was officially declared. It didn't make me feel different. I asked Sylvie if she did. She didn't answer for herself - instead she spoke of her dad. "Mum'll

149

never get over him. She's worse now it's finished with.''

"Maybe you ought to tell your mum -'' I stopped - what could she tell her - that Sid was a hero? Hard to think of him charging away at Germans with a gun or in a tank rolling over deserts, sending the sand up over dead bodies with a determined look to him, a look that let the Germans know what for 'cause Sid wasn't that sort of person - Sid had never got in arguments with anyone except when he was playing cards.

"We ought to celebrate - it is the end of the main part of the war. I bet London'll be exciting.''

"You mean you want to go?'' She sounded uncertain.

For a minute I saw how wild and gay it'd be - dancing round Eros in Piccadilly Circus - poor boarded-up Eros - and streamers and flags fluttering high above the smart West End Shops. "Shall we?''

"Go on our own?''

"We could -''

"I don't think mum . . .''

"It don't matter.'' I didn't really want to go to London - not with dad being by himself.

That evening we went out anyway - got ourselves 'victory' done-up and out we went -

The Kettering streets were decorated with bunting so's they seemed like old women with too much make-up on. There were giant portraits of the Royal family smiling into nowhere and Churchill's bulldog face biting the fat cigar. Mr. Evans was whistling "There'll Always be an England'' while he tacked red, white and blue twisted paper around the frame of his shop window and Mrs. Lee decked herself out in "a booty of a frock I've been keeping for this day'' and tippled along the pavement in very high heels looking like a hen with its neck poking forward. The 'cow' opposite kept her curtains drawn tight and Mrs. Evans remarked, "She'll never get over her Jim being lost at Dunkirk.'' I didn't know that and wondered if mum knew -

Sylvie said we should get tiddly. I thought so too - I was sixteen now and sixteen opened all sorts of forbidden doors - seemed like all my life I'd been waiting for sixteen and now it had come I ought to get started. We bought some cheap sherry and Sylvie drunk first straight from the bottle. I took a large gulp. It wasn't sweet like

150

the cherry brandy grandma used to make for *Pesach* and which
Melanie, Sarah and me would sip with the grown-ups watching,
laughingly telling each other we'd grow up to be *shikkereh shiksas*.

"How long till it works?"

"Depends how much you get down you," Sylvie answered.
"D'you want to get prop'ly drunk then?"

I hadn't considered it but it was what one ought to do on Victory
in Europe day. Besides, I'd got a lot to get through with the
divorce and all and if drinking was as good as the gentiles seemed
to think, maybe I would take it up. I had another long swallow.
"C'mon then. It'll be all over time we get on our way!"

The last of the children's street parties were being cleared away.
A pair of red 'sausagey' balloons bounced rebelliously up the road.
I chased after them but they didn't want to be taken and gently
moved themselves on each time I went to grab.

"Where we going?"

"Anywhere you say!" I answered recklessly.

"The Star and Garter?"

"We're not old enough."

"We look it."

It wasn't the time to bring up how I felt about pubs - didn't they
always bring trouble? Wasn't that how mum had met Jim and
wasn't it where her cowboy had got ruined for life? No, reckless or
not, pubs it would not be.

That wasn't how the rest of the town was thinking - it seemed
that everyone, soldier, sailor, airman, civilian, was drinking them
dry. Laughter, real and forced, talk, loud and victory-cocky, snatches
of piano where, as mum would have put it, the right hand had never
been introduced to the left, jarred out from the engraved glass doors
- pushed into the shut-up streets and all the while the drinkers
drank and all the while they talked and boasted, swore and flaunted
the hard-won victory each at the other.

"Shall we try The George?" Sylvie offered.

It was full. People weren't bothering to dance properly, just
holding to each other, a multi-coloured ball of humans stranded
into a creature from under the sea, gently turning this way, then
that. A husky soldier, the pores of his blotchy face large and
sweaty, grabbed me and stuck a hard kiss on my mouth. Before I
could complain he was gone, back into the sea, seeking another

pair of lips. "Shall I get us a drink?" Sylvie shouted, over the band who'd started "Roll Out The Barrel". - "Yes!" I yelled back, our small bottle now finished. Everyone was singing -

"Roll out the barrel, let's have a barrel of fun,
Roll out the barrel, we've got old Adolph on the run,
Zing, boom, terrarel, let's have a song of good cheer,
Now's the time to roll the barrel, 'cause the gang's all here!"

There was clapping and cheering and strangers congratulated strangers who this night were all blood-brothers and sisters, all sharing in bringing about this waited-for day. It was probably like this all over England - all over Europe - even for the ones who'd just waited, even those who'd done nothing but make a lot of money out of it - capitalists, big and not so big, now all kidding themselves they'd done their bit, their patriotic bit so's they too could sing out, "We've got old Adolph on the run . . ."

Sylvie was weeping. She groped for my hand while a girl in an emerald-green, sequin-covered dress sang into a microphone a song familiar and sad and romantic,

"We'll meet again, don't know where, don't know when
But I know we'll meet again some sunny day,"

I tipped the glass of gin. It was vile - my eyes started watering.

"I didn't mean for you to get upset as well," Sylvie began. I let her think they were sympathy tears.

"Let's go eh?"

The outside air slapped us in the face. Sylvie grabbed me as I swayed. "You look ever so funny." She giggled - a tipsy giggle which spun the both of us into a laughter session shrill and fast as spinning tops and just like tops we couldn't stop till we'd spun ourselves out.

She slipped a high-heeled shoe off, rubbing at her cramped toes. "Shall we think of getting back . . ."

"Not yet!" It hadn't been my idea of a celebration. We walked on, treading carefully, towards the market square - all to bed, not knowing a thing about wars started or finished. The stalls were bare, their metal supports like skinny arms held up to the moonlit sky. A Yank, jacket off, was sprawled across one, his drunken snores loud in the tidy square. "We should have done something Sylvie." I felt more and more let down by our night out.

"We got tipsy." She leant against the side of a stall.

I felt a great dare starting up in me - just the way it used to in school when I'd have to show off before the rest and mimic the teachers soon as they'd left the room. I was climbing onto a stall. "What you doing?" Now my voice was announcing, "I'm going to give you ladees and gentlemennn . . ." same as the Chairman at the Working Mens' Club - ". . . an evening of enterrrtainment!" And for all that a policeman had passed and said, "Now then Miss, walk along please", I couldn't have done so.

It began - my grand performance - for Sylvie, for the large moon above us, for the snoring G.I. who, if he did hear anything, would probably think he was dreaming. I started with the impersona-tions - Mae West, W.C.Fields, Greta Garbo. Never had the voices and mannerisms of these old friends sounded so for real - so although I was mouthing the phrases I was as a ventriloquist's dummy, not active but a machine, working at another's will.

"You've missed out Shirley Temple," Sylvie protested.

"On here?" So the boards of the rickety stall clattered and vibrated as my feet tapped out the old routine, the one I'd watched golden-haired Shirley do over and again.

Sylvie clapped. "What about Al Jolson?"

It was down on one knee then for "Mammy" followed by "Sonny Boy" and I gave it all the pathos and sentiment that being tipsy adds. I loved it - every magical moment, as magical as the flashing images on the Silver Screen itself and the night with its spotlight stars and the drink in me and the knowledge that we'd beaten the Germans so that now they couldn't get to me and mum and dad and turn us into slaves or corpses made me wildly free.

"Say, thas' great!" a voice called from the night. Walking uncertainly towards us and carrying a paper Union Jack on a thin stick was the Yank, awake and ready for more of the free show. "I'll say this for the little ol' town, they sure know how to lay on the works . . . for a little cele . . . cele . . . cel'bration!" He came up close and leaning forward, kissed the tip of my shoe. "Lemme help you down honey." Before I could speak, his arms were around my waist and I was lifted down and set on the ground right

153

up close to him. His breath was like he'd drunk the Star and Garter and Rising Sun empty.

"Thanks . . ." I pushed him away hard. "C'mon Sylvie, dad'll be looking out for us."

"Dad?" she said, till I gave her a quick dig. "Oh yeh, DAD!" We walked away fast then started running in case he decided to follow.

"Wasn't such a bad night after all was it?"

"Smashing!" Sylvie said. We walked home, she to her 'posh' bit of the town and me to the opposite end. The smell of bonfires was still strong in the air.

The postwoman got used to pushing thick, important-looking letters through our door during the next few weeks. Mum would read them carefully, fold them back into their proper creases and replace them respectfully in their fawn envelopes.

"You won't be too nervous at the hearing will you?"

"You've told me what to say over and over."

"Yes, I have haven't I? Sorry."

What you sorry for I wanted to ask - for me - for the way I was going to have to perform my piece about you and Jim in bed when I took you up tea in the mornings? Or maybe it was dad you were sorry for - for his life with no point to the "till death us do part" bit - or didn't that come into the Jewish marriage ceremony? - I'd have to ask someone -

"At least he won't be able to make any more of his surprise visits. We'll have peace," she went on. I hoped that dad would find peace too but I didn't say so.

Sharon was beautiful, as though it was her right to be. She was seldom fretful and as the weeks passed I found myself loving her as though she was mine - my own baby.

When Jim came he'd take them both out, pushing the pram, daring all to look with critical eyes, while mum, so small against his six foot, walked beside him, all self-consciousness, almost nervousness she showed when alone, gone.

"He adores her, you can see it can't you?" she'd say after he'd gone - then the fear that kept her chill would be put aside.

"D'you reckon you'll like America?"

"That's a funny question. 'Course I'm gonna' like it." There

154

were other questions I had, like what about me when you go, if you go - I never really knew if Jim didn't like me because I was me or because I was dad's child. No matter how I tried I couldn't like him, not the way mum wanted.

She crossed off each week on the big calendar hanging beside the fireplace. Those pencilled-off crosses in black seemed like a dark omen and I felt sick at the thought of what was ahead.

The day of the divorce hearing there was a summer storm - thunder and lightning, just like the Gods, Jewish and Christian, were showing their disapproval. Me and dad hurried past the man selling papers outside the Law Courts - everywhere splashed and my stockings got spattered - I wetted my hankie and rubbed at them so's I wouldn't show dad up when my big turn came. It seemed like a poster-size dream - us being here - in this marble hall of a place, "washing our dirty linen in front of the *goyem*" as grandma would have said. "You stay together for the children" - always she said it - everything for the *kinder* - no matter if your husband chased the *shikses* - no matter if he gave you a slap in the face if you questioned it - no matter if you bore child after child, some to survive, some to die, you stayed together - there was no other way.

Dad's solicitor was hearty and pumped my hand up and down as though expecting water to gush from me. "Won't be too bad my dear," he assured, like you tell someone who's about to have an operation. I should smile, I told myself but my jaw had become stuck. Everywhere was marble and grey stone so that our footsteps sounded out sharply like they did on the films with Fred and Ginger. Dad and him were mumbling in serious tones while I considered this cathedral of a place.

It was stately beautiful, cold, dignified so that not for all the world would I have dared sneeze or laugh or speak in a loud voice. "This way," the solicitor said and we followed his dark suit across the hall to a central stairway with a small balcony above it. I looked up, expecting mum to appear - to see her leaning over and giving a nod to a hidden orchestra so that music would start and she would sing in her rich contralto one of the arias from "La Boheme" or "Tosca" - a piece dramatic - a song right for a place as this - for an occasion as today.

155

"Like Westminster Abbey," I whispered, following the grey suit and clutching dad's hand like I was six instead of sixteen. He didn't answer and his black, polished shoes with the laces tucked in, not in a bow the way other people's were, walked a few steps behind grey suit with a manner of obedience so that he wasn't dad the rebel at all but a pall-bearer, dark and ashen at his own funeral.

"It's small in here isn't it?" Dad made a curt nod, his mouth just a line as we sat side by side on the wooden benches of the court. I tried concentrating on what was being said - phrases of legal usage - words like "Respondent" and "Petitioner" and "Co-Respondent" and I half-listened and stared at the books, old and leather-bound in the bookcase on the side wall and almost got up to see what books the judge kept and the talk went on and I took in the oak panelling and was suddenly remembering our oak sideboard, the one dad had crashed the barley-twist candlesticks on, the one with the angry gash and I was glad we had taste also so that we were every bit up to the court and the black-gowned barrister.

My name was called and I was moving forward, towards where the judge sat up on his throne, the golden lion and white unicorn above him and on his head his wig was tilted slightly to a side so that I had to stop from calling out, "Shall I adjust it for you sir, 'cause although I'm not a properly trained hairdresser, I know about such things." I pulled at the jacket of my tailored costume, grey also with a thin white line threaded through it, formal, right for an occasion such as this. From his seat dad made a sickly smile and I wasn't sure whether it was to give me courage or because he was satisfied with the fit of the jacket.

The judge was speaking - then the barrister - and then it was quiet - quiet too long and I realised they were waiting for me, my reply. The judge spoke again, and the barrister, like a puppet, spoke after him and once more they all looked at me.

"What did he say about the baby?" the barrister was asking, seeming ill-at-ease like it was him in the witness box, not me.

"Who?" I asked stupidly, panicking, because it wasn't like mum and me had rehearsed it.

"The question refers to the Co-Respondent," the judge was informing me from on high, "you understand who that is?"

"Oh yes," I said, enthusiastically, 'cause by now I knew that was Jim.

156

Then again the question, "Did he say whether or no the child was his?"

"'Course!" I said back. What a stupid question - was this what dad was paying out good money for and what Jim was going to pay him back for like mum said -

"You may stand down now," a voice said and I waited, expecting them to ask more but they didn't and somehow I felt cheated 'cause I'd rehearsed my part so well -

There was more sorting of papers from bundles and low mumblings and serious faces and now dad's solicitor was pumping the arm of the barrister and dad said we could go and did I fancy Lyon's for tea? He was shaking a bit and there was a damp film on his upper lip much like dew on a young plant leaf first thing in the morning. I put my arm through his and he seemed grateful that I did. When we got out the taxi though his hand was shaking again as he paid the driver.

We queued at the self-service counter which was a disappointment - I'd expected it to be the same as when we went there once before, with 'nippies', their backs straight as the King's Guards, bringing wide trays to your table with pots of tea and extra hot water and oval-shaped crusty rolls with a slight indent in the centre and real butter pats.

"Have one of these." Dad pushed a plate with Madeira cake and Bath buns towards me. He poured himself a second cup of tea but didn't eat.

I cut my cake in slices like I remembered from Miss Arnold's and dad watched as though it was the first time he'd seen anyone do that. "What do you do with yourself? Do you go out much?" I asked, realising I sounded too chirpy. He stared at the cake and still not looking at me said, "Did you know, they have the most wonderful coffee-houses in Berlin?" I prodded the slices into a crossways pattern on the white plate. He stared at them and for a moment I thought I should leave them as they were. "I went to an exhibition," he went on, not really talking to me, "a while back . . . photos they were . . ."

"Umm?" I said through my Madeira cake.

"Photos," he repeated.

"What of?"

"Daily Express put it on. They got a reading room . . . must

157

show you . . . in Regent Street . . ." He drained his cup. "This exhibition you couldn't have come, too young - children not allowed -"

I swallowed my cake and disturbed the pattern on the plate.

"I wouldn't have wanted . . . I mean, you should know . . . as Jews . . ."

"What?"

"Photographs . . . of Belsen and Buchenwald. You couldn't imagine . . . no-one could . . ."

He went on, talking without pausing, telling exactly how he'd seen it - on the walls, the black and white records of what had taken place, all in all its detail. You shouldn't be telling me this, I wanted to say, aren't I too young? Didn't you say children weren't allowed? - But then I'm not a child am I - 'specially after today -

"P'raps I shouldn't have said nothing to you . . ."

"No. I ought to know." I didn't eat the last finger of Madeira cake.

There were flowers on the table at his flat and on the window-sill, a gay arrangement trying to block out the colourless walls of the buildings at the back. The living-room and bedroom were small but everything was neatly arranged - books side by side, shoes coupled under a painted chest-of-drawers, shiny metal shoe-trees stretching into each one. He lit the fire. It was orderly too. Neat fine sticks, criss-crossed over crunched-up paper then a match and a whole newspaper page held close to the fireplace "to draw it" and when the flames were leaping, small bits of coal set with care on the glowing embers.

In the morning he was up early. "Here, breakfast, like the aristocracy." He'd laid a tray with a proper tray-cloth and one of the flowers from the vase was set across the sugar bowl. He looked tired - "Sleep well? I did" - How could I make the little time left nice for him - ? With sudden inspiration I was telling him of Miss Minch and Cynthia and how I was always running after them and maybe if I laid it on strong he'd get whipped up about exploitation and spark out - then I could go home just remembering his shiny button eyes.

"You can come up often now the bombs and everything's done with, eh?"

"Umm."

"Your mother . . . she's O.K.?"

"Umm," I repeated. "Good about the election wasn't it?" It was my last attempt - if he didn't get going about the Labour victory, he was finished, done with for certain. I bit hard into my cold toast. Then he got started. Soon he was waving his arms about, pointing to each side as though the room was filled with onlookers, listeners who would follow his words and tell themselves how fortunate they were to be in the company of such an informed person - an orator - a man who, if he'd had the opportunity would have made a superb Member of Parliament. I made up my mind to think of that all the journey home.

And that's what I would do - not remember him as he was at this moment - holding to me while the engine steam hissed impatiently and people shoved past, anxious to find a seat on the train.

"Don't talk to strangers," he warned and I remembered all the times he'd said that when I was small and running an errand or going to school.

I pulled myself from him. "Bye, dad."

"Here!" He poked a ten-shilling note in my pocket. "You'll come again, soon?"

Slowly the great wheels moved and we pulled away. The lady opposite me took off her green, felt hat and was leaning slightly from the window. She lifted the hat in a graceful sweep of a wave. P'raps I ought to have waved from the window too but I didn't want to see dad as I knew he'd be looking - anyway, I didn't have a hat.

CHAPTER TWENTY

August - December 1945

"Why'd they do it - when we were winning anyway?" We'd just heard the Americans had dropped the first atom bomb on Japan.

"How do I know?" mum said. "I don't understand war - never did and I never will. Still, I suppose some good comes from it."

159

She looked at Sharon as she spoke. "No matter what's ahead I'll never regret having her."

She didn't need to say - I knew - I knew also how apprehensive she was right now - many Americans had gone and it could be Jim's turn any day. Each time he came she hovered about him, trying to soak up the look of him, as if the more she took in now the better it would help when he was gone.

Miss Minch's takings were down, same as in the pubs, same as everywhere where money could buy anything - even in war-time. So the painted, gum-chewing women strutted about out of habit, without Yank on arm, living on recent memories, still swinging their walk even if they now looked sideways at the unglamorous figures of the British servicemen suddenly come into their own.

"Pat'll be getting worried." Now she was washing the child, gently soaping her.

"What about?" I asked.

"Her husband - won't be long before he's back and that'll be the end of . . ." The back door opened - Pat was there. Neither of us had heard her coming. "Give me the towel will you?" mum flustered. Pat walked straight past us, for once not hiding what she felt.

"She heard."

"I don't think so." She began whispering words to Sharon - Yiddish words - *fagala* - *choochala* - as though the part-Jewish, part-Irish-American-Indian child understood.

"I wonder who he is."

"Who?"

"Pat's boyfriend," I whispered, seeing again the fat man in the alleyway, old enough it seemed, to be her father.

Now she was dressing the child - "Whose daddy's going to see his pretty babba then?" Sharon smiled as though she understood. The child seen to, she began on herself. "Look at my hair - take her while I do something with it." The iron curling-tongs were put to heat and when ready tested on a scrap of paper - if they made a scorch-mark they were too hot and would have to stand, open as a yawning mouth, until cool. Now though they were just right, so the hair was sectioned off and carefully wound into the tongs, held so for a minute, then released into an immaculate sausage of a curl and this repeated until a glossy bunch of grapes tilted onto her forehead.

I lay on my bed. Pat had gone out, her underwear thrown on the bed, not put neatly to wash as usual but abandoned like refugees, one stocking clinging to the cotton bed-spread, its partner heaped snake-like on the floor. Why wouldn't she ever take mum up - challenge her and tell her straight out what she was thinking?

It was muggy, a sticky evening with the air squashed up tight and no spare for anyone. What would it be like in Hiroshima now? Atom bomb - what did it mean? Maybe if I multiplied all the bombs dropped on London would that be it? And if it was didn't it seem more the sort of thing the Germans would have done to us - not what we - or our allies, the Americans ought to be doing? I'd have to write and ask dad 'cause one thing for sure, whatever faults he had he understood about people killing each other -

I was sleepy - hot and sleepy. The roses on the curtains had become faces with black, smudged noses, swaying on long, green necks. They were elegantly curved the way swans' necks are and they were gliding the way swans do, across a lake and now they were blurred as though a fine mist layered the water and I concentrated hard so's I might still make out their shapes -

Mum was screaming. I sat up quick. "No!" she shouted, over and over. Then her voice was low and it was just the mellow Louisiana drawl I could hear. I stayed where I was. It was a long airless night.

By the end of that week the 384th had moved on, to France, to "Keep the Show on the Road" - their bomber group motto. "Will you come back in with me?" mum asked. In no time it was as always - both of us in the big bed, she snuggling for some second-class comfort in the night and me pretending I didn't hear the many times she wept.

She wrote, every day, assuring him of her faithfulness, her unchanging love and her hand was fast as she filled the pages, fast with the panic inside her. When she wasn't writing or with the child she'd be at the piano, the songs always including "Yours". But it was the letter-writing that gave her most ease. Once written the letter would have to "catch the very next post" and as Pat passed the main Post Office each day, she it was who would be asked to, "Drop this in the post-box to catch the next collection would you?" And Pat, with a nod and smile would place the sealed envelope inside her jacket against her own breast, then straddle the cycle and pedal, a strong, shapely messenger of love.

"Just my bloody luck." She indicated the calendar with the weeks marked off - the days till the decree would be final. "If only . . ." She couldn't finish - say - if only Jim could have married her before he left -

"It'll be O.K." As I said it I didn't know what would be and what did O.K. stand for anyway? I took to waiting for Jim's letters too, watching, waiting for the postwoman - sometimes catching her on my way to work and she also became used to it so that as we passed each other she would nod and pat her postbag if there was something for mum. Then all would be well - for a while - till the days passed and nothing, then blackness would cover each day, for both of us - all of this I watched, with pain, with fascination - Would I ever feel this way about a man?

Yet it would have been nice to have someone. Sometimes when Cynthia dashed off for a date after work I'd feel envious - how anyone like her could have a boy-friend - her with the bossy manner - the gawky looks - then I found myself thinking of Sylvie - what might have been - maybe her ending up on a ranch somewhere in Texas - ?

The war was all over - the Japanese had surrendered. Inside me I knew I ought to feel shame at being happy when all that way away such a terrible thing had been let loose on a lot of people but all I could think of was I'm glad it's finished -

Fay and Sylvie came round - to celebrate - but none of us could get in a celebrating mood. "Mother's already talking of going back," Fay told us.

"What about you?" mum asked.

"It's not easy. Mother thinks all I have to do is go live with her." We could see that was the very last thing Fay wanted. Me and Sylvie left them talking. We walked to the recreation park, past the Aquascutum factory on the corner where so many different armies had been billeted - British, American, the Pioneer Corps - a hotch-potch of dark, intense faces, Slavic faces, who smiled devilishly as you passed - we went on - past the row of small cottages where the old couple who grew cabbages in the front garden lived.

"I'm fed up," Sylvie said. "It's alright for you, you like all this

162

green grass stuff - me, I've had all the grass I want -''

"I miss London." I offered it defensively as we wandered in-between the swings. A bit of breeze was pushing them so that their heavy chains cranked in an awkward Tower of London sound. Two women passed us, one kept looking behind as though expecting someone to be following. No such luck, I almost yelled across, the Yanks are all gone. We strolled on, without purpose, like the two women and I thought about the West End and theatres with neon signs of actresses' names in high letters and Lyon's Corner House as it always was with splendid, shining chandeliers and the red buses with lights full on and headlamps spreading on the roads so that when it had rained puddles glistened and petrol rings lay like dead rainbows and busy people dashed across them, intent and full of the idea of themselves as city dwellers. "What'll your mum do, do you think?''

"Dunno'. What'll yours?''

"I don't know either.''

"I'll probably go anyway," Sylvie said and once again her manner was that of a woman.

Mum pulled a browned petal from one of the roses. The movement jarred the others in the vase to drop to the table. "There's a letter from your father." She sounded resentful - that it was from him to me instead of one from Jim to her. I made to go upstairs. "What's so secret?" I tore the envelope with a flourish and read his words deliberately aloud. "Doesn't change does he? As balmy with his *meshugge* politics as ever!''

She was right. It was tight-jammed with no thought of me who would read it, who would have to take it in - let it make its mark on my mind, so that in years to come I'd think a thought or say something and really it wouldn't be me but my father - I read the rest silently. 'Take my word, this atom bomb is a dress rehearsal . . . Yanks preparing for another . . .' I made a tight ball of the pages - who did he think he was, writing to me this way? Just when everyone was thankful the war was done and planning for long, peaceful years - I had a lot of sorting out for the future as well - I didn't want to consider what might or might not be - hadn't he seen the Movietone News of Hiroshima and Nagasaki and hadn't he realised that no-one, ever, in their sane minds would drop another

163

bomb like those? I got my writing-case, which Paddy had earned the money for, working, building the long runways for the Fortresses to take off from, the planes with bombs, ordinary, normal bombs to drop on Germany, to kill lots of Germans with so's the world would be safe again, for me and Sylvie and little Sharon. 'Dear Dad, you shouldn't forget we owe the Americans a lot, plenty gave their lives for us . . .' I blotted the paper, remembering how Jim would scream out in his nightmares of lifting shot-up boys from cockpits after their missions - I put the pen through the page. How could I tell him that - how much we owed the Yanks - dad, who knew better than anyone.

On Saturday night I nearly told Miss Minch I was leaving. "Be better if you waited till I know what's going to be," mum said when I got in. She fussed around Sharon. "I mean, soon as Jim's sent back to the States he'll get things organised for me, for us, to go over . . ."

"Don't know if I want to."

"You want to stay here then? With your father? Is that what you want?"

"Maybe."

She lifted Sharon. "We'll like it, won't we my angel? You'll see your daddy and we'll live happily ever after . . ."

"You'll never grow up! Never!" I slammed the door on her.

I sat in the parlour like an uninvited visitor, staring at the piano - the walnut family piano - sturdily it stood, sure, proud, why couldn't we be like that - ? Were all humans as complicated as us - ?

I stayed on at Miss Minch's - waiting - waiting for the letter that would come for mum - the letter to tell her to speed herself to him - to him with the easy walk and the easy smile and that's all she needed to make her world right.

And it did come - a letter in blue paper which she read over and over, first quietly mouthing the words, then aloud the special bits - '. . . anytime now honey we'll be together . . . write me more than you do . . . I'm just living for your letters . . .' She fluttered the paper, the thin, blue paper as though it were a fan and I waited for her to fan her cheeks cool. "Did you hear? You heard that?" She laughed and she cried and Sharon was kissed and I was hugged. Then she calmed - "What did he mean? I should write more than I do? No-one could write more than I do - why hadn't he got them all?'' I tried to assure her - wasn't he on the move - probably her letters were still catching up with him - first through France and now - ''Of course! Why am I such a fool! You're right. Why are you always right?''

She hadn't noticed the other letter I'd lifted from the hall mat - dad's. Now I read it alone, holding it with both hands, giving it all attention, trying to free myself from the thought of Jim, trying to disentangle myself from the cat's cradle of loyalty that had become twisted up with mum. At the end he'd asked his now usual enquiry, 'How's your mother?' and 'How's the child?'

The world was alive again for mum - the gloomy, wintry weather, cold and damp, seemed unnoticed by her, everyone was good and beautiful - Pat ''wasn't such a bad lodger'' and Fay was ''A loyal, true friend . . .'' all now came under the umbrella of her warmth and love -

''What's got your mother in such a good mood?'' Pat asked it evenly the way she always asked everything, as though half in shadow, without the full light on her intentions.

''She's just heard from Jim in America.''

She lifted her fine eyebrows in the slightest of movements. ''Oh? Bet she's pleased.'' She began spreading a slice of bread with butter, thickly, more than she'd have dared if mum was there, then she considered a jar of fish-paste and a pot of Bovril, side by side on the table. She chose the Bovril.

''Will you still work on the buses when the men get back from the war?''

''Shouldn't think so. Have to look for something else, like selling dresses or quarter-pounds of pear-drops.''

I thought of that time she'd given me that large pear-drop and how much I'd liked her for it. ''Not fair that, why shouldn't you keep your job if you like it, even when the men do get back?''

''Why shouldn't I?'' She picked a crumb from between the space in her upper front teeth.

It was still dark in the morning when I heard her unbolting the door on her way to the wash-house.

Mum said over breakfast that Fay and Sylvie were taking the old lady back for good. ''Fay's going to wait a bit till she can find somewhere for her and Sylvie on their own.'' I went to the cupboard

165

under the stairs to wash. I didn't want mum to see me crying.

CHAPTER TWENTY-ONE

February - March 1946

Sylvie, Fay and the grandmother were leaving for good. I stood with them on the platform, waiting for the train. Mum wouldn't come - the sudden change in Fay's plans - to "wait for a bit", was too much for her.

"I'll write lots," Sylvie said miserably.

"Me as well."

For once we had nothing to say to each other. A poster on the wall with a loose corner flapped a bit. 'IS YOUR JOURNEY REALLY NECESSARY?' it said. Fay was fussing, turning up the collar of the old woman's coat, grumbling because there was only a Force's Canteen.

"Look." Above us the pagoda-like glass roof sparkled with the hard February frost. "Pretty."

"Umm," Sylvie mumbled.

A girl and two boys waited also, a large trunk between them labelled to an address in London. The bigger boy stamped his feet, more with impatience it seemed than at the sharp cold.

"Remember when we first came here?"

"And we thought no-one would take us in?" she reminded me.

"It wasn't so bad."

She didn't answer. There was lots I wanted to say - I ought to say - The train was there - suddenly and noisy like it had galloped the last bend and now was breathlessly snorting frothy grey, yellow and white gusts.

Fay pushed her mother up a high carriage step into a Ladies Only.

"Tell your mum I'll write . . ." Her voice was unsteady. "Soon as we're sorted you can both come . . ."

The boys struggled with the trunk - an elderly porter shoved them aside and took over with a strength that had never left him.

"Sylvie . . ." She placed a kiss somewhere on my face, then was on the train - the platform was desolate - no-one seemed to be getting out at Kettering. The doors banged and the horse of a train got itself up once more, steaming, impatient to be away to the capital city. I stood alone, while the steam spread and lost itself about the station and the train moved slowly off. My hands were cold - I'd forgotten my gloves. I walked home.

"Fay said soon as they're sorted we can go and stay."

"That'll be nice." Mum's voice was like a machine.

"The train was late, as usual."

"Oh?" She went to the mirror. "I don't look my age?"

"I hope I'm like you when I'm older."

She sat, away in her thoughts, idly tracing the check tablecloth with her forefinger. If only Fay hadn't left right now - now when mum needed her - when it had been more than six weeks since she'd heard from Jim. I put my hand on her shoulder. "I'm sure it's just his letters have got lost, remember, same as those of yours did?"

"P'raps." She stood up. "He wouldn't let me down . . . you know . . . I know . . . he never would . . ."

"Why don't you make yourself nice and go to pictures? It's Bette Davis, you like her."

"Yeh, no good sitting round the house all the while. You're right. Mustn't get morbid -" She took her comb and swept the fringe in place, then eased a curl forward, still to do its coquettish bit, and this from long habit, with no enthusiasm.

"O.K.?"

"O.K." I replied. She went for her coat - it would be a relief to have her out of the house - then I needn't act and could give in to my own despondent feelings.

"Alright, I'm off. You know when to put her to bed."

"Mum . . . go!"

She looked so small and vulnerable standing there in the high doorway, the bit of fur collar around her neck. "Bye then."

It was quiet again. Now I let free my miserable imaginings. What had happened with Jim? Like mum, I couldn't believe he'd let her down, not when he'd written and built up her hopes like he had. If he didn't want her why write at all? It didn't make sense - I heard the front door open - probably Pat in from work - but mum

167

stood there. She unclipped the fur collar. "Didn't feel like it. Sorry."

Miss Minch was getting worried now that her shop wasn't the busy little salon it was. I saw too the diplomat side of my employer, chatting and laughing as she worked, enquiring after family, health, love-life, until it seemed all these things were fundamental to her own well-being. Cynthia was becoming more spiteful, a special jab of hers was to ask me what I was doing after work on a Saturday knowing too well all I had to look forward to was an evening stuck in with mum and Sharon. Sharon - she seemed the only brightness in our lives - now she was trying her first steps, pulling herself around the furniture - she'd fall, then impishly look at me waiting for me to pick her up - I was her slave and she knew it -

"Come on, I know what you want -" I lifted her, swirling her above me so that she chuckled and I wanted more of this, so infectious was its innocence and sparkle - I shook her and like an obedient elf she chuckled more, kicking her feet and I got tipsy with the sound, shaking her more till she squealed with delight. At last I put her down, the rosy face staring up at me, all for the game to go on and on - "You are the living image of your daddy aren't you?"

"Yes, she is, isn't she?" Mum was watching from the doorway.

She was up first now, mornings - glad for daylight - waiting for the post. We would take our first tea of the day silently, as two people grown old, with nothing to discuss.

The letter-box snapped shut and the fall of the envelope was heavy. She was in the hallway first then back in the kitchen holding a long fawn envelope.

"Aren't you going to open it?" She made no answer. "Shall I?" It had a London postmark with handwriting old-fashioned and formal so that our address took on an unfamiliar dignity. I read it, with care. "Mum . . ." She kept her head down, the misery of the world upon her. "Mum . . . it says, 'The said decree made final and absolute . . .' " She snatched the page, reading it with care, missing not a word. "Great isn't it eh? Free I am, after all this bloody time . . . free . . .."

Why aren't you happy then I ought to have asked, except it was

168

a pointless question.

She wrote him again - telling the news - she was a free woman, that word repeated itself and each time she said it there was a bitter overtone so that the word became sharp as lemons.

Outside of us the world was trying to get itself together. In the papers all we seemed to read about were food shortages - it didn't even help knowing the Germans were having it worse than us. At the cinema it was newsreels of displaced people and ruins and the horrifying remnants of concentration camps. The Nuremberg trials were going on and more details told of "crimes against humanity" and the eyes of the men who had committed them as they sat in the dock were as frightened as the eyes must have been of those they'd destroyed such a short time before.

It was a foggy night, unnaturally quiet, the way fog seems to muffle all living sound. I got through the grey thickness of it finding our street by memory, as a blind person does, then counting each door to our house by saying aloud the numbers as in a child's game. At our door I nearly said Hurrah, but once in I felt something badly wrong. "Mum!" There was no answer. "Mum!" I repeated, louder. Sharon's garbled chatter came from upstairs. It was dark in the bedroom and chilly. I switched on the light. She was on the bed, Sharon beside her, playing with her Teddy bear. At the brightness of the light she stretched her arm across her eyes but not before I had seen them red-rimmed. "What's wrong?" I moved her arm. "Is it Jim? Is he dead?"

"Dead? No . . ." She shivered, I pulled the blankets around her. She pushed them off and sitting up leant against the dark oak of the headboard. "He came round . . ."

"Who?"

"Her man . . . hers . . ."

"Whose?"

She put her fist to her forehead, trying to remember. "Hers . . . Pat's . . ." She whispered the name and it was full of loathing and also of fear.

"Why? What did he want?"

She gripped my hands, squeezing them with such strength I couldn't pull free. "Do you know what she's done? Why? In God's name what would make her do it?" She closed her eyes

169

again.

I shook her impatiently. "Mum! Are you going to tell me!"

The story came, slowly, and as I listened I too became tight with disbelief that one human being could be so vindictive to another - for Pat and her lover had fallen out, she told him she'd never see him again and he, in turn full of spite had come to mum to tell what his dimpled girl-friend had been up to - what she had laughed at and done with the letters mum had given her - the loving letters of those past months, the ones that should have been posted to Jim - all torn up and burnt up and laughed over in the small hut on the allotment which had been the secret meeting-place for them - where they had met and made love on the wooden floor and where Pat had read aloud, then ripped and burnt the letters.

"It can't be . . . no-one would do such a thing!"

"She did. I believe him."

"But why?"

A low moan started from the deepest part of her and its sound made me cold. I lifted Sharon from the bed - best leave her alone to sob and scream. Downstairs I sat the child in her high-chair then turned the wireless to full volume but still I could hear her. Sharon banged her small fists on the tray of the chair. I wanted to bang my fists also - hard - harder - I became brim with anger such as I had never known. I went upstairs, now to the back bedroom and pulled open the drawers of the dressing-table. There, seductive and still with her scent on them, lay the neat folded pile of panties and cami-knickers, the blue, artificial silk cami-knickers the colour of the big doll-eyes. So many times I'd watched her dress, admiring the chorus-girl legs, the straight, masculine back, strong and freckled, the firm breasts, small like apple-halves with the stalks on - and all of her was hard and strong and why hadn't I seen it - the hard streak of her?

I tipped out the drawers onto the floor, wanting to stamp on her things, crush them, crush out the sound of mum in the next room and now my voice was mouthing curses in Yiddish - curses that father knew - curses that my people had known for many years and how had these curses originated? Had my people suffered at the hands of so many as mum was suffering now at the hands of this woman - this *shikse*?

At last I had her suitcase closed and into a cardboard box pushed

170

shoes, brushes - anything left that was hers. I dragged them down and set them on the back doorstep. Then I bolted the door and drew the curtains.

"What you doing that for?" mum asked. She held a mug of coffee with two hands tight - the way old people do to stop from shaking. Her lovely eyes were almost closed-up and her face blotchy and as she spoke a sob would catch in her voice.

"She's not coming in - ever - she's got to go - at once."

"Pat?" There was immediate apprehension in her. "You can't!"

"Can't? Can't? She's a bitch! A bloody, wicked bitch!" Again I sounded like father.

"She'll get the police!"

"Let her! I'll tell them - let everyone know what she is!"

Now the coffee-mug was shaking so that the brown liquid tipped down her dress. "I don't want no fights - what about the neighbours?"

"What do they matter? Always you worry about them -" Now she was at the door, sliding back the heavy bolt. I pulled her away. "Leave it!" She started crying again. "Mum, I don't want to bully you . . . trust me. We can't have her here like before, can we?" I turned off the light and we waited, like two burglars in our own home.

Her footsteps sounded on the flagstones at last. The barn door creaked as the bicycle was put away, then up the back path her light feet stepped. The door-knob was turned, then turned again, then the large key was put in the lock and the door pushed, then rattled, then pushed again, harder. Mum put out her hand - I gripped it. There was a tapping at the window - a pause - then a knocking. "Is anyone in?" she called out. Mum's breath was fast. "You're to leave us . . ." My voice was shaky - ". . . and never come here again."

"What's wrong? Open the door!" I heard the panic starting in her and felt a thrill of satisfaction. "Why's my things out here?"

"Go away," I repeated.

"Away? Where? Why?"

Mum pulled away from me, starting for the door. "No!" I shouted. Sharon was saying, "Mum-mum-mum . . ." Now the voice, close up to the wooden door - "Has anyone . . . been making trouble?"

"Your boy-friend's called if that's what you mean." I waited -

"He's told us everything" - Through the wall as though it was glass I saw the dimples now tucked away - the eyes no longer calm as a doll's - "You're wicked! We don't want you here!" My heart was thudding. There was no sound from her side. We waited - at last her footsteps walking away, slow -

"She's gone?"

"She's gone," I answered. I switched on the light. Mum sat down, grey-faced. "You alright?" But now the footsteps were hurrying back. There was knocking at the door - now more timidly - "My wireless . . ." I rushed upstairs. The small wireless was still under her bed. I took it, made to go back down - but no, this would be better - pay her back even more - I lifted the window. "Pat!" I called out, "Here!" I threw the wireless to the ground below - its crash gave me real pleasure - I slid the window down tight and put the catch on in case by some wild manoeuvre she might fetch a ladder and climb back in while we were all asleep.

"What shall I do?" Mum had lain awake most of the night. So had I.

"I've been thinking. You've got to talk to him - Jim - phone, tell him."

"All the way to America? How can I?"

"Where's your spirit? Mum, you've changed . . . you used to be . . ."

"What? What did I used to be?"

"You want him still?"

"How can you ask . . .?"

"Well?"

"Yes . . . what's happened to me? I will speak to him . . . explain everything. God only knows what he must have thought all this time . . . he lived for my letters, same as I did for his . . ."

"He got some - the ones I posted."

"Yes, of course! There were those!"

We planned as though for a major battle - when would be the best time to phone - what the time difference was - what to say - "I'll have to speak quickly - the cost" - If only I was rich enough to have told her - speak - take as long as you need - to sort it out - convince him of your love - that nothing has changed - so's you'll be happy again like when he was with you.

She drafted and re-drafted what she would say, then went to the red phone kiosk outside my old school and booked the call - her long-distance call which would make everything good once more, to the Air Base in Nashville, Tennesee.

She was elated. The idea that soon she would be speaking with him transformed her so that no more was she the aged woman, dry without hope but young and vibrant again.

When I got in on the Big Night she was wearing her best silk dress and her hair was curled - I almost told her, it's a nonsense - he's not going to see you -

"Hurry and eat . . . then we'll clear up . . . I'll see to Sharon . . ."

"Mum, the call's booked for half-past-one in the morning, it's only just turned seven."

She looked at the clock, as she would do over and over. "As well to be ready . . . it's a great business, phoning all that way." It had been a long time since I'd seen that lemonade sparkle in her eyes.

Mum was shaking at me, pulling off the blanket I'd thrown across myself. "Wake up, it's time to go. Dress warm, it's bitter out."

While the town was all asleep we pushed the pram with Sharon also sleeping, to the phone box. Outside I waited, the cold wind nipping my ears. Mum within, was tight, excited, her hand shadowing the phone, waiting, then the double ring and her eager "Yes?" and the panes of glass misted with her breath till inside was a misted image like a night dream. Sharon poked a hand from the covers. I pushed it back against her small warm body. I could hear the muffle of mum's voice, pushing out words against the speeding seconds, question after question. The paper with the carefully rehearsed phrases fell from her hand and now there was a gap of silence - now more words and all the while I longed to pull open the door and hear all, know if it was going well - but I didn't dare - this was her night -

Suddenly she shouted "No!" A pause, then again, "It can't be!" I pulled open the heavy door and she was repeating his name and I knew by the way she said it, he wasn't there any more. She slipped suddenly to the floor and the ear-piece was left swinging from its cord.

"Mum . . ." I stroked her face as her head rested awkwardly against the heavy-framed pane. Her cheek was cold. I made to lift

173

her. "No . . . no . . ." she murmured. "Try and stand . . . we can't stay here," I tried - "He . . . doesn't . . . want . . . me . . ." She gripped my collar. "He's with the wife again . . . he divorced her didn't he? With her and the children . . ." She pulled my collar tight. "How could he?" - "Ssh, mum -" I covered her hand. "He hadn't heard from me he said and he thought, can you believe it . . . he thought . . . I didn't want him . . ." I dragged her up. "Come, you're freezing."

We went home, through the moonlit streets - a 'bomber's sky' - funny how the war left you with a whole lot of new sayings -

I poked up the dead fire. "Get undressed mum, I'll make you a hot-water bottle." We waited for the kettle to boil. Outside, the footsteps of someone walking unevenly drew nearer the house. They stopped and I heard peeing against our wall. Then he went off singing, "Yourrs till the starrs lose their glorreey . . ."

CHAPTER TWENTY-TWO

March - April 1946

"Won't you get up, for a little while?" Mum was in bed, as she'd been for the past two days. She raised her arm weakly for me to leave. I didn't know how much was the effect of shock or if she was just still drugged from the tablets the doctor had prescribed - "Two of these at night and the green and yellow ones, two, three times daily." At the door he'd added, "She shouldn't be left alone more than is necessary." I paid him and almost asked, what about my job and it's the only money we've got now besides the allowance for Sharon and how much longer would that be paid?

I opened mum's purse - seven pounds, fourteen and sixpence. That wouldn't last long. I thought and thought - if only there was someone I could go to - ask advice from. It seemed the only thing was to try for yet another lodger, p'raps two if we could get them. Mum wouldn't like it - after Pat she swore she'd never take anyone in. I put an advert in the Leader and Guardian for a 'Mature, responsible person . . .' and hoped to God, like mum said, we'd be luckier this time. For the present though I didn't tell her.

"Will you try and eat something?"

She didn't answer. She looked like a painting I'd seen once in a book in the library, of a youngish woman it was, sitting in a rocking-chair the same, her clothes olive-green and yellow, her face shadowed - "The Young Widow" it was called -

"I'll have to go to work soon."

"Go . . . I can look after Sharon . . ."

"The way you are?" I sounded impatient. She turned away, covering her face. "Mum, look at me." I told her of the advertisement. As I expected she was angry. "How can you think of it - after what's just happened . . ."

"But how we going to manage?"

"I wish Fay hadn't gone . . ."

"Shall I write and ask her to come and stay for a bit?"

"You mad?" She threw it at me, for the first time since that dreadful night showing a bit of the mother I remembered. "D'you think I want her to know my shame? How could I face her - face anyone?"

The following morning she dressed to go out. "I won't be long," was all she said. I watched anxiously, as she went up the street. It was warmer, softer now the first spring winds had left us. Next door the sister was sweeping the pavement - she too watched mum - opposite the "cow" was cleaning her parlour window - On mum walked, trying to act the part, the role of a woman still loved and wanted -

How could he have done this? She would have kept faith till death - and beyond - whatever is beyond. She would never get over him, I was sure, he was the only man she'd ever really cared about, put before herself - and look where it had got her.

I felt old also, like my life was all used up. I was seventeen, the war was done with and I felt older than mum.

She was back. "This'll help anyway." She placed three pound notes down. "Pawned my old wedding-ring," she said in answer to my look. She touched the gold watch on her wrist, the one Jim had given her. "Meant to get something on this as well -" She sighed. "Couldn't part with it."

I went for the rations from Mr. Evans and collected my shoes from the cobbler. There wasn't any change.

175

We got just one answer to the advert - not many people needed to be staying in Kettering now.

"Well?" I asked.

"He writes a decent enough letter . . . polite." She wrote back, "just to look him over . . ." The following week Mr. Levine called.

He was bright and his brightness was at once attractive the way all things bright are so that I thought of brass buttons and the best of summer and the faces of children at birthday parties. His look focused first here, then there, missing nothing, his nose wrinkling at the same time so that he was almost smelling it too like an animal. He seemed about fifty and most and not least, spoke with a distinct Jewish accent - not common like the stall-holders in Petticoat Lane but with the slightest thickening of the "t's" and "s's" and with a nasal overlay. He removed his hat and I was certain he wore a toupee - so, Mr. Levine, you're worried about your age, I thought.

"The room's upstairs, at the back." He followed mum, chattering about the weather, shortages, the town now the Americans had gone. He seemed to know about everything and nothing could stop his talk. "Very nice," he said, down in the parlour again, "a nice quiet house. I can offer references." He drew hand-written papers from an inside breast pocket and they were well-creased so's I could see they'd been pulled in and out of his jacket many a time. Mum read them, her expression showing nothing. "About meals . . .?" he asked. "I'm a good cook," mum said, her face still set.

"I'm sure you are. I am, excuse me if this sounds vain, an observant man. The moment I walked in I said to myself, Jack, here is a place where they know what good food is." He paused, giving mum the chance to smile or appear grateful but she stayed as she was, anxious to get it all done with and him away. He must have sensed it for now he asked, "May I move in at once? Is it convenient?"

"Rent's in advance. Two weeks."

He counted from a wad of notes. Mum gathered them, trying not to do so hastily. He shook both our hands, then left.

"He's lively!"

"Wonder what's brought him here," mum considered. Fate, I thought.

176

We got busy, polishing the back room, checking the blankets were clean and aired, the windows done. All at once I was very grateful to Mr. Levine - mum was thinking of something else.

He moved in, bringing two cases with him, well-scuffed at the corners as though they'd scraped up and down many a staircase. Soon his silver-backed hairbrushes were royally sitting on the old dressing-table.

"D'you think we'll keep him?" I asked mum after the first week.

"Expect so." After the first business of settling him she was depressed again. Mr. Levine was too sharp not to notice - she hardly spoke at meal-times and let his jokes pass unlaughed at - but nothing spoiled his good humour for long - although sometimes a shadow blurred the brightness it was as a cold wind which catches you out and makes you hold your breath.

A second letter came in answer to the advertisement, from a lady. "Where'll we put her?" I asked.

"There's the old single bed - we can put it in the parlour." She wouldn't look at me - "I'll let her call anyway and see what we make of her."

Lizzie was ugly. She was also very friendly - so much so that it seemed she wasn't aware of her ugliness. Her complexion was rough with large, open pores. Her teeth were uneven and her hair obviously home-dyed a streaky chestnut-auburn. Her posture was bad so that although not old she had an ageing bulge of her upper spine which you couldn't call a hump but if you looked at her sideways on, her back seemed to wave in and out. I liked her at once. It was bubbly when she spoke, cockney bubbly - I hoped mum would have her. We showed her the parlour, now called, "bed-sitting room" - mum apologised about the piano. "S'alright, might fancy gettin' up in the night to have a tune," she joked.

We took her and she took us. "You been here all the war?" I asked. "Yeh, been a presser, on the Hoffmans - heavy great things they are, doing army overcoats - expected the push but the foreman's kept me on for civvy suits - must like my looks eh?"

Mr. Levine and Lizzie brought warmth and life back to the house. Meal-times they'd chatter and Lizzie would laugh at Mr. Levine as, perspiring, he related story after story - of people he'd known, situations he'd got into and then out of and he'd change his voice and facial expressions till it was like all these people he'd known were in the room with us also. One thing he wouldn't do was talk about the Blitz. We knew he came from London too but if ever we started talking about the bombings he'd change the subject fast.

"It's nice having them, isn't it mum?" She was sitting still for a change, something she seldom did lately for once idle, thoughts of Jim would return to torment her.

"I'll never understand, not if I live to a thousand."

"What?"

"How he could have believed I didn't want him."

I put my arms about her. "I don't know either mum. No-one could have loved him more than you did." She leaned against me and I held her so, trying to visualise how it had been for Jim, far away, when the letters had stopped.

Dad wrote, asking when I was coming up again - I didn't answer - I didn't want to see the nothing look of him - the look that said I've finally given up what I most wanted to keep -

Mr. Levine was a mystery - most days he'd be up early and out, not getting back till late evening and then in a good humour as if he'd made more than the most of the daylight hours. He never referred directly to his work - just to "business associates". He spoiled Sharon, magicking bars of chocolate for her which she'd quickly eat, smothering herself in a dark, creamy mess. Mum would protest then but I saw she was grateful for this man's attention to her child. It seemed to me that just now and then Mr. Levine would look at mum a shade longer than he should as she passed him his tea or half-listened as he recounted yet another 'story of the day'. He took to carrying in the water too and never, ever, did he use the chamber-pot - somehow Mr. Levine could hold his pee inside of him till morning. All of this showed me he was definitely trying to make an impression on mum.

"He's nice isn't he?" She didn't answer. "Mum, Mr. Levine, he's nice."

"Nice? Yes."

"Wonder if he's ever been married."

"Who knows . . ." She lifted Sharon from the floor. "Come my *fagala*, come . . ." She put her on her lap, stroking the hair,

178

kissing the small face, wanting no talk of anyone. Soon she was looking deep into the child's eyes, trying to recapture those eyes of the father - those eyes with the smudged lashes -

"What d'you reckon he does?" Lizzie was interested in Mr. Levine. "Know what I think?" She put her face near mine. "I reckon he's been a black marketeer all the war - that's why he changes the subject when we ask what he does." I hadn't considered that. "Only to look at his togs - that flashy tie-pin - that costs a few bob I know. Still, if that's the case, gives him a bit of a dash don't it? I mean, that's important in a feller, a bit of go - initiative, don't you reckon?"

I didn't see it Lizzie's way - top of my list how a man should be were intelligence, then nice manners and tall, fair-haired looks.

"I wonder if he's ever married . . ."

"Looks a real bachelor," I said, repeating mum's words.

"I dunno' - bit perky for that."

She was probably right - thinking back to Mr. Parmer and the dull, unspeaking life of a monk till we'd come and shook it all up. Lizzie sucked lightly on her finger, contemplating Mr. Levine further.

I began seeing Mr. Levine through Lizzie's eyes - even if he was a black marketeer did it really matter - it was "having a bit of go" that was important in this life - why, wasn't that what dad used to say - except dad didn't have it. Yes, Mr. Levine was a 'do-er' and being a 'do-er' was just what mum needed - of course he hadn't seen mum at her best - her sparkling, cheeky best but with someone like him I bet she'd soon be her old self. P'raps it was meant to be, Mr. Levine being sent to us, like it was right for mum to have a bit of luck - *nuchas*, before she got too worn out to appreciate it. Yes, it was a chance for her - the more I thought about it the more sure I was she wouldn't miss out on this opportunity -

She had just done us a real tasty dinner. Mr. Levine was cutting and prodding at his food with obvious pleasure, now and then pausing to push a spoonful into Sharon's mouth, near the table in her high chair. Lizzie scraped at her plate. Mum alone was without appetite.

"Compliments!" Mr. Levine told her, "You are, no question about it, an excellent cook!"

"Don't know how you do it," Lizzie joined in, "with things as

179

they are - worse than in the war -''

"I dunno' about that," mum answered, taking no pleasure in their praise, giving out a meagre portion of herself - her real self that was bonded in with him - far away -

"It is, I believe, time to make a little suggestion," Mr. Levine announced. "I've had a bit of good fortune, business-wise, and when one has such luck it's right that one should share it. So, why don't we all have a little fun and give our cook here something of a break?''

Me and Lizzie looked at one another. "What have you got up your sleeve then?" she asked, trying to be coquettish.

"If you're all willing, I'd like to treat us to Sunday lunch at The George!''

Lizzie showed her uneven teeth. Mr. Levine smiled broader. Mum stayed silent. We all waited. "You're not . . . orthodox?" he asked her. Until then he'd not let on he knew we were Jewish, same as him. Mum shook her head, still saying nothing. Lizzie and me joined in the coaxing of her and finally she gave in.

It was a pity Cynthia had now left Miss Minch's - it would have given me such satisfaction to tell her of The George outing - she who'd always bragged about places her parents had taken her before the war - hotels for tea and week-ends at Rye in Sussex with its cobbled streets and sometimes it seemed that Cynthia's life had been thrown up against mine just to show that mine had, after all, been a poor thing by comparison.

Lizzie brought fresh hair-dye. "Slap some on the partings at the back for us will you?" Soon she was redded afresh. "Look O.K. does it?" I told her yes. You'll never touch mum for looks I wanted to add - even though she can't hide the heartbreak she feels, somehow it makes her wonderful green eyes even more attractive. P'raps that's what Mr. Levine saw -

Mum was out with Sharon, after a lot of coaxing from me. It was a gentle evening, the days longer now and lately she'd hardly stepped from the house. I sat by the open back door, reading.

"Good is it?" Lizzie brought a chair, setting it by mine. I didn't want her company just then and turned slightly away. "I don't read much - nice out 'ent it? Been a nice month - said on the wireless this month's been good - beginning of the month was the warmest April day since - when'd he say? Eighteen-forty was it or

180

'41 -?''

I shut my book. "It is nice."

"You and your mum, you never asked no questions when I come here. I'm grateful."

"Neither did you."

"Not my place is it?" She re-lit her cigarette which was almost burnt-out and half-whistled out the smoke. The light breeze quickly lifted it, spreading it in several directions. Lizzie coughed like a miner, drawing on her 'fag' - "I'll tell you anyway, I don't mind." She drew in again, swallowed more smoke and once more coughed hard. "I've made a stupid mess of my life." Her frankness surprised me so that at once I became interested. "Yeh, got married at eighteen - ran away from home, such as it was - all romantic stuff - Gretna Green - not that mum and dad cared whether or not I was making a mess of me life - no, what they couldn't stomach was the idea of me being a rebel." The fact of Lizzie being a rebel was something I'd never thought of. "When you've a mug like mine and a bloke like him, good-looking - all my mates fancied him - asks you to get married, you grab, and that's what I did." She waved her hand in the air as she spoke and a small piece of glowing ash fell from her cigarette. "Comes the war he joins up - fancied himself in the R.A.F he did - only in three weeks, he meets this W.A.A.F. - blonde, slim, you know - spun him round till he didn't know if he was coming or going." The cigarette was ending. "Hang on . . ." She went to get a fresh packet from her bag. "Don't start this habit, filthy it is. Where was I? Oh yeh, well, to cut it short, we ended up divorced. Didn't think I d trust no-one again." She twisted the cigarette between her fingers watching her own action as though it was the most fascinating thing in the world at that moment. "Chester was a Yank, second lieutenant, opposite of my old man - ugly really - heart of gold - give us the north star if I'd asked. Dressed me up - looked like I'd walked out of Harrods - got me a ring - said I'd go to New York when everything was over. Still waiting ain't I?''

I put my hand over hers.

"I cried every night for a month - then I thought, sod it, always another fish in the sea." The breeze had blown up. She shivered. "Better go inside." I sat on, thinking of Lizzie, her lieutenant, mum and Jim - and also of Mr. Levine.

Sunday morning was like Charing Cross station in the rush hour. Mr. Levine was up first, shaving in the outhouse, bravely assuring us it didn't matter because it was "nearly summer anyway." Lizzie decided to wash her hair yet again and kettles were refilled and the water bucket topped up and Mr. Levine carried it in, lather still on his face. Then he wanted to "put a knife-edge crease in my trousers, seeing as I'm accompanying three ladies today." Lizzie at once offered, "I'll be only too pleased to do them for you Jack." I noticed that "Jack" and wondered when he'd given her permission to use it -

"Going to put your silk, flowered dress on mum?"

She turned a page of her book, "The Constant Nymph", pretending to read. "Shan't be going. Sharon's got a cold."

"You promised! Sharon's only got a sniffle!"

"I've told you." She wouldn't look at me.

"*I* want to go."

"I'm not holding you back."

"You've *got* to come!"

" 'Got' - 'got' - there's no 'got' about it. I'm staying here and that's that."

Lizzie was in the parlour and Mr. Levine upstairs, happily whistling. I lowered my voice. "It's a good chance."

"What chance?" Her expression was innocent - white and untouched.

"Mum, in time, when you're more over the shock of what's happened - don't you think - what I mean is - couldn't you imagine liking anyone else - a man I mean - ?"

The face she turned up to me was filled with horror, then anger. "You mad?" She got up, moving from me as though I were a cobra. "Leave me alone! How can you? You, who ought to know more than anyone . . . just how much . . ." She was breathless now, agitated - at once I was ashamed. "As for him - has he said anything? What has he got hatched up eh? All his smiling and fawning, all the while thinking he's on to something!"

"He's not! He didn't say . . . he don't know anything! I just thought . . ."

"Thought? What did you think? You don't think." She lifted Sharon and hurried from the room, upstairs.

Mr. Levine came down. He must have heard her but still kept a smile on. He had a red carnation in his buttonhole like my uncles used to at weddings. "Ready are we?" He stood before me, immaculate as a tailor's model in Burton's window, eyes ashine as a small boy's on his first circus visit. I told him mum wasn't feeling well. If he was disappointed he hid it. Lizzie swaggered in, "tarted up" as she said with a self-conscious bubble of an apology for keeping us waiting. "Well, well," said Mr. Levine, taking her all in. "I'll do then?" Lizzie asked, pushing her luck a bit I thought. Mr. Levine took a small cigar from a tan, pigskin case, placed it carefully between his cherub lips and lit it with his shining lighter. "You will, indeed you will."

At twelve o'clock the taxi arrived. I went to mum. "You won't change . . .?"

"I'm alright. Go." Lizzie was calling for me to hurry.

The front doors of The George opened slowly and easily for us on their strong, oiled hinges. All inside was the same - easy, comfortable, in an old-fashioned sure-of-itself way. I'd always wanted to see inside of this part of the large hotel - often, passing it on my way to and from Miss Minch's I'd get a whiff of people coming in and out, people with cash in their wallets, in their crocodile-skin handbags, in the tips they gave to porters ordering taxis. Farmers doing well came here and officers on leave and Yanks with fancy girl-friends who knew a thing or two about where to go when they were on to a good thing.

The head waiter led us to our table and the moment I sat he pushed my chair in under me. He did the same for Lizzie which took her a bit by surprise - then he handed her a large menu. She stared at it, blinking fast. "Do you ladies trust me to order for you?" Mr. Levine gallantly offered, taking the menu from her. His eyes scanned the copper-plate writing of dishes, Lizzie watching his every move. "What do you think of consommé to start with?" I'd no idea what consommé was but said yes at once. Lizzie nodded. "And to follow, roast duckling, potatoes and petit pois?" Now I nodded vigorously, madly hoping petit pois was something I didn't hate - "Apple tart to finish with?" he went on. It didn't look much like they'd heard of rationing or food shortages here.

We had our consommé, which turned out to be just soup while Mr. Levine chatted same as if he was at home about places he'd visited, "in the course of business" - the north of England, the south coast, Bournemouth particularly he lingered over, "very Mediterranean the atmosphere," he took a deep breath, "bracing, like heady wine. I wouldn't say no to retiring there when my time comes."

"I'm sure that's a long way off yet," Lizzie said gaily. Mr. Levine laughed and so did she. For a moment I remembered mum - why couldn't she see what a jewel of a man Mr. Levine was?

The duckling was gorgeous - I felt sure it was the sort of thing King George had for his Sunday lunch. It was all so English - it made me consider whether or no Mr. Levine had been brought up in a *frum* household, anyway at this moment I didn't care - it was all smashing, I was having a good time and even if Mr. Levine hadn't been *barmitzva'd* it wasn't going to spoil today.

He refilled our wine glasses and Lizzie became very talkative. Any moment I expected her to let out about her American. Unexpectedly the talk went serious - the war - "the senselessness of it all" as Mr. Levine put it - and now Lizzie listened, her face grave, as he spoke, in a way I wouldn't have expected, of the Nuremberg Trials - he'd followed every bit about them in the papers, the reports - pleadings for the defence, "as if there could be any defence! And Ribbentrop - he bursts into tears! Tears!" He pulled a handkerchief angrily from his top pocket and instantly its immaculate creases were undone as he mopped at his face. "Now - what happens? British troops rounding up Jewish 'terrorists' " - he said the word like it was bitter medicine - " 'terrorists', in Palestine. I don't know what they expect." I wanted to ask who? Who expected what?

"It's terrible Jack," Lizzie agreed, "a bloody shame."

He refolded his handkerchief. "Come, this won't do, we're supposed to be having ourselves a good time." He put the silver lighter to another cigar. "Tell me," he asked, "what d'you intend to do with your young life?" The question was so direct I went hot. "P'raps I'm a shade blunt. Let's put it another way. What would you like to be?"

"Clever!"

He gave a gusty laugh. The head waiter turned. "She's sharper than ever I was at her age," Lizzie put in.

"And you Lizzie, what do you want?"

"Just to be . . . happy." She looked directly at him.

184

"And why not?" He tapped the still, grey ash from the cigar into the heavy, glass ash-tray.

We had another taxi home. Me and Lizzie sang "My Old Man" while Mr. Levine relaxed on the wide leather seat. Our driver, an oldish man with a military moustache going back to the First War said, "It's a fair while since I've had such a merry party aboard."

Now I had to face mum. I hurried from the taxi first. "Where are you?"

"In here," she answered. She was in Lizzie's 'bed-sitting room', at the piano. "I was just trying to remember some of my old songs," she said, looking awkwardly at Lizzie.

"Anytime. Didn't I say you could if I wasn't in?" Lizzie said, still full of the wine and Mr. Levine. Then he told mum one of these days she must let them hear her repertoire. Mum sat on the piano stool, her hair needing washing, her eyes bare of mascara.

CHAPTER TWENTY-THREE

May - June 1946

"It's up to you if you want to go. I've never stopped you seeing him."

Mum had a poor memory when it suited - I nearly said what about when she told me to threaten he'd lose me for good if he didn't agree to a divorce. Dad had written, a pleading little note - it had been too long since I'd visited - there was a Bank Holiday for Victory Day at the beginning of June - 'Why don't we take the chance to see each other?' It was a restrained few lines. Anyone reading it knowing nothing of the man would think how civilised, how proper the father should behave so, take his responsibility seriously, keep contact with this only child, this daughter, whose loyalty was always first to the mother, despite what she did, always the mother - would they have believed if they were told, of the unpredictable moods, the frenzies, the screams when he'd trailed mum in the streets, telling the world Sharon was "a Mexican bastard!" Best put that away - all thought of it - I answered, saying it'd be nice.

"What'll I tell him if . . .?"

"If what?"

". . . he asks about you . . . and . . ."

"Tell him." She set her mouth in that tight little kiss shape.

"Tell him?"

"What can he do? I'm not his wife anymore." 'Course she wasn't - hadn't the Probate, Divorce and Admiralty Division of the High Courts of Justice issued a piece of paper saying so?

I told Lizzie I was going. "That's good luv', should keep in touch - your dad's your dad - not that I'm the one to talk - you enjoy yourself. I'll take the little 'un to the park eh?"

Lizzie was good with Sharon. I told her so. She went to speak, then stopped. "What?" I prodded. "Keep a secret?" I nodded. "I've got a lad. My sister took him when the marriage went bust. He's fine with her - now and then I visit, send Easter eggs, Christmas - you know -"

"Lizzie, wonder if Mr. Levine ever had a family?"

She fumbled in her bag, seeking yet another cigarette. "Filthy habit this, don't ever take it up - I've said before haven't I?"

"What d'you think?"

"About what?"

"What I just said - Mr. Levine."

She sat herself on the piano-stool, spreading her hands across the keys. "Wish I could play like your mum. Talent she's got. I heard her once, right up the street, coming home from work, singing, sad and lovely as well it was -"

"She nearly was an opera singer."

"Go on?"

"You know something don't you?"

"Know?"

"About Mr. Levine. That's why you keep changing the subject."

"Curious as a wagon-load of monkeys you are!" She went to the door, listened and satisfied he wasn't about spoke in a low voice, "Ever notice anything - about how he walks?"

"His sciatica you mean - how it makes him walk stiff -?"

"Sciatica my eye! He ain't got no right leg. Lost it in one of the raids - not only that . . ." She drew deep on her 'fag' - "He's had a wife - kids - lost them all" -

186

For a few mad seconds all I could think was where did he put his false leg when he took it off? "Lizzie, that's terrible . . . his family I mean."

"Never know do you?" She stubbed her cigarette hard. "Yeh, you go enjoy yourself - life's short -"

I lay on the bed thinking of Lizzie and her little boy - Mr. Levine and his tragedy. The sun stretched into the room, its last evening rays all out of tune with my feelings. Yes, it'd be good to go to London now, be there with the celebrations and people happy instead of tragic and morbid, all having someone dead or lost to them for always. Yes, best think about London - London at peace - no Blackout and Piccadilly Circus sparkling with coloured BOVRIL and SCHWEPPES TONIC WATER neon adverts - newspaper sellers with bill-boards with good news in large black letters and people going about enjoying themselves easily - not all a-scramble in case the next day would have them blown to bits or sent off to a foreign land. Yes, I would enjoy going - it'd be a relief to leave mum's wretchedness whenever she spoke of Jim or heard a song that had been 'theirs' -

The day was bright and I was ready to go. "You look smart," mum said. I knew I did, with my best dress on, my sandals whitened and freshly-washed hair caught at the sides with imitation tortoiseshell combs.

"You'll be fine. Lizzie'll keep you company."

She kissed me, hard. "Hasn't been a picnic for you, I know - but you're all I've got now . . ."

"Sharon . . ."

"She's different. I depend on you."

The journey was quicker like the train also knew the war was all done. If only the bit where he met me at St. Pancras could be got over quickly too - that first kiss and the clinging and the handkerchief dabbing at his eyes while he assured me it was the smoke from the engine and "always makes your eyes run don't it?"

This time I got in first with "How posh you are!" I would set the mood, the festive, light mood so that pulling and probing would be pushed away - or at least put off -

He held the edge of my elbow - he'd never done that. His suit was smart, of light brown with a darker over-check. It went better

187

with him than the usual navy blues and dark greys. "Thought I ought to get myself up like a bloody capitalist to take my grown-up daughter out." He was easier. P'raps it wouldn't be so bad this time.

He talked non-stop on the bus to his flat - the new Labour government would give people like us a chance - sometimes wars bring about changes a dozen revolutions couldn't - he didn't think much of Atlee - "weak - a bit crafty - weasel-like" - I looked out of the window, half-listening, and names new in his political vocabulary sped past my ears same as the shop-fronts - Herbert Morrison, Ernest Bevin, and then good old Ramsey Macdonald was dug up and cursed afresh. "Nearly there," he was saying and now it was talk of the newly-painted living-room and the second-hand Ascot water-heater - "Smashing it is, right over the sink - no boiling-up kettles" -

We were in his street, narrow as I remembered it with an ugly assortment of small workshops squeezed in beside a sombre warehouse, opposite them the four blocks, three storeys high, of much-stained dark grey stone. We climbed the steps to the second floor. Two boys reading comics were stretched across the space outside his front door. I stepped over their legs, following dad into the flat.

"Tea first! You'll have my bed, like before!"

"I'll be alright on the bed-settee," I said.

"No, no, you're a lady now. See, I got cheesecake and mandelbrot."

"Like grandma used to bake."

"Like your mother's mother used to make."

Downstairs the wireless was loud. He talked fast, like the machine-gun fire in all those war films. "Sylvie's here now," I told him. "Oh?" he said and straightaway went on talking about his own things and I knew there was still no woman in his life. "Glad you like living here," I said as a stranger might, trying to be polite.

"Go on, eat!"

I put a large piece of cheesecake in my mouth - there was nothing else like it - and only a Jewish baker could make it so - proper cheesecake, lemon-sharp with fat sultanas - worth coming just for this.

"Have you thought more about what I wrote?" he asked.

"Any more of that gorgeous cheesecake?" I wriggled from his watch and cut deep into the creamy-yellow till in its richness it crumbled. "Well?" he repeated. "Think you'd like to live here, with me?"

"Don't know," I said through a full mouth. Downstairs turned off the dance-music - seemed they also were listening for my answer. "Your mother O.K.?" Still fascinated with the cheesecake like a pig of a child I told him yes. "That's good. And the child?" I told him fine. He nodded his head the way old Jewish men do when they're considering on beyond what you've told them, weighing it up against their own experience. "What we doing tomorrow?" I asked. "Is she going away?" he persisted. He was watching the enamel clock with a small chip out of its base on the mantlepiece. "No," I answered. He moved to the mantlepiece and wound the clock till there was no slack in its mechanism, then he shook it, compared it with his wrist-watch and set it back in its place, dead centre. "It's late. Better turn in."

His tobacco smoke soon filled the place and once when I woke in the night, strange in the unfamiliar bed, I couldn't work out why Mr. Levine's cigar smelled like dad's pipe.

Dad was up early as always, listening to the news. He knocked cheekily at the door. "Tea's made - ready for a day out? D'you know, beats me what people'll do - just said on the wireless, thousands of them, already out in the streets, waiting for the parade to start - slept out since Thursday some of 'em - more than I'd do."

He sat on the bed, eager, happy to have me. "So, what do you fancy?"

"Can we go?"

"Where? Go where?"

"As well - to the parade, same as everyone else."

He scratched his head - at the top, so's he looked like Stan of Laurel and Hardy. "You serious? You know what it'll be? The Royal Family decked out like they were costermongers on a trip to Southend and Churchill taking the salute as if it was him alone won the whole bloody war -" I held up my hand, "I don't care! I *want* to see them!" He stood up. "Get dressed then - if that's what you want -"

Trafalgar Square was filled with people and it wasn't yet half-past eight. They were everywhere, even sitting astride the bronze

189

lions - men, women, in red white and blue, children wearing paper hats and blowing toy trumpets at you as you squeezed past them. He shoved and dragged me through it all and across the road to Admiralty Arch. There on top of the high gates three people had entwined themselves, like a daring circus act - all to see the procession the better. "Wanna' ticket for near the front?" a cockney voice asked dad. "Bugger off!" he told him, sweating, his face with two bright red patches on the cheeks. "Don't think this was such a good idea . . ." But it was just as I'd hoped - and it felt good, being at the centre of this mass of people, alive, happy and showing their feelings in such an un-British way. It felt like when I used to get them singing down the brewery, a feeling of togetherness even though in our blood and our bones we were far apart as the earth and the moon - it felt so good and it was what I'd missed -

It had been very late when dad and me finally got back. Now as the train rumbled towards Kettering I closed my eyes. I was still tired but my mind bubbled with thoughts of the previous day. How would I begin to tell Lizzie and mum about it all? If I used words like "stirring" or "a nation together" I'd sound just like Churchill or the commentator on the newsreels - and yet it was that - stirring - and it found parts of me I didn't know about. As I'd watched the columns of marching army men and naval men, the A.T.S. and civilians - the Wardens, Firewatchers, and then the fireman and Land Army girls, all cheered as they drove past on their tractors, and the miners with their helmets and lamps who got the biggest cheers of all, I was proud I was part of it - proud and thankful my grandparents had decided to come here, for although England had a lot to put right, like dad always said, still I was glad -

The sun on the window warmed my face and shoulders, welcome after the long hours of yesterday's rain. Now fields were spinning by, rain-battered also and dad's face came to me through the window - "You'll come again, before too long?"

It was unexpectedly chilly when I got home. Mum was preoccupied and worried. "Would you believe it, we got through the whole sodding war and now, not enough coal to go round." Maybe I should tell her about the marching miners - "Mum . . ."

"Sharon's got a chesty cough . . . she ought to be kept extra warm . . ." I was sent straight to Mr. Evans to scrounge wooden boxes. I was soon back.

"Only one? That all he'd let you have?" Still there were no questions of what it had been like for me - nothing about dad - "Best get this box chopped up hadn't we?"

Mr. Levine got back to find us all sitting about with thick jumpers on - even Lizzie was glum. "What's all this?" He rubbed his hands briskly. Mum told him and Sharon, just like she understood, coughed even more. "Who would have thought such a cold snap would catch us out this time of year?" He took a flask from his pocket and unscrewed the top. "Here." Mum shook her head. "I insist," he said authoritatively. He poured some into the silver top. She swallowed it. "A drop for you too." He tipped the dark gold liquor into my empty cup. "I've never had whisky," I told him. "It's brandy, and now's a good time to try." I drank some. It burnt my tongue and throat. Was this what men liked and women too, some of them? "Horrible!" He laughed, then poured some for Lizzie who drank obediently. "Thanks Jack," she told him familiarly. It looked to me as though he and Lizzie had made a certain amount of progress over the week-end. Then with a brisk "Leave it to me," he departed. Mum went to bed with Sharon "to keep warm . . ."

"Want to come in mine for a natter?" Lizzie offered. I went, eager to tell someone of my outing.

"You should have gone on the stage like your mum said to - you make it all so real when you tell things - a gift you've got . . ." She means a *mitzvah* really, same as the *boobahs* always said about mum. She pulled her cardigan tighter around her thin body. "Tell us some more then."

So I told - all the bits I'd hoped mum would want to know - about the people who'd slept on the pavements for two nights before the procession to get a "front-row view" and the military-looking man who'd made sure of his place by camping out with bed and equipment - and the stalls in the side streets and the hawkers with cockles and pies - "I've never had a good pie since I come away," Lizzie interrupted. And I told of the people there from all over the world - all nationalities - all shades of brown - and how the military man commented while they marched past - "That chap's Fijian and here's a bunch from Borneo" - and he and the others had clapped and dad muttered about the "colonialistic

191

attitude" and I just ignored him and clapped along with the rest. Then I told how the crowd kept speculating whether the Russians would be in the march and how dad pricked up his ears, saying if anyone should be, they should - and the military man had agreed, saying, "Damn spunky, those Ruskies" - That had set dad off and the whole Battle of Stalingrad was gone over, with him and dad discussing the tactics and the battle for Moscow and Marshal Zhukov until everyone about told them shut up -

"Did you see the fireworks?" Lizzie asked. "It said on the wireless they was lovely."

So I told her just how lovely they were, and the searchlights playing on the clouds over the Thames after dark and the firefloats sending up coloured fountains of water and the gasps of delight of the children and the cheers and dancing in the streets long into the night and on I talked - on and on -

"Time you and me got to bed," Lizzie said suddenly. I hadn't realised how long I'd been talking.

There was a rat-a-tat on the front door early next morning. "Got a barrow-load of wood for this house Miss," a broad, earnest-faced lad said, balancing the long handles of a wheelbarrow piled with broken timber. Mr. Levine had "fixed it up".

"I'll miss him," mum said, as we sat cosily around the crackling flames that evening.

"Mr. Levine? He's not leaving? Has he said?"

"Not yet. He will though."

"How d'you know that?"

"Got eyes in my head that's why. Him and Lizzie." She said it easily - no trace of envy - no disappointment for what might have been -

"Think they'll be happy?"

"He'll suit her and she'll suit him." She made no mention of love - it was, for them a suitable match - a coming together of two souls, bashed a bit by life, by circumstance, and ready now for a bit of peace - comfort - of one to the other. "My Jim had the most beautiful body." It came out suddenly. "Did I ever tell you - just how beautiful his body was?"

Just as well you're not getting Mr. Levine, I thought, him with his false leg and all -

And not long after, they stood before us, Lizzie glowing in the morning sunshine, almost pretty. "Lizzie and I have something to announce," Mr. Levine said, stretching his arm to hold her hand.

"Oh yes," mum said.

"I'm sure you've seen - how could you fail to notice - Lizzie and me have become, attached, well, I suppose one could say . . . love at our age . . ."

"So we're gonna' make it legal, without delay," Lizzie stuck in. I kissed her. "I'm glad."

"Congratulations," mum said.

"Fancy yourself as a bridesmaid?" Lizzie asked me.

So they married on a peaceful June morning and there was a tasteful arrangement of pink and red roses and tall gladioli on the table at the Registrar's Office and strangers on the pavement smiled and were curious the way they always are at weddings and Lizzie wept a bit and Mr. Levine patted her arm and all in all it seemed proper - a "happy ever after" except Lizzie wasn't beautiful and Mr. Levine was old. Maybe grandma wasn't so wrong when she said that *nuchas* can come to anyone -

Mum wasn't there - Sharon's cough gave her a good excuse - I was glad she wasn't for wouldn't she have been thinking, but for a few months this might have been her and Jim.

The couple went off to Bournemouth for a short honeymoon. "Be happy!" I called after them as the train became a small caterpillar sliding away. There were spots of rainbow confetti bouncing madly along the platform, then onto the railway lines - some scuttled upwards to be gone for always - I waited till the tiniest speck was out of my sight.

"Went off alright did it?" Mum tried to keep her voice even. "Umm." She blew her nose hard. "It'll be O.K. something'll . . ." I started. "Don't for Christ's sake say 'turn up'!"

"Someone's sure to need a place to live."

"The town's getting emptier by the day. P'raps we ought to be thinking of going back."

"To London?" And I could leave Miss Minch - after all these wasted years - still with no qualification and earning just ten shillings more than when I started. "D'you know what Miss Minch asked me? If I'd like to go to be a trainee maid for this rich friend of hers - thought it'd be a good opportunity she said."

193

"You didn't tell me!" mum flashed out.

"Told her it wasn't what I'd got planned for myself." I didn't tell mum what I'd thought was, you can tell your high-falutin' friend to stick her lady's maid job right up her County arse-hole! I wasn't reared in the East End for nothing.

"Maybe I ought to try for a job," she began, uncertainly. "I could get a second-hand typewriter - practice - get my speed back -"

"Sharon - you can't leave her . . ."

". . . you could stay home . . . you don't like it at Miss Minch's . . ."

"No!"

"You're good with her . . ."

I pulled off the amber beads, the ones grandma had left me, the beads mum let me wear just for special occasions. "Thanks." I placed them in her lap. She got up and holding them fast left the room.

"Bunt . . . ing, bunt . . . ing." Sharon had her arms held up to me, wanting her song, asking to be lifted for the game where she held tight to my hands and I swung her round and around - swinging and singing - our game, kept for only when mum was out of the room -

> "Bye baby-bunting
> Daddy's gone a-hunting
> To get a little rabbit-skin
> To wrap his baby-bunting in
> Bye baby-bunting."

She chuckled, sure of herself in our game, unknowing of mum's worries, innocent of why she'd been born. What when she was old enough to ask questions? What could mum tell her?

Mr. and Mrs. Levine returned from Bournemouth looking very well. Just before bed-time he became unusually self-conscious and dabbed at his forehead several times. Lizzie, with the confidence of a wife of many years, took charge. "What we thought luv'," she looked straight at mum. "Seein' as how we're spliced as the sayin' goes, can I go in with Jack?"

194

"It'll only be for a week or so, until we find a place of our own," Mr. Levine added.

"It's natural. Why not?" mum replied, looking past Mr. Levine where the back door stood open wide. "The garden's still nice, despite all the wind and rain."

Through the wall that night, as I lay beside mum, I heard the low mumble of their talking - sometimes Lizzie would let go a small private laugh, followed by his high-pitched, almost womanish giggle.

"Don't worry." She kept her back to me. "Mum?"

"I'm tired."

It was ages before I got to sleep. Just as I was dozing off I heard the bed-spring in a rhythmic movement, that same regular movement that I knew from the time that Jim was with us.

CHAPTER TWENTY-FOUR

June - July 1946

"D'you miss Sylvie?"

"That's a funny question. Like me saying do you miss Fay?"

Mum was bundling together some of Sharon's baby clothes. "Slip these along to Mrs. Evans, she's always after jumble for her church fund-raising." That done, she started on a pile of old love books. Lately it had been turn out and burn up and "I ought to have got rid of this years ago . . ." Now it was, "You better go through your drawers - you hoard almost as bad as me."

"Why now?"

"Just that . . . if we do leave here, think of the rubbish we'll have to get rid of." She went to busy herself upstairs.

"Wait mum. Why'd you ask about Sylvie?"

"No reason special . . . 'course you miss her, letters aren't the same and neither of them is exactly a Colette when it comes to the written word. We've got no-one we can call close anymore. Who is there I can really talk to - trust - no-one." She sat herself in the rocking-chair, pushing back and forth, working up her discontentment.

It had been bad since Mr. Levine and Lizzie had left. Now our

195

problems didn't have to be acted away - now it was all there in front of us - the past, the present - and the future threatening so that I woke at dawn wishing it was still night and I might sleep away my fear - was this why dad had hidden beneath the bedclothes all those times?

"It's no good. We're going to have to go back." She said it as though it was a funeral oration.

"This is our home . . ."

"Home? This is a prison! Every time I poke my head out the door, they point at me, sneer, the 'abandoned woman' -"

"It's not true."

"Even Mrs. Lee asked why I was staying on. And him, Mr. Evans - owe him money I do - me, who's always managed to keep out of debt no matter what."

I wanted to say, something'll turn up, that old phrase that put heart into the down and the desperate - is that what they said to someone as they stood on the gallows - ? She sat rocking and the chair squeaked slightly with each forward movement - I'd never noticed that -

She stopped still at last. "I've written to him." I knew she meant dad before she said. "Your father. Asked him to take us."

"No." I could barely hear my voice so I wasn't sure if I'd spoken it or thought it.

"Listen."

"No! No! No!" I shouted.

"For God's sake!" Now she was talking fast and broken phrases came through the screen of my anger and confusion - "desperate" - "loved" - "lonely" -

"You hate him! You don't want him!" The words threw themselves at her and I needed to find more to spite her again and again and they came and their sound and their meaning shocked me while I was mouthing them but I couldn't stop.

"That's enough!" She was shaking and staring at me as if at a creature unknown. Still the anger controlled me so that I cared nothing for this shadow of a thing before me - nothing for this weakling for whom I felt such contempt, who had no fight or courage, who thought of little but her desires and needs, who was obsessed with them - and again, as so often before I wondered why I had had such a mother thrust upon me and not someone calm and

196

strong and wise the way a mother ought to be.

Sharon was screaming. "Look at her . . . control yourself . . ." She lifted her. "There . . . there . . ." she said over and over. Now my tears came so that I was as Sharon, knowing nothing of this world of adults, where they played a part for so long as it suited them so to do. "Where you going?" She called it after me.

I ran, the way I always did when meeting Mary, to the park - between her street and mine, past the row of cottages with their ironstone walls and the vegetables growing strongly in the end one's front garden - where the summer delphiniums were deep blue and high - past the polished knockers of brass and the clean white curtains all telling of order and no conflict within. People with children passed, children flushed with play - a dog ran on and its movement rushed past my bare legs and on I also ran, eager to reach the park, green with summer rains, startlingly green through the black, iron railings - just to reach it - lie down upon its dampness, feel it hard and certain beneath me - a safe, tidy hardness -

"My turn!" a girl's voice called and her call, like a ball, bounced over my head and calls of other dark-haired, dark-eyed children in a ring sounded out - "Eenah-deenah, abba-dasha . . ." the lead into the chant, the rhyme of special significance - our rhyme, the rhyme of our group - the happy, quarrelling, laughing gang - my gang - and oh, to be back with them, to have known nothing of this place and this war where people did terrible things to each other and families were pulled this way, then that - and oh, to be again as I was - throwing the ball in a make-believe world -

"Give us a push." A boy was looking down at me. "What?" His feet were beside my head and his shoes were scuffed. He leant, offering his hand. I took it, pulling myself up. He reached to just above my waist. His cheek was scratched and his shirt unevenly buttoned so that a large piece of material bellowed between the second and third opening down the front. The scratch had bled and now was all stuck dry. He led me to the children's playground and without a word got on a swing. I pushed. He gripped the chains, stretching his legs forward, working the swing higher, then his body leant forward, his legs and feet tucked in behind until the swing came back and again I pushed like a servant. A man with a dog on a lead watched - the dog, a golden retriever, had its tail up and spread with the wind which was stronger now and the wind

197

pushed the swing to me and I strained it away again and all the while my new master said nothing.

Now he jumped from the swing and pulling me, took me to the see-saw. "Get on." He waited for me to slip across the wooden end-seat. "You first," I told him. He hesitated, unwilling for me to be boss but I stayed firm and walked to the opposite end and on he sat, his feet astride, crouched like a squatting frog till I eased down my end and up in the air he went - sudden - "Bounce it!" he called. Down I went, close to the ground, my feet pushing hard on the asphalt, then up I went and down he came, taking his hands daringly from the handle. "Hold on!" I called. He laughed and the wind took his laugh and scattered it till it reached the bowling-green where the golden retriever was and the animal turned its head. Fickle again, my friend was off the see-saw and scampering to the 'umbrella'. This time he didn't call me for he knew I would follow and he stood on the circular seat making it tip like a heavy flower wind-blown. "Push," he ordered again. I leant against the dark iron bar, then slipped onto the seat also, closing my eyes, swaying with the to and fro, wanting the evening here to last and last - My side had tipped down again. "Where are you?" My call got lost in the rustle of the laburnum leaves.

The first of our trips to father began. To start with, just going for the day - leaving early, him waiting at St. Pancras, then the three of us bundled in a taxi while he grandly gave instructions to the driver. It would be brim with pleasure - lunch in a proper restaurant, a promenade then along the Bond Street and Piccadilly shops, him bragging he could copy any of the elegant outfits displayed. Then again he would tell of the tale of the titled lady placing an order with his guv'nor's West End showroom for a jacket - "black it was - with a peacock in braid to be stitched on the entire back - Imagine! Machining black on black - enough to make you blind!" Mum had heard it so many times - she would switch off, gazing at the clothes designed for elegant women - women who had little else to do but eat in fancy restaurants and ride about in taxis.

Dad was happy - hadn't he every right to be - hadn't he shown her forgiveness - compassion - ? And in his well-being he talked and joked, seeming to see little of mum's strain or my unease. He wheeled Sharon along the streets in her push-chair, proudly as if father of this beautiful child and soon she was holding her arms to him to lift her. This he'd do, talking gently to her in a manner I'd never before seen in him. Mum watched all and if her heart was breaking she tried to hide it for if he saw and acknowledged it she'd never be able to keep her word - to go back to him.

On the train home she'd stay silent, dad's gifts untouched on the seat by her. Each time we returned she'd be wearing something new - he insisted she wore at once whatever he saw for her in the shops - a straw hat once, pale golden, with a veil, short, and darker spots of gold on it of fluffy material so that it seemed specked with lost bumble bees. "Doesn't your mother look nice?" he would ask and I would think of the words Jim would have used - "a beautiful doll" or "my Queen" - but how could I teach dad to say those things? Anyhow it wouldn't have sounded right coming from him.

Each time we returned home she would withdraw a little more so that we didn't return from the big city and the shopping sprees like schoolgirls with new possessions but as old women after a funeral, heavy and doubtful whether or no we could get through the next few days without weeping and wailing. And each time we returned I felt more certain that before the end of the month, when it was time for us finally to go, she would back out.

"Isn't it time you gave Miss Minch notice?"

"Suppose so."

"You can't live in London and work here can you?"

"No."

"We're going." She tossed it out wilfully. "D'you think I wouldn't?" She scribbled on yet another list. "Got to get rid of most of this furniture . . ." Her tongue flipped at the corner of her mouth, something she did when concentrating. Around us were the things that had once been cared for by Mr. Parmer's mother - the deal table, the yellow vases.

"Not the rocking chair?"

"There's no room for it."

"You'll miss the garden."

"I will."

And what of the things I would miss? London was dirty, the flat small and miserable, the street mean and dark and it would be like before - us living in one grey place after another.

Dad wrote again. He'd organised transport - 'I'll be up to help

199

you get the last few things . . .'

"He can't come! I'm not having that!"

"It'll be easier . . ."

"You lost your reason? Think I want everyone seeing him - me and him - after . . ." She was searching for the handkerchief she never seemed to have.

"Here . . ."

She took mine, blowing her nose hard. "They'll put two and two together . . . what d'you think they'll say when they see us moving and taking stuff with us eh?" Now she was weeping with no attempt to keep up the act.

"Mum, don't. I know it's hard."

"Do you?" She spoke quietly now. "I pray to God you'll never experience what I'm going through."

It was raining again, spluttering into next-door's water-butt. Mum was writing a list of last jobs to do - the electricity people to read the meter - ration books and identity cards to be changed - should she say a proper goodbye to Mrs. Lee? This she asked aloud.

"Mum, there might be a way around it."

"What?"

"I've been thinking. You know the way the G.I. brides put adverts in the papers when they leave for America saying goodbye to their friends? You could as well."

At once a spark lit her face. "D'you think so? Oh, that would be one in the eye for the old cow opposite! Would it work? But what would I say?"

"Thought you always came top in the class for composition," I told her lightly. I left her, sitting at the table, sucking the end of a pencil like a kid. There was no water left and same as always I went to fetch some - at least with dad I wouldn't have this to do -

"How's this sound?" She began to read, pausing now and then to scratch through a word and replace it with one better. 'To all my friends I have made . . . during my stay here. I want to say a fond goodbye . . . now that I am leaving . . . to join my husband . . .' She threw the pencil to the floor. "How . . . can I . . .?" She stretched her arms down on the table and lay her head over them, shutting me out, shutting the world out. It all seemed so cruel - so unfair - I lifted her shoulders till she was looking at me with those

200

sad, lovely eyes, those eyes that had brought her to so much sorrow. "Be strong - for Sharon . . ." She looked up at me. "For . . . Sharon . . . yes . . ."

Between us we finished the advertisement, then propped it on the mantlepiece to post, the way all letters were.

I gave Miss Minch my notice. She wished me a weak "luck" after the first shock had left her eyes. I had been a "willing worker" - I almost laughed out, thinking what dad would say when I told him. She enquired of my "plans for the future" - I said I was "probably going to study" - that'd show her - offering me a lady's maid job -

I asked mum if dad would pay for me to study something. "Study? What?" She had a smell of smoke on her where she'd been making a bonfire of six years of 'rubbish' - She looked at me steadily then eased herself down, wearily. "Trouble is, you're like I was, clever and don't know what to do with it."

"I do!"

"Good then . . ." She got up. "Better finish that burning up -"

It was our last evening. Saturday at seven-o-clock 'sharp' the removal van would come to take us and our 'bits' back to London. "Where you going? There's still things to do." Mum was fussing as she would till the last moment. "Just for a breath of air," I called back. I needed to make my own goodbyes.

"Lovely day it's been?" Mr. Evans called from the window above his shop.

"Yes, it has!" I called back. I longed to tell him a proper goodbye and the truth of what was really happening for didn't he deserve it - him who'd let mum have extra on the rations and who hadn't pushed her when she owed him and the sing-song in his voice - All this I wanted to thank him for as I walked on up the street. Before turning the corner I looked back and he was at the window still. I waved and he waved back.

I passed the school, its bell-tower neat above the large, square entrance porch. How many times had I jostled and giggled my way through the heavy swing doors? And how many times had I come out again, flushed with a Credit Mark or down because I'd just missed one - ? I could almost hear Mary's laughter and the hand-claps of the girls that time I'd sung songs in the air raid. P'raps I

201

should visit Miss Arnold before I left - just to say what shall I do Miss?

A group of men, rosy with beer and good spirits were outside the gates of the Working Mens' Club. "I'll bet my last shilling on it!" a heavy-mouthed one said to the others. They stayed arguing as I passed, unnoticed. Were they there that night I'd given my one and only professional performance and p'raps mum was right and the stage should have been my aim -

"Paper Miss?" He was pitched outside The Rising Sun, a wiry, alert figure, shirt-sleeves rolled up showing a tattooed arm with a snake twisting upwards through the grey-white hairs. The paper he held out was head-lined 'NEXT U.S. A-BOMB TEST AT BIKINI LAGOON'. I stood still, the paper stuck before me, like a foreigner trying to comprehend words in a language strange. He shook the paper at me. I found a coin and took it from him. The sound of the bolt being shunted back from the door of The Rising Sun jerked me back to the times mum had gone there - to play the piano - be at the core of the hard, quick excitement that happens when people live full because they don't know how much living might be left - and somewhere far away a mother and father were grieving a son left simple as a babe, made that way in a pub brawl, not in battle - not with a yell and a thrust at a strange man's belly but in a pub full of laughing, drinking people, cracked on the head by a man wearing the same uniform as himself.

On I walked, the paper lightly beneath my arm, inside, its pages formal columns of discord - of print words mocking the years of war - 'ANTI-JEWISH RIOTS IN POLAND, 36 REPORTED KILLED' - 'U.S. QUESTIONS REPARATIONS TO RUSSIA' - I turned to go home. A young woman was walking towards me. She was pretty and held tight the hand of a small boy. His skin was the colour of very dark honey and his hair the close crinkle of the negro. She stepped towards me, a suggestion of defiance in her step - "So what?" it said. I knew that mum would never be able to stare out the world in this way, even though Sharon was white and pretty as a doll in the front of a toy-shop window. Just as well she was going back to dad.

"You've been a while." She sat with her hands in her lap, the finger-nails still with dirt in them.

"I'll go up and see if anything's been forgotten shall I?"

The carpet was still on the stairs, worn through its cord on the edge of the treads - the same dreary beige and brown cord that had been here since we came. There was no need to lift it for where we were going there was no staircase, just two rooms and a kitchen. The rag rugs Mr. Parmer's mother had hooked from their old clothes were in their places beside the beds and would someone else's feet step on them and would they be taken down and beaten and beaten for oh, would the dust never stop coming from them? And sometimes, if something reminded me, like the colour of a lady's dress or the touch of cold lino under bare feet, would I pull to the front of my mind the old rag rugs? There was one large, cardboard box left out for the last of my things. In the small top drawer was the glove-box of black, lacquered wood with the design of soft, pink roses across the lid. I opened it. Inside my pencils were lined at rest. Beside the box was the green leather writing-case Paddy had given me - big Paddy who taught me Irish dancing and - what kind of a first kiss might he have planted on me?

Down in the garden in the creeping night light next-door's cat jumped from the roof of the wash-house and with a knife-movement of his head looked up at me looking down at him. His intense eyes brought to my memory how once I'd teased Sylvie about a cat hypnotising you if it stared at you long enough - five seconds even would do it I'd said and now it must be all of that so quickly I turned, just in case it did put me to its will.

"Finished?" mum called. I went down and had tea with her. Soon after we went to bed. We had to make an early start in the morning.

****

203